THE AMENDMENT

MELANIE MORELAND

MORELAND BOOKS, INC

THE AMENDMENT by Melanie Moreland
Copyright © 2019 Moreland Books Inc.
Registration # 1162043
Ebook ISBN # 978-1-988610-26-9
Print book ISBN # 978-1-988610-25-2

MORELAND BOOKS INC.

Edited by

Lisa Hollett—Silently Correcting Your Grammar

Cover design by Melissa Ringuette, Monark Design Services

DEDICATION

*The Amendment is a journey of love, forgiveness, and understanding.
There is only one person I could dedicate it to.*

This book is for my Matthew

*Because with him
Forgiveness is offered
Support is never ending
and
Love surrounds me every moment of every day.*

Always and forever yours—M

RICHARD

I t was late when I finally pulled into the driveway, sighing with relief at being home. I used to love traveling for work, but now, I found I dreaded going. I hated leaving Katy and my girls.

My flight had been delayed leaving Toronto, then again departing Calgary, and it had been a long day. I reminded myself to speak to our travel specialist who handled our bookings. I wanted direct flights—no more stops.

I noticed although the house was dark, two lights shone in the night. The one over the front door for me and the muted glow coming from the nursery window. That meant Katy was awake with Heather, no doubt feeding her.

I pushed open my car door and stretched. The streetlamp glinted off something white, catching my eye, and I glanced toward it with a frown. I jogged down the driveway, confused at the half-dozen campaign signs on my lawn. All the political parties were represented. With a curse, I yanked them all out of the grass and carried them to the garage, tossing them into the corner. I grabbed my small suitcase and hurried into the house.

I took the steps two at a time, stopping to drop my bag into our room, then headed next door to the nursery. Exhaustion, stress, and the tension of the day drained away at the sight before me.

Dozing in the huge cuddle chair was my beautiful wife, Katy. Cradled in her arms was our baby, Heather. Tucked beside them was my Gracie. She lay across her mother's lap like a starfish, taking up as much room, and no doubt her mother's attention, as possible. A discarded bottle lay on the floor. They were a beautiful trio, and my little girls were both growing up far too fast for my liking.

I bit back my amusement watching them. I pulled my phone from my pocket, snapped a couple of pictures before I crossed the room to try to help settle my girls in their proper places.

I eased Heather from Katy's arms, whispering assurances to Katy as she stirred. "It's okay, sweetheart. I've got her."

"You're home," she mumbled. "You're late... We waited."

"I know, baby. I'm sorry."

She tried to pat my face and missed. "S'okay."

Chuckling, I held her hand, kissing the palm. "I'm here now."

"Missed you."

Her words warmed my heart. I pressed a kiss to her head. "I missed you."

"Hmmm." Was all I got.

"Is she all fed?"

"Yes, all fed. Again."

I grinned. Heather had a voracious appetite. Constantly hungry and impatient when she was made to wait for her meal.

"Okay, stay there. I'll be back."

She smiled, sleepy and content, letting her eyes drift shut.

Heather snuggled close to me, and I stood by her crib, not wanting to tuck her in quite yet. She was a warm, sweet-smelling weight in my arms. I rocked side to side in the motion that always soothed her, loving how she felt nestled to my chest. Finally, I laid her down, stroking the wild hair away from her forehead. She had inherited my cowlick. If she was anything like me, it was going to drive her crazy.

Once I made sure she was settled, I went back to the chair, studying Gracie. She was a light sleeper, and I knew there was a good chance once I tried to move her, she would be awake, and nothing short of one of our Daddy and Gracie raids on the ice cream tub would lull her back to sleep. We would sit at the table, her on my lap, the ice cream tub in front of us, and I would feed her tiny mouthfuls and listen to her babble on about some great event in her day, trying not to grin like an idiot the way her lisp made some words sound.

"It wath tho funny, Daddy! I laugh and laugh!"

Luckily, she must have been exhausted, because she stayed asleep through the lifting, carrying, and re-tucking into her little princess bed. Bending low, I kissed her curls, my love for her bursting in my chest.

Then I returned to the nursery. With no children on top of her, Katy had curled into a ball and was sound asleep. I tried not to laugh. She probably wouldn't remember me coming home or talking to me, albeit briefly, when she woke up in the morning. I bent, sliding my arms under her and carrying her to our bed. Her side of the bed was straight and tidy. She had obviously been sleeping on my side, the pillow wrinkled and bunched, the blankets thrown back. She always slept there when I was gone. She said it was the only way she could sleep when I was away. My side of the bed, dressed in one of my shirts, and clutching my pillow.

I pulled back the blankets on her side and slid her in. I left her sleeping, grabbed a long, hot shower, and got ready for bed, slipping in beside her. In a second, she was nestled against me, her head on my chest and her leg tossed over mine—my own personal starfish. There was no doubt Gracie had inherited that from her.

I wouldn't trade it for anything.

She shifted, lifting her leg, her knee rubbing over my groin, making my cock stir. Maybe she wasn't as sleepy as I had thought.

"Katy," I warned. "Don't be starting something you're too tired to finish."

She burrowed closer, running her hand down my chest, her voice low and raspy from sleep. "I missed you so much."

I lifted my head, peering down at her. Her eyes were drowsy and narrow but still filled with adoration. She had a way of looking at me that made me feel ten feet tall. As if I could do anything. Be anything for her.

I tugged her up my chest, my lips close to hers. "I missed you too, baby. I always miss you."

Her hand slid under the waistband of my sleep pants. Nude sleeping had stopped once Gracie began to walk. She was adventurous and had no trouble climbing into our bed in the middle of the night.

Katy's hand closed around my hardening cock. "I missed this, too."

"We're both happy to be home."

She sat up, throwing her leg over my hips and gripping my waistband. "Up," she commanded.

I arched, and she dragged my pants down, lowering herself until we were skin-to-skin.

"Jesus, Katy, you had underwear on a few minutes ago."

She tossed her hair over her shoulder. "My undies exploded."

"Exploded?"

Her voice was raspy and sexy. "They heard Richard VanRyan was back. Boom! They were gone."

"Is that a fact?"

She stretched over my torso, the heat of her sliding along my cock. "Yeah."

"I hope you weren't hurt during the blast."

"A little scorched. I'm sure you can put out the fire." She kissed me, her lips devouring mine, hungry and urgent. I gripped her hip and wound my other hand into her hair, kissing her back. The taste of my wife, the feel of her skin on mine, was like nothing else. I loved these moments with her—when it was simply us. Together.

I eased back, gazing up at her. Her quiet beauty overwhelmed me at times. I stroked her soft skin, spreading my hands over her stomach.

She bit her lip, for the first time not meeting my eyes as I ran small circles over the gentle curves of her. She stilled my actions, her fingers restless on top of mine.

"Hey," I called quietly. "Katy, baby, come back to me."

She lifted her eyes, and I shook my head, knowing exactly what she was thinking. I traced the light lines that bothered her so much along her hips and stomach. It wasn't very often she was insecure with me anymore, and this was something I needed to address, once and for all.

"These don't bother me, Katy, and they shouldn't bother you. They don't make you less beautiful—only more so to me. They're part of you. Part of us. You have them because for nine months you cradled, nurtured, and carried our children—*my children*—inside you. These little lines are proof of the strength you have. Tiny reminders of the wonder that your body is to me." I raised myself up and kissed her, pouring all the love I felt into the kiss. "Of the wonder you are to me."

"How do you always know the right thing to say?"

"It's not the right thing, Katy. It's the truth."

"I love you," she whispered.

"Good." I winked at her. "Because I'm about to fuck you, and I need you to be with me on that."

She grinned, her dark moment passing. She pushed me back to the mattress. "Oh, I'm with you, VanRyan."

She shifted, lifting her hips, and my cock slid along her folds, the heat and wet making me hiss. She sat up and engulfed me fully.

I slammed my head back into the pillow. "Fuck!"

"Yes," she moaned and began to move. "*Yes.* Fuck me, Richard."

I matched her rhythm, thrusting up into her. "Katy, baby, you're *wild* tonight."

"I've been thinking about you all day." She rolled her hips, leaning back and taking me deeper. "Thinking of you inside me. Oh God, Richard…"

I flipped her over, staying inside, and drove into her mindlessly. She whimpered and cried out, her blunt nails digging into my shoulder. I covered her mouth with mine, needing her taste and her silence. I didn't want Gracie wandering in right now. I would scar my daughter for life, because there was no way I could stop fucking my wife.

Katy stilled, screaming her release into my mouth. I rode it out, my orgasm crashing in around me, tightening my balls, sending shards of pleasure down my spine. I thrust one last time, groaning her name as I came, hard and shaking.

Then I collapsed on her.

She wrapped her arms around me, her touch a gentle balm to my soul.

"I love you, Katy."

I felt her smile against my skin. "I know."

I chuckled, pulling myself away. I tucked her into my side, tugging the blankets over us.

"Everything okay while I was gone?"

"Yes. Jenna and Laura came for a visit and checked on us. Graham called to make sure we were okay. How was the trip?"

"Good. It went well."

"The BAM boys behaving themselves?"

"For now. Becca sends her love. There are some gifts in the suitcase for the girls."

"Oh, lovely. I miss her. Is she okay?"

"Seems to be."

"Is Reid treating her well?"

I snorted. "The boy is head over heels for her. He'd give her the world if he could, so yeah, she's fine."

"I need to call her and check up on her. Make sure she's all right. I know she's still settling. She sounded stressed last time I spoke to her."

"She's gonna come home for a visit soon. I'm sure she was busy the day you spoke. If she needs to talk before, she'll reach out."

"Nope. I'm going to call her. She might be worried about bothering me. You know what she's like. I want her to be okay."

I sighed, knowing there was no point in arguing with her—it was a lesson I had learned in our time together. Katy was stubborn—a fact I adored about her. She loved my old assistant Becca and missed her greatly. Another fact I adored about my wife—the way she cared for people.

I remembered what I had seen when I'd pulled up to the house.

"Hey, what are all those bloody political signs on the lawn for?"

"Oh. Well, the candidates asked, and I didn't want to say no to anyone, so I let them all put up a sign."

"I hate those things."

"So, take them down."

"I did. I tossed them in the garage."

She laughed. "They'll probably put up new ones."

I groaned. "Damn it. How can I stop it? Cover the grass with poison ivy? Fence it off and station a guard dog inside?"

"A little drastic, don't you think?"

"You have a better suggestion?"

"Maybe you should put up your own sign."

I was confused. "I'm not running for anything, Katy. I don't have a damn sign."

"That would work."

"What would?"

"*Richard VanRyan. I'm not running for anything. I just wanted a damn sign.* We could print them and put them everywhere."

I started to snicker at her silliness. "Maybe I will. I need to come up with a better slogan, though."

She giggled. "Richard VanRyan. Panty exploder."

I had to turn my head into the pillow to stop the loud peals of laughter. Only Katy could make me laugh this way. She was the first and the only one to be able to do so.

"I don't think that's exactly PC."

"You have something better?"

I thought about it, then grinned.

"Sure. Richard VanRyan—I'm kind of a big deal."

It was her turn to be amused. "Whatever." She rolled over, still laughing. "Such ego."

I wrapped my arm around her waist, dragging her back to my chest. I nibbled on her earlobe. "But I am, Katy." I thrust my hips into her, letting her feel how big a deal I was.

"Oh, go fuck yourself, VanRyan."

I snickered at her favorite expression. "I would rather fuck you." I lifted her leg over my hip, tilting forward, pushing against her warmth. "I think you would too."

She pressed back with a groan.

"Fine, Mr. Big Deal. Make it worth my while."

I bit down on her neck. "Oh, baby. Challenge accepted."

2

KATY

I woke up to an empty bed, the sheets still warm from Richard's body heat. I rolled over into his spot, burrowing into his pillow. It smelled like him—warm, rich, and decadent. Citrus and ocean breezes mixed with a darker hint of musk. He always smelled wonderful. Even when I'd disliked him, he had smelled good.

I sat up, drew my legs up to my chest, and wrapped my arms around my knees. I glanced at the clock and grimaced. It was barely past seven, but I could smell coffee and knew without a doubt, Richard would be in the kitchen with the girls, giving Gracie cereal and feeding Heather a bottle as he sipped his coffee and listened to Gracie tell him everything he had missed.

I was never sure who missed whom more. Gracie was a daddy's girl, and she had him wrapped around her little fingers. He had endless patience when it came to our girls. He never lost his temper, his voice always held such tenderness when he was with them, and his eyes glowed with his love. It was a far cry from the cold, uncaring man I had first known. Once he had opened himself up to love, allowed himself to feel it, he had transformed completely. When he had fallen in love with me, my entire life had changed. He became everything I could have imagined in a husband and partner, and now a father for our girls. His career had flourished, our married life was rich and full, and I was happier than I ever thought possible. I glanced at the picture that sat on my dresser. It was one Richard had taken of Penny and me.

Penny Johnson had rescued me from the streets and gave me everything I needed in life: a home, love, and stability. She became more than my caregiver—she became my friend, protector, teacher, and mother. Losing her to Alzheimer's had been a crushing blow. I wasn't sure I would have been able to cope if it hadn't been for Richard.

In the photo, she was cupping my cheek and talking, her face alive and vibrant in one of her rare clear moments. I missed her every day, but I knew how thrilled she would be to know how happy I was with my life. She had adored Richard and helped make him the man he was today. With her, he found the ability to love another person—to open himself up to feelings he had long denied. It was her passing that brought us together in every sense of the word and helped get us to where we were now.

Thinking of her brought a tear to my eye, and suddenly I needed to see Richard. I pushed off the blankets, and rushed through my morning routine, hurrying down the steps toward the kitchen. I could hear Richard's low laughter and Gracie's voice chatting at him. Heather was gurgling, no doubt wrapped in Richard's arms. He rarely let either of them out of his sight the first couple of days after he had been gone. I walked into the kitchen, smiling at the sight before me. They were all together at the table, bowls of cereal and oatmeal eaten, the banana peel still on the counter from Richard slicing it up on Gracie's cereal.

They were both on his lap, his arms holding them close. Gracie was talking, Heather sleepy and content, safe and secure in his embrace. He lifted his hazel gaze to mine, the expression in his eyes tender and content.

"Hey, sweetheart. We've been waiting for you."

Gracie slid from his knee and rushed toward me. In her hand was a new stuffed toy Richard had brought her. He always came home with a present for each of us. I held out my arms, scooping her up and raining kisses over her chubby cheeks, making her giggle. I walked to Richard and pressed a long kiss to Heather's head. Richard's head fell back on his shoulders.

"What about Daddy?" he asked. "Does he get a kiss too?"

I brushed a kiss to his mouth, whimpering when he caught my neck, pressing my face closer to his and deepening the kiss. He slid his tongue along mine, caressing the skin on my neck, his touch possessive and firm.

I stood slowly, our gazes locked. Gracie giggled.

"Daddy, you kissed Mommy."

His gaze never left mine. "I did, baby girl. I like to kiss Mommy."

"Me too?"

Standing, he smirked and blew a raspberry on her cheek. "Yep. You too."

He tucked Heather into her infant seat, making sure she was strapped in, then lifted Gracie from my arms. He grinned at me. "Daddy needs more coffee to keep up his kissing strength."

I laughed. Richard could do anything—except cook. His coffee, no matter how often I showed him how to make it, was horrendous. His cooking skills were limited to cereal, pancakes, and toast. Our most used appliance was the Keurig machine. He would be lost without it since he needed caffeine as soon as he woke in the morning and he was always up before me.

I turned to start the coffee, and he tugged me back, kissing me one last time.

"Morning, Katy," he murmured. "I love being home with you. I missed you."

I cupped his cheek. "We love having you home. We missed you too."

"Are you okay?" he asked. "You look sad."

I lifted my shoulder. "Memories," I confessed.

He knew on occasion that thinking of Penny made me sad. He always understood. With a gentle smile, he pressed a kiss to my forehead as he slipped a small box into my hand. "For you."

I flipped open the lid, gasping in delight at the delicate pearl earrings resting against the dark velvet. Small pink, black, and cream beads hanging from white gold threads glinted in the light.

"They're beautiful."

"As are you."

I turned and kissed him, our mouths moving together perfectly. "I love your presents, but I especially love that you're home. That's always the best gift."

He wrapped his arms around me, holding me close. "Thanks, sweetheart. Home is the best gift for me too."

An hour later, he appeared, dressed in a dark-charcoal suit with a silver-gray tie. He tugged on the sleeves of his white shirt, the embossed RVR on his cuffs peeking out.

"I can't get these damn cuff links on, Katy," he grumbled. "This pair never seem to cooperate for me."

I set down my coffee and slipped the heavy silver disks into the sleeves, fastening them. "There."

He inspected his sleeves, pleased. "Thanks, sweetheart."

"Will you be late tonight?"

He shook his head, smirking as he grabbed my coffee from the counter beside me and stole the last few mouthfuls.

"Damn it, you still make the best coffee."

I rolled my eyes and waited.

"No, in fact, unless there's some big emergency at the office, I thought I'd come home around three and start the weekend early. Maybe we can take the girls to the park and out for supper somewhere."

"I'd like that."

"Zandini's?" he suggested. "We haven't had pizza in a while, and Gracie loves it there."

I chuckled. "So does Daddy."

He lifted one eyebrow in amusement and kissed me fast. "Yes, he does. I want to spend the weekend with my girls. I've missed you all too much."

I cupped his cheek. "A family weekend sounds perfect."

"Great. I looked at my calendar and next week is going to be crazy. Graham has me booked solid. You have a sitter for Thursday, right?"

"Yes. The dinner?"

He nodded, a grimace crossing his face. "Graham is certain we're going to grab a few awards for the campaign for BAM. Otherwise, I'd skip it."

I studied him for a minute. "Why?" He usually enjoyed the dinners and spending the evening talking with his peers about marketing and strategies.

"David will be there. From the rumors I've heard, things aren't going well with his company. That will make him especially nasty. I don't want him anywhere near you."

I stroked along his jawline, feeling the tension simply talking about David caused him. "He's in the past, Richard. He can't hurt us now."

He huffed out a long breath, not meeting my eyes.

"Hey."

He looked up, wary.

"What is it, darling? Tell me," I insisted.

He slid his arm around my waist, pulling me close. His breath tickled the hairs on my forehead. "Seeing him, being in the same room as he is, reminds me of the man I was before. The bastard I was to you —to everyone. It reminds me how close I came to becoming like him. I hate even hearing his name, never mind being around him."

I hugged him close. It was rare, even now, that Richard showed his vulnerable side.

"I know he's going to bait me. Make his snide remarks—remind me of my past."

I held him tighter. "Nothing he says will make any difference."

He laid his cheek on my head. "I worry I'll slip back into that behavior someday," he confessed in a low voice. "That I will lose everything I hold so dear to my heart."

I tilted up my head, meeting his worried gaze. "No, you will not.

You will *never* be like him, Richard. You've totally changed. You were lost and alone before. You have me now. The girls. The Gavin family. We would never allow that to happen. *You* would never allow that to happen." I studied him, worried. "Maybe you should tell Graham you don't want to attend. He would understand."

Our eyes locked. Anxiety was evident in his stance. "Katy..."

"I love you," I insisted. "I love you with everything I have. I love the man you are."

"I know." He stroked my cheek with his finger, but he still looked worried.

"David baits you because you have something he will never have, Richard. Happiness. You're fulfilled and complete. At the end of the day, you have a home and a family that loves you. He's alone and miserable."

His tension drained away. He stood straighter, and the frown lines eased from his face.

"You're right. I have everything he wants and will never have. He can't affect me because I won't let him. I have too much good in my life."

"Yes, you do."

He lowered his face and kissed me, his mouth moving with mine gently. "Thank you, sweetheart. I don't know what came over me, but thank you for listening and being there for me."

"I'll always be here."

He kissed me again. "Then I have everything I need."

RICHARD

"Is that everything, Mr. VanRyan?" Sheila, the woman who owned my favorite flower shop, inquired.

"Yes. Those will be delivered this morning?"

"Absolutely."

"Perfect. Thank you." Satisfied, I ended the call, the music returning to the speakers in my car. Katy would have flowers arriving by lunchtime.

I had no idea what had come over me this morning. I'd dealt with David on several occasions since leaving his firm. We attended many of the same functions, and we often competed for the same business. I ran into him on occasion in the same restaurants. Victoria wasn't a huge city, and the marketing world was small, so it was inevitable. I would acknowledge him at the dinner and move on. Why knowing I would be seeing him next week suddenly bothered me, I couldn't comprehend. However, as usual, my Katy had been there and offered me precisely what I needed to sort it out in my head and be able to move forward.

She was correct. The man I had been was gone. The person I was back then when I worked for David and lived his cutthroat ways no longer existed. I had a real life now and the one thing David would never possess, because he was simply incapable.

Love.

It made me richer and stronger than he could ever be.

Sometimes, I simply needed reminding.

Katy descended the steps, her deep-red dress swirling around her knees. The off-the-shoulder look was sexy, and the cut of the dress hugged her curves. She was perfect.

Gracie clapped her hands in delight. "Mommy, you look tho pwetty! Doesn't she look pwetty, Daddy?"

"Yes, she does. Beautiful, in fact."

Katy lifted Gracie from my arms. "Thank you. Are you going to be a good girl for Mrs. Thomas?"

Gracie bobbed her head eagerly. Mrs. Thomas had been a staple in our home since Gracie was born. A grandmotherly sort, she doted on both our girls, and us as well. She lived a few houses over—her husband was retired and enjoyed golf. She preferred to stay busy and had a small group of parents in the neighborhood she babysat for. I made sure to pay her enough and treat her very well, so she was always available for us. It was easy since she reminded me a little of Penny and I liked how she cared for my girls.

All of them.

"We're gonna do a puthzel."

I grinned at the lingering lisp in Gracie's voice. It was slowly disappearing, and I hated to see it go, although I knew it was part of her growing up.

I hated that part as well. It was happening too fast.

Katy rubbed her nose on Gracie's affectionately. "I made a treat for you to share too."

Gracie threw up her little arms. "Yay!"

"Give Mommy a kiss goodnight," I instructed. "Then Daddy needs one, and we have to go."

Kisses, snuggles, and more nose rubs later, we were headed to the dinner. Katy slipped her hand into mine.

"You're wearing my favorite suit. You look very handsome."

I squeezed her fingers. "Thought you'd like it." I winked. "Hoping if I show you a good enough time, maybe I'd get lucky. My good looks should seal the deal."

She chuckled low in her throat and turned to the window. "Such ego. Go fuck yourself, VanRyan."

I laughed, feeling my tension ease as I steered the car toward the banquet hall. Katy always knew how to get me to smile.

"God, I love you, Katy VanRyan."

She looked at me, her beautiful eyes bright in the dimness of the car. "I love you. And I'm right beside you. Okay?"

I lifted her hand to my mouth and pressed a kiss to her knuckles. "Okay."

The noise level was intense, the lights too bright, and the dinner, as usual, ho-hum. Looking at the two awards, however, sitting on the table and knowing it was my efforts that brought them to The

Gavin Group was an incredible high. Graham had been lavish in his praise, accepting the awards and making sure the entire room knew who made them possible, even making me stand up and take a bow. Katy was so proud, she wept—silent drops of joy that told me how she was feeling. I kissed them away, then kissed her mouth.

"Does this cinch the lucky part at the end?" I asked against the softness of her lips. I felt her wide smile.

"Definitely."

"Win for me."

I waited in line at the bar, accepting congratulations. I ordered a round of drinks for the table and waited patiently for them to be ready, glad for a quiet moment to myself.

"How does it feel?"

I stiffened at the voice and turned my head slightly. David Anderson stood beside me. He looked older, the deep furrows on his forehead more pronounced. His hair was thinner and his mouth in a perpetual glower.

"Excuse me?" I replied coolly.

"That's three years in a row you've won Gavin's company awards. Three years you've brought acclaim to Graham. How has he rewarded you for that?"

I turned and faced him fully, keeping my voice low. "How he has rewarded me is none of your business, David. If you recall, I won you a few awards in my time with your company—which you never bothered to thank me for. Suffice it to say, his rewards are far more generous than yours ever were."

"I can offer you a partnership. I'd even throw in VP. You'd get the title, the prestige, and the money. The whole package."

I was dumbfounded at his brashness. Galled that he would do this here and now. Burning rage set in.

I leaned forward, ice dripping from my tone. "There is no amount of money, no title, nothing you could offer that would ever entice me to come back to work for you. You and your company are pure poison, and I want nothing to do with you."

He regarded me with contempt, his tone filled with derision. "You used to be such a shark, Richard. Top of your game. Working for Gavin has made you soft. You need to be challenged. I can do that."

I barked out a laugh. "*Soft?* Just the opposite. I know who I am now. I work in a company that thrives on positivity. They have pride in their work and the campaigns they put together. Their reputation is stellar. I'm proud to be associated with The Gavin Group. That itself is reward enough. As for being challenged, I think the awards I won tonight speak for themselves. They were won with integrity and team effort."

I spun around, hoping like hell the drinks were ready, when David spoke again. "He'll never make you a partner. He'll use your talent and pat you on the back, but you'll never really be one of them. He only promotes family." His voice grew pitiful. "You might make him a lot of money, but you'll never be family."

My hands curled into fists, but I refused to respond. I accepted the tray of drinks and elbowed my way past David. If I spoke again, things would get ugly, and I refused to embarrass Graham that way.

"Get in touch with me when you change your mind," he called after me.

I ignored him.

3

RICHARD

The next morning, a knock at my door diverted my attention from my laptop. I glanced up to see Graham leaning against the frame.

"May I come in?"

With a grin, I saved the work I was doing on my computer. I indicated the chair in front of my desk. "It's your company, Graham. I think you can go anywhere you damn well please."

He smiled and sat in front of me. "I didn't want to interrupt. You looked very intense."

"Tightening up an idea for the BAM boys. Becca had a great concept, but it needed a little tweaking. I think they'll like it." BAM was one of our largest clients and based in Toronto. Although Becca was their point person and brilliant at her job, Bentley, the owner of the company, liked me to stay involved. Given his status with our firm, and the relationships I had developed with the men at BAM, I was happy to do so.

"I have no doubt. You seem to thrive on their campaigns." He shifted and ran his fingers down the perfect crease of his pant leg. It was an uncharacteristically nervous gesture for Graham.

"What's up?" I asked, picking up my cup and taking a sip of coffee.

"I wanted to congratulate you in private. You were very successful last night."

"*We* were. Becca was a huge part of my work, as was everyone else here." I cocked my head to the side. "You taught me that, Graham. Teamwork. Because of *this* team, I'm doing some of the best work I have ever done."

He steepled his fingers together and rested his chin on them as he regarded me.

"I saw David talking to you last night. You seemed, ah, perturbed when you came back to the table. I didn't want to bring it up last night, but I'd like to ask you about it now."

I leaned back, studying Graham. Unlike David, his appearance hadn't changed much. He was a bit older, but then again, so was I. We both had a few more silver hairs on our heads now. Unlike David, however, Graham's countenance was smooth and unruffled, although his eyes looked troubled.

I waved my hand. "He was being his usual arrogant self. He thinks I've gone soft and need a challenge."

Graham lifted one eyebrow. "A challenge? Has he counted the awards you've won since coming here?"

I snorted. "This time, he offered me a partnership and VP to come back. Name my own terms. He's upping the ante."

It wasn't David's first offer, but it had certainly been his boldest to date.

Graham tapped a beat on his chin with his index finger. "Were you tempted?"

I was caught off guard by his question. "Not even remotely. I have no interest in working for him again." I huffed out a long breath. "You know the kind of man I was before I worked here, Graham. I have no desire to fall back into old habits, no matter what carrot he's dangling. I love my life. My family. My job." I paused as a thought struck me. "You weren't really worried about that, were you?"

"To be honest, I'm more worried you'll decide to fly off to Toronto. Bentley would love to add you to his company. He has been very straightforward about that many times. All you'd have to do is say the word, and you could write your own ticket with him."

"At what cost?" I said. "Drag my wife and children across the country—away from everything familiar and move to a city I like to visit but don't want to live in? Leave the company that changed my life and gave me all the good things I now have?" I shook my head. "No, Graham. I'm not interested in leaving. Now or in the foreseeable future. You taught me a very valuable lesson called loyalty, and I'm sticking right here—with you."

Our gazes locked, the air thick with tension and seriousness. I needed to break the ice.

"Unless, of course, you want to get rid of me. Then I'll take Bentley up on the offer. David can go fuck himself. He wants the awards. Screw that—they belong here." I winked.

Graham chuckled, my words concluding the serious moment. He leaned forward, resting his elbows on his knees. "You are a very important, vital part of my company, Richard."

"Thank you."

"You also know, aside from Terence, all the VPs in the company are family."

Terence Gifford came onboard with Graham at the creation of The Gavin Group. He was Graham's oldest friend and his most trusted ally outside of his family.

"I'm aware, Graham. I knew that coming in, and frankly, it would have upset the old Richard. But now, I've figured out there are more important things. I meant what I said to David. I'm proud of the work I do here. Proud to know that one day my kids can see a campaign I put together and be proud *of* me. I never had that satisfaction at Anderson Inc. It was simply a game of survival."

He nodded in understanding and spoke again. "Terence is leaving."

"What? Is he okay?"

"He's fine. More than fine. His son and wife are expecting twins. They live in Edmonton, and Terence and his wife Jill have decided to move there and be close for their grandkids."

"So, he's retiring?"

"Yes."

"Good for him."

There was a pause. Graham leaned back, now relaxed and confident. "We had a family meeting yesterday afternoon. We discussed Terence and the void that will be left with his departure. We're going to change things up. Spread out his duties and make some adjustments. And we're going to hire a new associate."

I was confused. Hiring a new associate wouldn't really fill Terence's spot. "Okay?"

"We'd like it if you took him under your wing."

I was even more confused. "Sure, Graham, whatever you need."

"He's a bit of a handful. Brad is Laura's nephew—not long out of school. He interned with a place in Calgary but has decided to come back to BC. I know Laura and her sister have hoped he would end up here. Her sister lives an hour away, which means he'll be close to her again. Frankly, I was never sure why he insisted on going elsewhere to work when he had the chance to be here, but he was always adamant on forging his own way." He paused, rubbing his chin in amusement. "Lots of talent—a great instinct for the job. Although at times, he gets ahead of himself. And he thinks he knows it all. Bit of an attitude, to be honest. Sound familiar?"

I chuckled. "Vaguely. I'm sure I can bring him down a peg or two."

Graham grinned. "Don't crush him. I am rather fond of the boy. However, I think he'd do well to work under you for the first while. See how to put together award-winning campaigns."

"I'll do my best."

He leaned back, crossing his legs. "I'm going to give him your office."

I sat up straighter, now feeling annoyed. I liked my office. "*What?* Can't you give him a different office? Where the hell am I going to work?" I sputtered.

His eyes danced at my reaction.

"In the corner office beside mine. Congratulations, Richard. You're the new VP of The Gavin Group and in charge of all Eastern Canada accounts." He snickered. "Bentley would have a meltdown if I pulled you from that territory. You do such an amazing job, I'm giving you all those clients to oversee. It's a growing market for us, thanks to you."

Shock was an understatement at his words, and for a moment, I was speechless. My mouth hung open, and I stared at Graham.

"Excuse me?" I finally asked.

He looked amused at my confusion.

"You heard me correctly, Richard. You are the new VP of The Gavin Group. You're moving offices, pay grades, positions, and you'll now own a small piece of stock in the company. Brad will work with you, and you can groom him and let him work on the smaller accounts to get some experience. I don't think he could have a better mentor."

"But-but you never…" I stuttered. "It's family. You keep the company within the family. I knew that when I came here and when you rehired me. I never expected…" My voice trailed off, amazement still rendering me incapable of coherent speech or thought.

He sat back, now relaxed and at ease. "I told you in our initial meeting that my company is family, Richard. That the people within the company are thought of that way. I meant it."

"I know. I've told you often how much I admire the way you run the company. You know what a difference it, *you*, have made to my life —both professionally and personally."

"That's the difference between you and my other staff, Richard. You have become a part of my life personally. Your family is an extension of my own. Laura dotes on your children the same way she dotes on our grandkids. Jenna and Adam think of you as a surrogate brother. Adrian admires you." He shrugged. "You have become…*more*." He paused, smiling before he spoke again. "Laura and I feel as though you're an adopted son to us, Richard—the same way Adrian did when he married Jenna. You have made me proud of the man you have become and the man I know you will continue to be. You deserve this."

I swallowed hard, my throat constricted. I had to blink several times before I could respond. With Katy and my girls, I was able to show my emotions. The tenderness and love I felt for them were easy for me to express. Katy had shown me how to be real with them. I was still learning when it came to other people. I could joke around with Maddox. Tease Jenna. Hug Laura and allow her to fuss over me. Graham's acceptance and trust in me overwhelmed me at times because of the deep sense of need it fulfilled within me. The paternal role I'd lacked my entire life that he filled with his encouragement and pride.

I cleared my throat, but regardless, the words were thick and heavy as I spoke them. "That means more than I can adequately express, Graham." A grin pulled on my lips, the irony not lost on me— words and ideas were my thing after all, but this was different. Personal and overwhelming. His trust and opinion were paramount to me. I met his steady gaze. "I won't let you down. Thank you."

"I know you won't. This is the right move for all of us. Call your wife and give her the good news. Come to my office later, and we'll sign the paperwork." He chuckled. "Some formalities that have to be done. HR, you know. They insist on this stuff."

Standing, I reached across my desk, extending my hand. "Thank you, Graham. This is unexpected and amazing. I'm excited about the entire concept."

He shook my hand, his grip firm and strong. He stood and walked toward the door. He turned with a wide smirk. "I'm glad you're excited, but you might not be thanking me once you meet Brad."

I wasn't concerned. I had dealt with lots of junior executives in the past. I once was one of them. I knew how to handle their brashness. Really, how bad could this kid be? If Graham and Laura were fond of him, and Graham was bringing him into the company, he had to have merit. He probably needed a firm hand from someone who didn't have a direct family connection. If he was going to be part of my team, I would oversee and encourage him.

I was grinning as I picked up the phone, anxious to share this news with Katy. Maybe we could get Mrs. Thomas to babysit and I would take her out tonight to celebrate. Dinner and a hotel room for a few hours so I could have her to myself. I grinned at the idea, liking the thought.

⌇

I stared at my wife across the table. The candlelight flickered, the dim glow casting shadows on the walls and highlighting her lovely features. Her beautiful eyes were filled with pride and happiness—and a little glassy from the champagne we had drunk to celebrate my new role.

"I'm so proud of you, Richard."

I tilted my head. "I couldn't have done this without you, Katy. All of this—my life, my career, my children—is because of you." I knew as the words left my mouth how true they were. Katy had been the turning point in my life, and without her, nothing would be worthwhile. Because of her, I had changed and become the person I was now. I reached into my pocket and pulled out a long, flat box, sliding it across the table. "For you."

She stared at the box, worrying the inside of her lip. It still amused me that, after all this time, she wasn't used to being spoiled. Every gift I gave her was greeted with the same surprise and delight. It didn't matter how big or small, she loved it. It made giving them to her all that more enjoyable.

"Take it, sweetheart." I pushed it closer.

Her eyes widened as she picked up the box and opened the lid. She lifted her gaze to mine then back to the box. "Richard..."

She removed the diamond and sapphire bracelet from the box, the gems glinting in the light. "It's lovely!"

I reached across the table and fastened the clasp around her wrist.

"The blue reminded me of your eyes, Katy. I love how they look at me—the way they see me." I held her hand, staring at the glittering jewels. "I wanted to give you something to mark today."

She blinked at the tears forming in her eyes. "Thank you, my darling. I will treasure it always."

I leaned close and kissed the tender, thin skin of her wrist. "I'll treasure you."

Her gaze was luminous as she regarded me. "Take me home, Richard. I need to be alone with you."

"I got a room here, and I told Mrs. Thomas we'd be really late. She said she'd sleep in the guestroom." I winked. "I want you loud tonight."

"Take me upstairs."

I signaled for the check.

~

We barely made it into the room. Katy was all over me in the elevator, her body molded to mine, her mouth hungry and demanding. I fumbled with the key, finally getting her into the room. I pressed her against the wall, lifting her and wrapping her legs around my waist.

"You want it dirty, sweetheart?"

"Yes," she moaned, sliding her hand between us and cupping my erection. "Hard, fast, and dirty. Fuck me, Richard." She nipped my jaw. "Take me."

I groaned low in my throat. I loved it when she let go. When she got vocal and told me what she wanted.

"Tell me."

"I want you to take me right here. Fill me with your cock." She dragged her mouth up my neck, sucking in my earlobe and biting down. "Play with me, Richard. Possess me."

I set her on her feet and, in seconds, had her out of her pretty little dress. I threw it over my shoulder, my suit jacket following it, and stared at her, my chest heaving with my labored breaths. Lace and satin covered her breasts, her nipples pebbled under the diaphanous material. She pressed her thighs together with a moan.

"I'm aching for you, Richard. Put out the fire."

I dropped to my knees, lifting her leg over my shoulder. "I will, baby."

Her head fell back against the door as I licked and bit my way up her leg, brushing my fingers over the dampness of the satin between her legs. I wrapped my fingers around the lace at her hips and tugged hard. It gave way under my strength, baring her to me. She slid down a little, widening the space, grasping at my head. I licked at her, moaning at her wetness.

"You want me, baby?"

"Please."

I didn't bother with more teasing. She didn't need it, and I was too impatient. I slid my hands across her thighs and opened her up to my mouth. I licked and sucked, latching on to her clit, swirling my tongue over it the way she liked. She cried out, grabbing my hair and pulling me closer. I buried deep, pressing harder. I slipped two fingers inside her, pumping, then added a third. She gasped, her voice pleading as she called my name. I slipped my free hand from her hip and, using her wetness, I pushed a finger into her tight ass, knowing how wild that made her.

She gripped my head, clutching at me frantically. "More, Richard! Oh my God, give me more!"

My cock grew harder at her pleas. I added another finger to her ass and began to finger-fuck her in earnest, my hands and tongue working in tandem. She thrashed above me, her voice keening, her body vibrating. My wife was beautiful in her need, her desire for me a total turn-on. I ached to be inside her, to feel her warmth and the way her pussy clenched around me.

She cried out, fisting my hair hard and moaning my name. I gentled my touch, drawing out her orgasm until she collapsed against the wall. Then I stood and met her gaze.

"Here or the bed, Katy?"

With a sexy smirk, she turned to the wall and spread her legs. "Take me here, Richard. Now."

I didn't need a second invitation. I held her hips, lifting her and sinking into her heat. She groaned as I filled her, reaching back to wrap her arms around my neck. I played with her breasts, pulling and pinching at her nipples as I drove into her. She was slick, hot, and perfect around me. I licked and bit my way up her neck, moaning hot dirty words into her ear.

"I love fucking you."

"Your pussy is perfect, Katy. And mine. All mine."

"Fuck," I groaned as her hand dropped and clutched at my ass, her blunt nails sinking into my skin. "Like that. Just like that, baby. So fucking good."

I slid one hand to her clit, pressing and stroking as I felt my balls begin to tighten.

"Come all over my cock, Katy." I moaned as I felt my orgasm start to wind its way through my body. "Come for me again."

She tightened around me, setting me off. I wrapped her up, thrusting and cursing as I shook and emptied myself inside her. Her answering whimpers were breathy and low, and she whispered my name like a prayer. I collapsed onto her back, leaning heavily against her, her body trapped between me and the wall. I kissed her skin, murmuring my adoration for her, and finally eased away, catching her in my arms and carrying her to the shower.

The warm water streamed around us. We didn't talk much, but we kissed and smiled as we soaped each other clean, letting the water rinse us off before wrapping up in towels and snuggling on the bed, the heated passion sated and contentment surrounding us. These were the moments I loved. Allowing both sides of myself to be free with Katy and feel her respond to me.

"You want to stay?" I asked quietly.

"For a little while. I want to be home when the girls wake up."

I pressed a kiss to her head. I was good with that.

"Sleep for a bit, sweetheart."

She snuggled closer. "I love you, Richard."

I held her tighter.

"With all my heart, Katy."

4

RICHARD

The next morning, I was still high from the evening with my wife. We had slept for a while, then I had made love to her again before we drove home in the early hours of the morning, dawn beginning to break as we arrived home. We snuck into the house like a couple of kids worried about being caught breaking curfew by their parents, and we tiptoed upstairs. Our girls were sleeping, safe and sound, and Mrs. Thomas snored away in the guest room, the monitor beside her blinking and ready to alert her should the girls need her.

I tucked Katy into our bed and went for a run. As I pounded the pavement through our quiet neighborhood, I contemplated my life over the past few years. How it had changed. How I had changed. Contentment and happiness were two emotions I never expected to find in this life. Love was another one.

Katy gave them all to me.

Her gentleness, the sweetness that resided in her soul, had transformed the terse, emotionless man I had been into a person I barely recognized—and respected a lot more than the person I had been. When I looked in the mirror, I liked my reflection. I no longer saw a bitter, empty, and jaded man. Now I was a husband, father, friend. I loved and nurtured those around me, and it was returned to me tenfold.

Five years ago, if I had been told this would be my life today, I would have laughed loudly at the absurd idea of it all.

Now, I was grateful and unable to fathom life any other way.

I showered, filled my travel mug with coffee, kissed a still-sleeping Katy goodbye, and headed into the office. I had a busy day ahead of me, including plans to go over for my new office space. Graham insisted it be remodeled to suit me, and I was excited to see the drawings. I knew it would be in keeping with the understated elegance of the building in general, but it would be brighter and laid out differently from what Terence had liked. He was older and preferred dim lighting and heavy furniture. My space needed to be open, with lots of room for campaign ideas I liked to have access to. A smaller desk. More comfortable, modern furniture. I had discussed it with the designer Graham liked, and she was coming in today to show me her sketches.

I sipped my coffee and looked over my day. I had a few meetings with clients, a new potential one in Toronto that Amy had set up a phone conference with, and I had a campaign I needed to finish. I pulled up the files on my computer to study the concepts. The client was proving to be hard to nail down, but I thought I had finally crafted the right images and words. I worked for a while, tweaking and adjusting, saved the file, and sent it to print.

My phone rang and I hit speaker, settling back into my chair with a grin.

"Mad Dog."

Maddox Riley of BAM, and one of my closest friends, chuckled. "I heard there were celebrations happening in BC. I wanted to call and say congrats on the promotion."

"Thanks, man."

"Were you surprised?"

"Totally. I never saw it coming."

"You deserve it, although Bent thinks you should turn it down and come here."

Bentley Ridge was the owner of BAM—our most successful client in Toronto and now completely under my jurisdiction. He often told me I had a job with him any time I wanted one. It was a standing joke between us since he knew I would never leave The Gavin Group.

"Tell Bentley to dream on. Besides—he gets the best of both worlds. He has Becca there, and I'm still overseeing the account," I pointed out. "He gets me without the pay grade."

"Or the ego," Maddox teased.

"Whatever."

He snickered. "How's Katy? She must be excited."

"She is. We went out to dinner last night to celebrate. I think she's planning something this weekend."

"Of course she is. Your wife is awesome that way."

"Yep. How is Dee? Still loving the condo?"

"She's great. The condo is perfect. We love it."

My office door opened, and a young guy sauntered in. Tall, lean, and dressed in an expensive suit, he had his hands stuffed into his pockets as he walked around, looking at my shelves.

"Hold up a sec," I said into the phone.

"Can I help you?" I asked the stranger with a glare.

"Nope, I'm good. I'll wait until you're finished."

"Is Amy not at her desk?"

"I think she's in the file room."

"Do we have an appointment?"

His smirk was wide. "Nope." He flung himself into a guest chair, crossing his legs and pulling out his phone. "We're good, man."

His too-long blond hair caught the light as he pushed it off his forehead. His light-blue eyes alternately gazed at his phone and at me. He was young—early twenties, if I were to guess his age. There was a brashness to his stare, and he seemed at home in my office.

I bristled at his arrogance, his interruption, and his lack of respect.

Who the hell was he?

"Listen, Maddox, I need to call you back. I have an unexpected visitor."

"No problem. Call the office later. I know Bent and Aiden want to say their own congrats."

"Will do." I hung up and studied the kid in front of me. His focus was on his phone, his thumb moving quickly over the screen.

I cleared my throat, and he glanced up.

"Oh, hey."

"Who are you, and why are you in my office unannounced?"

His smirk was wide, and he leaned back, resting his arm across the back of his chair.

"Uncle Gray said to come find you, so I did. I wanted to check out my new digs."

Uncle Gray? New digs?

Jesus.

This was Brad?

"Uncle Gray?" I repeated.

He leaned forward, resting his forearms on his thighs. His hair fell into his eyes, and he flipped it off his forehead, only for it to fall back. His words confirmed my fears.

"Yeah. When I was little, I couldn't say Graham. Gray came out, and it stuck."

"I thought you were arriving tomorrow."

"I got here early. Wanted to check out the place." He sat back again, flipping his phone constantly between his hands. "I heard we'll be working together. I wanted to introduce myself and say hey."

I was silent, studying him. When I spoke, my voice was low and controlled.

"And you thought the best way to say 'hey' was to barge into my office, unannounced, interrupt a personal call, and make yourself at home? You really thought that was the appropriate approach?"

His grin faded. "Uncle Gray said the office was casual."

I stood, tugging on my cuffs. "Casual is not the way you're acting. Rude is. You knock and wait to be told it's okay before you come into any office in this place, do you understand? Even better, you check with the assistant."

He pushed his hair back again. "She's in the file room."

"Then you show some manners and wait."

"Oh yeah, okay. My bad."

My bad? That was this kid's apology?

"And so we're clear, we're not working together. You haven't earned that right yet. You work *for* me. Until I've moved, this is my office, not yours, so remember your place. And when you're referring to your uncle, it's Graham during business hours, not Uncle Gray. Your family ties holds no weight for me."

He swallowed, suddenly still in the chair. "Of course. I apologize."

"Better," I acknowledged. "Now, I have work to do. Go find Graham or Laura, and they'll direct you to HR. Get your paperwork done, and come back and see me—knock this time before you come in. We'll talk about *my* expectations."

With another hair flip, he headed for the door.

"One last thing," I called.

He turned.

"Get a damn haircut."

He left, pulling the door shut behind him. I sat down, staring at the closed door. I was somewhat amused, a little annoyed, and mostly confused.

What the hell was Graham thinking?

I t wasn't long before I had my answer. Graham appeared, pausing in my doorway, lifting his hand to knock.

"May I come in?" he asked, his eyes dancing.

I waved my hand. "Funny."

He sat across from me, still grinning. His wife, Laura, followed him in as he sat down.

I stood and greeted her, accepting her kiss on my cheek and smiling at her. You had to smile at Laura—it was impossible not to do so. She projected a warmth I had tried to fight against at the beginning, but now accepted and liked.

She sat beside Graham and spoke first.

"I understand Brad made an appearance this morning."

"Appearance is one word for it."

Graham chuckled. "A grand entrance is more like it, from what I heard."

"He said that?"

He shook his head. "Amy overheard most of your conversation." He quirked his eyebrow. "I told you to knock him down a peg or two, Richard. Not bulldoze him."

I was about to defend myself when I saw the amusement in his eyes and the way Laura's lips quirked.

"I simply gave it to him straight." I ran a hand over my chin. "Did he complain already?" If he had, we were going to have major issues going forward. I didn't need him running to Graham every time I told him off, which I had a feeling was going to be often for the first while.

Graham shook his head. "Nope. Other than to tell me he had met you and had an errand to run, he didn't say anything."

I looked at Laura. She returned my gaze, amusement in her expression. "He said he thought maybe you got off to a rocky start." She paused. "Then he asked me where the closest barber was."

I had to laugh. Graham and Laura joined in, all of us sharing a brief moment of humor.

"His mother will thank you, Richard. She's been trying to get him to cut that hair for years."

"I may have been a little harsh," I admitted.

Graham shook his head. "Nope. He was rude walking in, and he did need a haircut. If I told him to get one, or if Laura did, he would shrug us off. But he listened to you. That bodes well for going forward." He leaned back. "Leave him a little spirit. He is very talented—he needs a strong hand and some guidance."

Laura leaned closer. "He's a good boy, Richard. His father died when he was seventeen, and he went a bit wild and never has settled. My sister has never been able to say no to him. He needs that. I think you'll help him find his place."

I blew out a long breath. "That's a huge responsibility, Laura. I don't know if I'm up to it, to be honest. My earlier lifestyle wasn't exactly exemplary. Wouldn't Jenna or Adam be better? They're family after all. They know him."

"Which is why it would never work. They think of him as that annoying kid they've known all their lives, and he doesn't see them as his superiors. You're removed enough, he does have that respect. I think you're the perfect mentor because of the fact that you weren't always the Richard you are today. You changed and grew. I think if you took him under your wing, it would benefit him a great deal." She hesitated, then spoke again. "Please, Richard. I'm asking this as a personal favor."

I studied her earnest gaze. "He gets no preferential treatment."

"None. Handle him just the way you did this morning."

Graham interjected. "Be sure to praise him as well when he does something right. You know how I feel about positive reinforcement."

"I can do that. I looked over some of his work you left me. It shows promise, but it's scattered. Unfocused."

He nodded in agreement. "You can give him that focus, Richard. I know you can."

I scrubbed my face. "Fine." I narrowed my eyes at Graham. "My office had better be spectacular."

He threw back his head in amusement. "Done."

~

Katy's delight was evident as she lifted Heather to her shoulder, rubbing her hand up and down her small back in a soothing motion.

"He's going to give you a run for your money."

I drained my wine and set down the glass with a groan. "I know."

Brad had reappeared after lunch, his hair short on the sides, and the top brushed back, no longer flopping into his eyes. He appeared in my doorway, and knocked, waiting until I waved him in. He sat down, his phone flipping in his hands, always in motion, and I realized it was one of his nervous tells. He relaxed when I commented on his hair, then I opened his portfolio and we began to review the few campaigns he had been part of. I pointed out different aspects, and we discussed why they had or hadn't worked. He had some great ideas, although his execution left a lot to be desired.

I studied him over my folded hands. "You need to stop trying to find shortcuts." I tapped the picture on the top. "If you had extended your train of thought here—removed some of the overkill, this would have worked better."

"I thought it was eye-catching."

I shook my head. "No, it's over the top and distracting."

"I don't see it."

I sat back. "That is when you get the rest of your team around you, and they help. We help. We work together here."

He shifted. "I'm not used to that."

"Neither was I when I got here. This place, the people, are different." I studied him. "Graham told me he offered you a job right out of school, but you refused. May I ask why?"

He was quiet. "I thought Uncle—I mean Graham—was boring. That his company was old-fashioned and dull, which is why I went to Calgary and got on with a different firm. I wanted to make a mark. My mark."

"Graham is anything except dull. This company is one of the most respected marketing firms in the country—the world, in fact. Dull isn't a word associated with The Gavin Group." I indicated the walls and the awards sitting on my shelves. "Their track record speaks for itself."

He stared, not saying anything.

"Never confuse integrity and class with being dull, Brad. Be proud to be part of this team. Use it and learn. This place will make you better." I closed the files on my desk. "This is an opportunity to grow."

He stood, contemplative and silent. He took the files I held out to him and headed to the doorway. He paused and looked over his shoulder.

"I hear you, Richard, and I get it."

"Good."

He glanced around my office, his lips pursed. "Still, I think this office needs a younger vibe to it. I'm going to add my own stamp here."

He walked out.

"I thought I got through to him, and the one thing he had to say was my office needed redecorating." I ran a hand through my hair, tugging on the cowlick. "I'm not sure how I'm going to get into that thick head of his."

Katy smiled, tilting her head as she studied me. "You will. He's young and trying to find his place. You're a tight team at GG, Richard. Even being related to them, he's coming in with nothing except his uncle's backing. He's going to push back because he knows who you are to Graham. *What* you are to him. Give him some time. Show him some of the patience you show Gracie."

I looked toward the end of the table where Gracie was dozing in her highchair. Applesauce clung to her cheek, her hair was wild and curly in ringlets around her face, and her hand still held the spoon she'd been eating from when she'd crashed. Or somewhat eating, since most of it seemed to be on her face and the area around her.

"She's far cuter," I mumbled and moved toward her to carry her upstairs and get her ready for bed. "And she doesn't talk back as much."

Katy rolled her eyes. "Give her time. That part is coming." She laid a hand on my arm as I passed. "You can do this, Richard. Lead by example, and Brad will find his place. Be as patient as you can be."

I dropped a kiss to her head and settled Gracie into my chest. She rubbed her cheek on my shirt, smearing applesauce on the white cloth. I sighed, knowing I should have changed before sitting down to dinner, but I didn't have it in me to care much. A soiled shirt was nothing compared to the feeling of having Gracie snuggled into me.

I decided Katy was right. I needed to take the patience I had at home and try a little harder with Brad. Once he settled in and I could help guide and harness his creative side, I was certain he would be a good fit at The Gavin Group.

Patience. It was a lesson it took me a while to learn, but I finally grasped it.

I could do this.

~

I shut my office door with too much force and whirled around, furious. Brad shifted on his feet, shoving his hands into his pockets since his phone wasn't within reach. I had thrown it against the wall in frustration.

So much for patience.

"If you ever do that again, I don't care who the hell your uncle is, you are *out* of here."

"I was trying to make a point," he mumbled.

I slammed my hands on my desk. "By interrupting and speaking over a potential client and telling him he was wrong? You never talk down to a client—ever!"

"But he *was* wrong. His ideas were crap!"

"That is our job!" I roared. "Taking his crap ideas and making them better! Letting him think he has something to do with the plan— keeping him involved and engaged. You fucking talked over him and made him angry. We won't even get a second shot at the campaign." I sat down, my chair rolling back into the wall. "Your attitude has undoubtedly cost us that chance."

I had left the boardroom for five minutes to grab something from my office to show the client who was having difficulties grasping a visual concept. I knew I had to give him a tactile image, and I had the exact picture on my desk. When I hurried back to the boardroom, I heard the raised voices and Brad overtalking the client and telling him how he was wrong and didn't know what he was talking about. The next line out of his mouth was the nail in the coffin.

"Leave the marketing to us. We know your product better than you do."

Big mistake. The client was furious. I did as much damage control as possible, but Brad had insulted the client and I wasn't sure if even Graham's influence could undo the destruction. The client had walked out in a huff, and I had lost it.

In the three weeks Brad had been at The Gavin Group, we had locked heads on many occasions. He thought me inflexible, arrogant, and opinionated. I found him cocky, fast to shoot off his mouth, and unwilling to listen. Yet underneath all the blustering and boasting, he was quite brilliant, which was what saved his ass. Still, I wasn't sure if I could stop myself from throttling Brad before Graham arrived back in the office from his meeting.

"Maybe his business wasn't worth us going after," he snipped.

My anger picked up again. "It was a five-million-dollar campaign."

He shrugged. "I've worked on larger."

I snapped. "Then go back to Calgary and work there."

He narrowed his eyes. "You think you're so great?"

That made me snicker. "I'm better than you, kid."

"*You* think so."

I indicated the awards on my shelves. "A lot of people think so. Including Graham. Show some respect."

"You show me some."

I was on my feet, yelling again. "I will when you do something to deserve it!"

"He was out of line telling me what to do."

I threw my hands in the air. "You were out of line!" I shouted. "This is his product—his baby—and you tell him we know it better? You're a moron!"

"Well, you're an asshole!"

My door opened, and Graham strode in, upset.

"I can hear the two of you all the way to the elevator. What the hell is going on?"

"Why don't you tell him, Brad?" I sat down, done with him. "Explain this to *Uncle Gray*."

Brad lifted one shoulder in a dismissive gesture. "A client didn't like what I had to say."

I couldn't stop the growl. "Because you talked down to him. You belittled a client!"

Brad opened his mouth to speak, but Graham raised his hand. "I already had a call from Marcus Whitby. A very unhappy one. He told me to straighten out my staff and to call him when it happened and he might take the call. Or he might not." Graham rubbed his eyes, and I noticed how tired he looked. "I should have known you had your hand in this, Brad."

Brad shuffled his feet. "His idea was totally without merit."

"That's why he wanted to hire us," Graham stated patiently. "To take his terrible ideas and turn them into gold." He perched on the edge of my desk and rolled his shoulders. I studied him, suddenly seeing the tension he was hiding. It was in the set of his shoulders and the lines around his eyes that I hadn't noticed until this moment. "Many of our clients come in here and want to share their thoughts. The campaigns we work on are for their companies—often, their lifelines. Their blood, sweat, and tears. We have to listen to them in order to understand what they want. Do we ever use their ideas? Rarely. However, they like knowing we heard them. It's part of the job and, sadly, one you seem to keep forgetting."

Graham stood. "Go to your office and cool off, Brad. I need you to really think if you want this."

"I do, Graham. I want to learn and to be here."

Graham held up his hand. "I need some time with Richard. I'll be along to see you later. Give us the room, please."

If Graham Gavin requested the room, nobody argued. Not even Brad. He left, closing the door behind him with a quiet click. Graham sat down heavily and shut his eyes. I waited, letting him gather his thoughts.

"Was this a mistake?" he asked.

I drew in a deep breath. I knew if I said yes, Brad was gone—family or not. Except somehow, I couldn't find it in me to do that to him.

"He is a pain in the ass."

"More than I expected." He cracked open one eye. "Even more trouble than you were."

I chuckled. "He is full of himself." I pushed a file toward him. "Still, when he grasps the idea and buckles down, he is good."

Graham opened the file and studied it. "This is good. How much did you have to do with it?"

"I suggested some, ah, trims. He came up with the slogan and the main concept. He goes over the top, but once he hits the sweet spot, honestly, Graham, he is good."

Graham glanced up, and I winked. "Not as good as me, but he'll do."

Graham rolled his eyes and tossed the file on my desk. "What should I do?"

"Chain him," I suggested.

"In the basement?" he asked dryly, lifting one eyebrow.

I laughed. "No, in the office. He needs to start at the bottom. He should work with Adam and Jenna. Learn what everyone does and their style. He needs to do some grunt work before we let him loose on clients again."

Graham stroked his chin. "Good idea. I thought he was ready. I'm thinking the company he was with let him run amok."

"I agree." I sucked in a deep breath and said what was on my mind. "I think his talent is in design. The drawings and ideas he renders are unbelievable. He expresses them much better with his hands than speaking them. Maybe his place is behind the scenes and not in front of clients."

"He'll hate that."

I shrugged. "Maybe not. He could oversee the entire department. Be involved in the campaigns but not the pitches."

He nodded in silence, seemingly lost in thought. "I'll talk to him."

"Are you all right, Graham? You look exhausted."

He sighed. "I am."

"Are you unwell?"

"No, but I think I need a break. A little downtime. I had planned on a few weeks off, but with everything going on with Brad, it seems the wrong time to take time away."

"Nonsense." In the entire time I had been at The Gavin Group, Graham had taken one vacation, and it was for a week. He preferred long weekends and the occasional four-day stretch away, but he never took a longer break. Hearing him say he wanted one was a shock.

"Between me, Jenna, Adam, and Adrian, we can handle it for a while. We have nothing huge on the calendar. You should take Laura and go away. Relax."

"And Brad?"

"You talk to him, and I'll keep him under my thumb another few weeks. Jenna will help. We'll keep him in line and encourage him in the design direction. You go and enjoy yourself. Spoil Laura."

He blew out a long breath. "I think I need it."

"Then do it. We need you here, healthy and strong, Graham. Take the time and come back better," I encouraged.

He stood. "I'll talk to Laura tonight and the kids. We'll meet as a group tomorrow, and I'll have my decision."

"Okay."

He held out his hand. "Thanks, Richard."

I shook his hand, his grip strong. "For what?"

"Your support and for not pitching Brad against the wall." He winked. "His phone is far easier to explain to Laura."

He was right. I watched him leave, seeing the weariness that surrounded him.

Graham needed the break. It was only a few weeks and would do him a world of good. I knew Jenna and Adam would agree and that Laura would be thrilled.

Brad...well, he would put up a fight, but I had an idea how to sway him.

I simply had to make it happen.

5

RICHARD

I ran a hand through my hair, tugging on the cowlick. I glanced at my phone, groaning when I saw the time. I was late again. I called Katy immediately, smiling at the sound of her gentle voice when she answered.

"Hey, you."

"Hi," I responded. "I'm late."

"No, you're not. I didn't expect you, so that means you're still on time."

I sighed, leaning my head back on my chair. "I have no idea what I did to deserve you, Katy, but I am grateful for it every day."

"With Graham and Laura out of the office, it's hardly a surprise you're working all the time. Jenna dropped by earlier and said everyone is burning the candle at both ends with her parents gone," she assured me.

I hummed in reply. I always knew Graham had a lot on his plate running the company, but without him here, I had discovered exactly how hard he worked. No wonder he needed a vacation. We had divided up his duties, and I left the daily running of the company to Adam and Jenna, and I took care of his clients and overseeing the other reps. Adrian helped out, yet it was enough to keep us working late every day.

And there was Brad. As Graham thought, he hadn't been happy about working more behind the scenes. He felt his place was in front, "schmoozing," as he called it. Jenna and I had sat with him, convincing him of the importance of the design aspect and praising his talent. When I mentioned the fact that one day he could head up the entire division and oversee it all, a light had turned on for him. He saw a chance to make his mark. His own stamp.

I had heard his unspoken reservation about working for Graham when we talked in our first meeting. The underlying reason he had chosen to work elsewhere. How could he live up to the greatness that was Graham Gavin? Because of the connection, even by marriage, he would be compared to him constantly. Graham was a legend, and following in his footsteps wouldn't be easy. Even Jenna and Adam had to fight to have their own identities when they started.

By Brad's handling the design aspect of the company, his talent would be recognized as his, and his alone. Once he grasped that concept on his own, he was more receptive to the idea. And as Jenna and I expounded on the vision, he seemed to understand it wasn't a demotion, but rather a chance to grow.

On top of everything else I was handling, I had been spending a lot of time with him. That meant time away from my family. I had missed dinners, bath time, weekends—all of which I hated to do, but Katy had been understanding and supportive.

"Is Gracie in bed already?"

"She's awake. You want to talk to her?"

"Yeah." I hit speaker and waited. Gracie's sweet voice burst through the phone.

"Daddy!"

"Hey, baby girl. Did you have a good day?"

"Aunt Jenna bring me a new baving thuit!"

"Wow, that's awesome. What color is it?"

"Yeddow an pink an puple."

"I can't wait to see it."

"You tome home, Daddy?"

"Soon."

"I miss you."

My chest warmed and ached at the same time. "I miss you, Gracie. I'll be home more soon, okay?"

"You tiss me when you home?"

"A million times."

"Otay. Lub you."

"Lub you too. Put Mommy back on the phone."

"She's smiling," Katy informed me. "She kept asking to call, but I didn't want to disturb."

"No," I responded. "Always call. Anything for my girls. Always. You know that."

"When will you be home?"

I scrubbed my face and looked at my desk. "A couple of hours."

"I'll have dinner waiting. It's beautiful outside tonight. You can eat by the pool and have a relaxing swim."

"It's only another week. Graham will be back, and life will get back to normal."

"I know."

"I'll make it up, Katy."

"You have nothing to make up, Richard. You're helping Graham. Jenna told me Laura said he looks much better and is getting anxious to come home. This is a blip in our routine. He'll come back, and things will settle."

I hated to remind her, except I had to tell her the truth. "I have a trip out east coming up. I'll be gone for a week."

There was a pause, then she spoke. "We'll deal with that too. Finish your work and come home to me."

As usual, her patience and acceptance astonished me. "I love you," I murmured.

"I love you. See you soon."

She hung up, and I stared at the phone, thinking. I looked at the pile of work on my desk and made a decision. As important as it was, *she* was more important. My family was number one in my life. As patient and accepting as Katy was, I could hear the sadness in her voice. I knew she missed me as much as I missed her, and we needed a little extra time together tonight.

I grabbed my briefcase and slid the folders inside. I was going home. I could kiss my kids, maybe feed Heather her last bottle, eat, swim, and make love to Katy. Once she was asleep, I could do some work. I wasn't sleeping much right now anyway, and I could be productive while my girls slumbered.

One more week, I told myself as I hurried to my car. One more week and our lives would go back to normal.

~

I smiled at Gracie sitting in her chair, spilling cereal and milk as she talked nonstop, excited to find me home in the morning. I sipped my coffee as I fed Heather, tucked close to my chest, content and warm. The decision to come home had been a good one. Dinner, a swim, and a few hours lost in Katy had been the break I needed. I worked late into the night once she was asleep, and when I was caught up, I slid into bed beside her and grabbed some much-needed rest. This morning, I felt calmer and refreshed and I decided to stay home and spend a few more hours with my family. I had a busy day of meetings all afternoon, but this morning I was being selfish. Amy had adjusted my schedule, assuring me she would handle it all.

"Try to get some cereal into your mouth, baby girl." I chuckled. "Daddy's not going anywhere for a couple of hours. You can talk once you eat."

She giggled, her expression happy, her eyes glowing. Katy was content and sleepy, watching us with her elbow propped up on the table as she rested her chin in her hand. Her dark hair was messy and fell around her shoulders in a mass of curls from my fingers tangling it as I made love to her. Her extraordinary blue eyes were filled with warmth as she watched us. She met my gaze and smiled. The smile she had only for me—one so filled with love, it took my breath away.

46

Even after all we'd been through, and the years we'd been together, it never failed to affect me.

Our eyes held a silent conversation. Mine one of gratitude and love. Hers one of understanding and tenderness.

"I'm taking the weekend off," I announced. "I'm caught up. How about we go on a picnic and to the zoo?"

Gracie squealed, dropping her spoon into her bowl, causing the milk to splash everywhere. The zoo was her favorite place. She loved animals, and I knew how much she wanted a pet. Perhaps Katy and I could discuss that soon. For now, though, I could take Gracie to the zoo and buy her lots of time in the petting area. She loved that.

Katy beamed at me. "That would be so much fun! Are you sure?"

I nodded. "I have to work later tonight, and maybe tomorrow, but I'm all yours for the weekend." I'd pay for it the following week—except I didn't care. I needed it. My family needed it. I needed it.

Her look of adoration and happiness was worth it.

Later that day, I cursed as I looked at my car, kicking the flat tire in frustration. How the hell did that happen? I bent down to examine it, muttering another curse when I saw the nail I must have driven over as I passed through the construction happening down the road on the way in this morning. After going in late, I had been rushed all day, and this was the last thing I needed. To top it off, a storm was brewing, and I could feel one of my migraines starting to build. Jenna was needed to cover another meeting and was unable to accompany me to this one, so I had no choice except to go. I wasn't sure how I was going to get through the afternoon.

I groaned as I pulled out my phone, calling Amy, explaining what had occurred.

"I need you to call CAA and get me a cab."

"Do you want me to cancel the meeting?"

"No, they're already not pleased it's not Graham. I don't want to cancel. As it is, I'm on my own since Jenna is elsewhere."

"Do you want to take my car?" she asked.

I glanced over at her car and shuddered. I would never be able to fold my long legs into the tiny Smart car she drove. I did it once, and my legs ached for a day afterward. Add in my headache and I didn't want to drive her car.

"No, get me a cab."

"I can take you."

I turned, surprised to see Brad standing beside me. I hadn't heard him arrive.

I frowned, hesitant.

"I can come with you and sit in on the meeting."

"Hold on," I muttered to Amy.

"Brad—"

He interrupted me, holding up his hand. "I know, Richard. I'll stay silent, but if you need something, I can help. You're using the design I created. Give me the chance. I want to see how the clients react to it. Please."

It was the first time I had heard him humble and asking. I made a fast decision.

"Cancel the cab, but get my tire fixed, please," I said to Amy.

"On it. See you later, boss."

I hung up and looked at Brad. "Don't make me regret this."

He shook his head. "I won't."

Almost three hours later, Brad and I walked out of the building. Both of us were silent as we walked toward his car. True to his word, Brad controlled himself during the meeting, speaking when I asked him to go through his concept drawings. As I suspected, when explaining the images he created, he shone. He was articulate and passionate while discussing his work, and he listened to the feedback from the client, quickly sketching out a few ideas as he spoke. The client was impressed with his fast thinking and grasp of his idea, and I felt a glimmer of pride at Brad's response and my own satisfaction that I had been correct. Design was where he belonged.

I slid into the car and rested my head on the cool leather. It felt good. My headache was building fast, and I hoped I could make it back to work before it hit full force. Once it did, I was useless. I dug in my pocket for the pills Katy had slipped inside earlier, ever watchful of my ongoing headaches when the weather changed. I swallowed them dry, desperate for the relief they would give me.

"Are you okay, Richard?"

I cracked open one eye and looked at Brad. He was grimacing, studying me.

"You're really, ah, pale."

"Bad headache coming on."

"Want me to drive you home?"

I thought about his offer and decided to accept it. I could lie down when I got home, take some more medication, and hope the storm passed soon. I could grab a cab back to the office and work later.

"If you wouldn't mind."

"No, it's not a problem."

I shut my eyes in gratitude. "Thanks. Take a left and head toward Mason Street."

"Got it. I've been to Jenna's, so I know where you live."

As we pulled out of the parking lot, the skies opened. Rain beat down in torrents, the wind picking up and pushing against the car.

"Wow," Brad mumbled.

"Careful," I uttered. "This road has a lot of twists."

"Yeah, I got it." He slowed down, and I relaxed. Jenna sent a text asking how it went, and I answered, telling her Brad had surprised me and done well. I turned to him, remembering Graham's mantra of positive reinforcement.

"You did well today, Brad."

"Yeah?"

"Yeah," I returned with a nod. "You were on point and polite. You handled the client well, and your response to his worries was perfect."

"You were right," he mused.

"I'm sorry?"

"I'm comfortable explaining my work because I know it. I know how to change it, adapt to what someone wants once I grasp the concept."

"It shows."

"I was angry at you when Uncle Gray told me what he had in mind. I knew it was your suggestion, and I was sure you were doing it so you wouldn't have to deal with me."

I didn't have the strength to argue with him, so I grunted in denial.

"Once I got over the anger, I realized I liked working with the design team. I understood their language, and they understood me."

"Good." I sucked in a deep breath as a wave of nausea hit me. The headache was going to be a bad one. I breathed in deeply for a few moments until the queasiness passed before I spoke again.

"You're talented, Brad. In a different way than I am. Than Graham is. But not less. Don't compare yourself or try to live up to him. Be your own person. You're as important to the team as anyone. I saw your talent, and I thought it was the best direction for you. It wasn't a punishment, and I'm glad you see that now."

"I do." He paused, his voice droll when he spoke again. "I still think you're an asshole for making me get my hair cut and breaking my phone, but you're all right, Richard. I actually think I owe you."

A chuckle escaped my lips, the effort making me grimace. "Get me home before I hurl in your car, and we'll call it even."

He sped up slightly. "Good plan."

Moments passed, the sounds in the car that of the rain beating down and the steady rhythm of the tires spinning on the wet pavement. I drifted, the medication beginning to take the edge off.

Brad's loud curse followed by the cacophonous squeal of tires and brakes startled me, and my eyes flew open. The car shuddered as the sound of metal screaming and twisting on impact filled the cabin of the automobile. My body jerked as the car lifted, glass breaking and shattering as we rolled. The airbags deployed, hitting me in the face and chest, the sound of them going off deafening and frightening. Pain exploded—my head, my entire body, screaming in agony as it hit me full force. The car stopped suddenly, teetering on its roof. I groaned, the sound filled with anguish and confusion.

I tried to open my eyes. To speak. Something warm ran across my face. I attempted to lift my hand to wipe it away, except I couldn't move. It felt as if my body were locked in a vise that was getting tighter every second, and I struggled to breathe. With an extreme effort, I forced open my eyes, blinking. I was upside down, hanging tethered from the seat belt. The airbag was pressed into me. I managed to look sideways toward Brad. He was unconscious and bleeding. Outside were people—screaming, running, shouting. I couldn't make out their words because of the loud ringing in my ears. I tried again to talk, to call out, but nothing made it past my lips except another groan.

"Help is on the way! Hold on!" Voices yelled. A woman shrieked, the sound tormented and painful.

The car rocked, tilting side to side violently. Pain ripped through me, slicing into my brain and exploding down my spine. Sirens came closer, the noise around the car growing.

I began to black out, the pain obscuring everything in its path. Like an explosion of shrapnel in my lower back, it radiated outward, unlike anything I had ever felt in my life.

Excruciating, sharp, and, piercing.

Images of my girls slipped through my head before I succumbed to the black. Gracie laughing, Heather snuggling into me. My wife holding out her hand as she greeted me. The images wavered, dissipating in a sea of agony.

One word slipped from my mouth in a long, low groan as I gave in. *Katy.*

6

KATY

I tucked Heather into her crib, brushing my fingers over her fat little cheek. Her lips pursed in sleep, and she looked so much like Richard, it made me grin. She had his eyes, full lips, and his smile, although she was more laid-back like me. Both girls had his cowlick—a fact that he found amusing, knowing how annoying he found it to be. Gracie had Richard's temperament, although she resembled me more, unless she was frowning. Then she looked like him, right down to the furrow between her brows. I had a feeling they would keep us on our toes for the next twenty years or more.

I peeked in on Gracie. She was sprawled out on her bed like a starfish, sleeping hard. I glanced at my watch, knowing I had thirty minutes of peace at the most. Probably more like twenty if I was being realistic. Heather would sleep a little longer, but Gracie would be up and raring to go in no time. She had been that way from day one. Down fast, up quick.

I walked downstairs, listening to the sound of the rolling thunder that had begun a while ago. I had noticed the dullness of Richard's eyes this morning and made sure he had some pain medication in his pocket. Storms like this always brought on one of his headaches, and with Graham away, he refused to stay home today, saying he would handle it. His stubborn streak was one thing I knew would never change, so I didn't argue with him.

I poured a cup of coffee, mentally planning dinner, when the doorbell sounded, and I hurried to the front door before it rang again and woke up the girls, interrupting my few moments of peace. Opening the door, I was shocked to find Graham and Laura on the doorstep.

"What are you doing here?" I asked, stepping forward to hug them. "You're supposed to be in the Caribbean!"

Laura chuckled. "We were until someone decided they were done with lazing on the beach and wanted to come home."

I studied Graham. He looked rested and relaxed. He met my gaze with a smile. "I had enough," he explained. "It was time to come home. There's no point in staying when my mind was ready to get back at it."

We walked to the kitchen as the rain picked up again. It hit the windows hard, the sound echoing in the quiet—tiny pebbles of water striking the glass with fury. I poured us coffee, and we sat down.

"Does anyone know that you're home?"

Laura sipped her coffee and shook her head. "We came right from the airport. We knew all the kids would be at work, and Julia is away visiting her parents with the grandkids, so we decided to stop here first. We'll see Jenna and Adrian tonight. Graham spoke with Adam briefly, and he's going to join us at the house later."

"The girls will be excited to see you when they wake up."

"We missed them. We missed everyone." Laura sighed.

"How is Richard?" Graham asked. "Jenna said he was burning the midnight oil daily."

"He's been busy," I acknowledged. "He'll be thrilled to hand the reins back to you, Graham."

"I thought I was going away at a quiet time. I had no idea how many new projects were going to happen."

I waved my hand. "Aside from missing his girls, he's enjoyed it." I glanced toward the window. "I have a feeling he'll be home soon, though."

Graham tilted his head in understanding. "His headaches."

"He refused to admit it, but I think one was coming on today. He had that look in his eyes when he left that he always gets when one is coming on."

"No doubt Brad will be dropping him off."

I was surprised. "Brad?"

"Adam told me that Richard had a flat tire and Brad drove him to his meeting. Jenna had checked with him and Richard said things went well, which she passed it on to Adam. If his headache was bad, I'm sure he'd have Brad drive him home. I'll arrange for his car to be brought home."

I smiled in gratitude. Graham always looked after us well. "Thank you." I glanced at the clock. "Do you know when his meeting ended?"

"A while ago. Traffic is bad with the weather. They'll be along soon." He shrugged. "Or perhaps knowing Richard and his stubbornness, he insisted on going back to the office to debrief. You know how he likes to write out his thoughts after a big presentation—headache or no headache."

We all laughed because it was true. Richard kept careful notes on a client's reaction, good or bad to a pitch, jotted down any information he thought would be helpful going forward, and other things he thought of in regard to the campaign or the people.

I heard Gracie's voice over the monitor calling for me, and I stood with a grin. "So much for quiet time."

Laura stood. "I'll come with you."

Graham's phone rang, and I heard his quiet hello as we ascended the stairs. I heard my phone ring, and I met her gaze. "It's probably Brad and Richard calling to complain about each other."

She smiled. "Perhaps."

"I hope it's not someone trying to call Graham about business already. You haven't even unpacked yet," I muttered.

She shook her head. "Probably Jenna. She was going to call to confirm the time for this evening. We're going to order in some Chinese and relax with everyone. Will you and Richard join us if he is feeling better?"

Graham's voice calling me made me pause on the stairs. Laura patted my arm. "You see what Graham wants, and I'll get Grace."

"Okay."

I hurried down the stairs, pausing when Graham appeared in the door. He was pale, his face drawn. "Katy, we have to go."

My stomach dropped at the tremor in his voice.

"Graham?" I asked, my voice shaking. The fear and worry in his eyes were blatant.

He gripped my shoulders. "There's been an accident. We need to go to the hospital."

"The-the hospital?" I repeated, unable to grasp what he meant, even though I had heard what he said.

"It's Richard and Brad." His voice shook. "It's bad, Katy. We have to go now."

My breath stuttered.

"Now," he repeated.

~

I shivered, unable to get warm. Graham frowned and pulled off his cardigan, draping it around my shoulders. I pushed my hair off my face, trying to gather my thoughts. I barely remembered the drive to the hospital. Laura stayed with the girls until Mrs. Thomas came home. Graham remained calm, taking control when we arrived at the hospital, speaking with the nurses at the desk, who directed us to the waiting room. We were still waiting to see a doctor.

"How long have we been here?"

"About an hour, Katy," he soothed. "The doctors are working on them."

The hurried click of heels on the floor caught my attention, and I glanced in the direction of the sound. Jenna and Laura were approaching, Adrian following behind them.

I met Laura's eyes. She reached out and pulled me in for a hug.

"Mrs. Thomas is at the house with the girls. She said she will handle everything, and you be here for Richard," she murmured. "Oh, Katy," she added when a sob escaped my throat.

"I'm going crazy," I replied. "No one has come to talk to us."

"They will."

Just then, a doctor appeared around the corner.

"Mr. Gavin?" he called.

Graham stepped forward. "That's me."

"I'm Dr. Davenport. I finished assessing Brad. He has a concussion, a broken arm, cracked ribs, and there are a lot of contusions and cuts from the glass. We're stitching him up, and we'll keep him overnight for observation. Luckily, his arm won't require surgery, but he'll be pretty sore for the next while." He drew in a long breath and smiled. "He was lucky. Given how many times the car flipped, he escaped serious injuries. With time, he should heal fine. Once he is done and moved to a room, you can see him."

There was a collective sigh of relief from everyone except me. My voice cracked as I spoke.

"My husband? Richard VanRyan?"

Dr. Davenport's eyes were sympathetic as he regarded me. "He is the gentleman who was in the car with Brad?"

"Yes."

"He's still being assessed by the trauma team." He paused. "That side of the car took the brunt of the accident. It was hit directly."

I whimpered, grasping Laura's hand. Graham wrapped his arm around my waist, holding me upright.

"We have the best neurologist and orthopedic specialists with him right now. He's in good hands. In fact, I'm going in to assist. One of us will be out as soon as possible to update you."

I couldn't talk. I heard Graham's voice speaking to the doctor, but I had no idea what words he uttered. I allowed myself to be led to the chairs, and Graham gently pushed me into one of the hard seats. He kneeled in front of me.

"Katy, we're here. Richard is being examined. You need to stay calm."

Tears clouded my eyes, panic gripping my chest. The lights around me were too bright, the noises of the busy hospital too loud. I struggled to take in a deep breath.

Graham grasped my hands. "Breathe, Katy. With me. You can do this. Focus."

I shut my eyes and concentrated on getting the air into my lungs. The movement became easier, and I felt the panic ebb somewhat. I gathered my strength and opened my eyes.

"Graham," I whispered. "What-what if…" I couldn't say the words. All my brain could focus on were those words. *That side of the car took the brunt.*

The brunt. He was seriously hurt. My Richard.

Oh God, how hurt? Was he dying?

Not Richard. He couldn't be taken from me. It was too soon. We hadn't had enough time together. We needed decades more time. Our girls needed him. My breathing picked up again, coming out in short pants.

Graham cupped my cheeks, his touch firm. "No, Katy. Don't even think that way. He is Richard *fucking* VanRyan. He's a fighter and the most stubborn man I have ever met. A car accident is not going to stop him. They are going to assess him and fix him. In fact, he'll wake up and tell them how to do it properly, knowing him."

A laughing sob escaped my mouth. "I have to see him. He needs me, Graham."

"Let the doctors do their job, Katy. As soon as we can, we'll get you to him. I promise. Okay?"

I met his eyes. His worried, understanding, pain-filled eyes.

"Be the strong woman Richard knows you are. For him."

I nodded. "I'll try."

~

A doctor appeared a short time later, his face grave. After introducing himself as Dr. Fletcher and stating he was a neuro-surgeon, he asked if I wanted privacy before speaking with me.

"No," I insisted. "You can say whatever you need to in front of Graham and Laura. They're our family."

He crossed his arms. I noticed the smears of blood on his scrubs, and my anxiety increased.

Was that Richard's blood?

"I'll make this as brief as I can. After getting the results of the CT scan, I can see your husband has sustained a severe lumbar spine injury, from L3 to L5."

"What-what does that mean?"

"He requires decompression surgery—immediately. We need to stop the bleeding into the spinal canal." He drew in a deep breath. "The compression of the spinal cord is causing paralysis."

I heard the shocked inhale of air beside me. I blinked at the term, unable to speak. Graham cleared his throat.

"Is that a temporary condition?"

Dr. Fletcher shook his head. "That is unknown at this time."

His words echoed in my head.

Paralysis.

"Is he awake?" I asked, desperate. "Can I see him before surgery?"

"No, he is unconscious. He has sustained other injuries, Mrs. VanRyan. There are broken ribs, lacerations, and contusions—" he paused "—and head trauma. His brain was swelling, and we had to take steps to stop it. We felt it best to induce a coma to give him the strongest chance."

"The best chance to stop the swelling?" I asked, my voice quavering.

"The best chance to survive," he replied.

My legs began to shake. Graham wrapped his arm around my waist again, once more offering his silent strength.

"What are his chances?" he asked, his voice tight.

Dr. Fletcher dragged in a long breath and scrubbed his face. "He is young, strong, with no other medical issues. His body will heal from the bruises and cuts. We need to get in there as fast as possible and relieve the pressure on his spine in order to give him the chance to recover from the trauma."

"*Will* he recover?" I asked, my voice barely audible.

He met my gaze. "There are no guarantees, but I'll do everything in my power to make sure of it, Mrs. VanRyan."

Laura spoke up. "Is there anything else you can tell us?"

Dr. Fletcher didn't answer her directly. "Let's get him through the surgery first. That is my one goal today. To keep him alive. His recovery will depend on what we find when we go in. I'll know more after that."

"Please," I said. "Please, can I see him?" I begged.

He hesitated. "All right—for a moment. I need him in the OR, Mrs. VanRyan."

A moment.

I would take whatever they gave me.

I stepped beside Richard's bed, my legs trembling, tears clouding my eyes. I signed the forms where the doctor indicated, anxious to get to Richard. The doctor had explained how much machinery Richard was hooked up to and warned me not to panic. *It's all there to help him, Mrs. VanRyan. The machines are doing the job his body can't do right now.*

I thought I was prepared, but I wasn't.

The room buzzed with activity, the entire team focused on getting Richard upstairs to the OR. I knew I had mere seconds before they whisked him away. I stepped forward, laying my hand on his forearm— one of the few areas not covered in wires or bandages. He was cool to the touch…and unresponsive. I stared at him, the tears streaming down my cheeks. His handsome face was a mass of bruises, barely recognizable with the swelling. A jagged cut stretched horizontally over his left eyebrow and disappeared into his hair that had been shaved. A breathing tube was in his mouth, taped across his lower face, and I could see more cuts under the white gauze. Everywhere I looked, there was trauma to him. Cuts, bruises, swelling, and bandages. Machines buzzed and whirred. Bags of blood and saline dripped into his veins, keeping him alive. He was pale and still—that fact unnerving since Richard was never still. I tried to focus on him, not the grisly sight of the room around me that told the story of how hard they had worked at keeping him alive.

"We need to take him, Mrs. VanRyan," a nurse informed me, her voice laced with sympathy.

I leaned as close as I could to him, my voice quivering.

"*Fight*, my darling. Come back to me. To us. We need you." My voice caught. "I love you, Richard, and I'm not ready to let you go. You can do this. *You can do anything.*"

The medical team stepped forward, and I clasped his hand in mine, careful not to press too hard with the cuts and bruises forming on his knuckles. "Please," I whispered, choking. "Come back to me. I'll be waiting right here." I rose on my toes and kissed his cheek, my tears dripping and mingling with the streaks of blood on his face.

They wheeled him out of the room. I followed as long as I could, silently weeping as the doors swung shut in front of me.

"Please," I prayed. "*Oh God, please.*"

"Katy."

I turned to Graham and Laura. They were distraught and pale. Laura held out her arms, and I went to her, sobbing on her shoulder, praying in my head.

"*Bring him back to me. No matter what else, please, God, let him live.*"

7

KATY

Time in a hospital waiting room ceased to exist. It could have been hours or days that I had been waiting. The pumped-in, recirculated air was stagnant and carried the medicinal smell I couldn't get out of my nose. The molded plastic chairs were uncomfortable and cold, the linoleum worn from miles of endless pacing as people waited to receive news of their loved ones. The vending machines hissed and groaned, spitting out undrinkable coffee and lukewarm cans of ginger ale or juice. The dull thud as a bottle of water rolled into the dispenser was almost constant since the room temperature was stifling.

Yet, despite the heat, I was freezing. Even with the sweater Jenna insisted on buying me in the gift shop and slipped over my shoulders, I shivered constantly, tremors running down my spine.

From fear or cold, I wasn't sure.

I kept praying. Begging God not to take Richard from me. From his girls. I couldn't imagine life for Gracie without the father she adored. Heather never knowing Richard and growing up without his love. My life without Richard.

It was unthinkable.

Adrian returned to the office to help Adam. Graham, Laura, and

Jenna stayed close. They murmured reassurances about Richard's strength. His determination and stubbornness. They insisted over and again that he would pull through and be fine. Recover and come home to heal.

I wasn't sure if it was me or themselves they were trying to convince.

All around me were families, like me, waiting for news. I watched relieved parents being led to the recovery room. Devastated spouses collapsing onto the hard chairs, overcome with grief.

Which person would I be? My chest constricted, pain lancing through me.

How would I cope without Richard?

I could hardly remember life before him. Briefly, I recalled working as his assistant and despising him, but then agreeing to his insane plan of a fake marriage to land a job with Graham. Slowly, we discovered each other, and I saw the real person he kept hidden. The one so capable of love that he surrounded me with it. He surrounded me with him. Despite our rocky start and the circumstances of our beginning, Richard had become the nucleus of my world. The center of the family we had created together.

Without him, we didn't work.

An anguished sob from across the room caused fear to ripple down my back at the sound of the woman's pain.

That can't be me.

Fight, Richard. Fight, my darling.

I bowed my head and prayed more.

Dr. Fletcher walked through the door, exhaustion written on his face. He pulled off his surgical cap and ran a hand through his hair. Graham, Laura, Jenna, and I all stood as a unit when he approached. Laura wrapped her hand around mine, her grip tight. She had been a rock for me the entire time, refusing to be anything except positive.

I tried to read Dr. Fletcher's face. I had no clue what he was going to tell me, but his expression was grave. My stomach clenched, and I had to reach for Graham's hand as well to stop from falling.

Dr. Fletcher stopped in front of me. "He pulled through," he stated simply.

Hot tears spilled down my face.

"He isn't out of the woods yet," he cautioned. "There was a lot of damage. He took a substantial blow to his spine and his head."

I could only nod, unable to speak. Richard was still alive. He was still here—fighting.

"He'll be in a special ICU and closely monitored once he leaves recovery. In the best-case scenario, he has a long road to recovery. After ICU, there will be acute care at first, then once he is stable, he will be moved to rehab. And all this depends on how his brain is affected. We won't know anything until he wakes up."

"Is he still paralyzed?" Graham asked quietly.

"Yes. It will take time for his spine to heal. The progression will be very slow."

"But he will recover?" I asked.

Dr. Fletcher met my eyes. His gaze was kind, and his tone was frank. "I won't sugarcoat this, Mrs. VanRyan. I don't know if he'll walk again. It will depend on how he heals and the effort he puts into recovery. Your husband suffered a massive thoracolumbar spine injury. It impacts all sensory and motor function of the lower back and spine. Surgically, we've done all we could. Now we have to wait and hope for the best."

I cleared my throat, swallowing the lump that kept forming. "You said the best-case scenario..." My voice trailed off, unable to complete the sentence.

Dr. Fletcher was blunt. "Your husband may not wake up. Or he might wake up but never recover the use of his legs."

A violent tremor went through me.

"Or he may recover some use, but never walk without some form of assistance. There could be lingering aftereffects on his brain." Dr.

Fletcher explained. "As I said, until he wakes, there are a lot of unanswered questions."

"He will wake up," I insisted. "I know he will."

He allowed a smile to cross his serious countenance. "Keep up the positive thoughts. He's going to need them."

"Can I see him?"

"Once he's moved from recovery, and only for a brief time. It may be a while before you can get in. I must insist on one person at a time and limit the number of people. Family only."

"These people are our family."

"Fine. There's a quieter waiting room closer to the unit you can go to. I'll have someone escort you," he stated. "I'll be checking on him frequently. If there's any change, I'll let you know."

He turned and walked away, pausing when Graham followed him and spoke in a low voice. The doctor listened, his gaze flickering to mine before he replied to Graham. Laura led me back to the chairs and sat beside me, while Jenna flanked my other side.

Graham and Dr. Fletcher shook hands, and Graham returned to us.

"Richard will have the best care. Anything he needs will be made available to him. Once he is out of recovery and ICU, I'll make sure he has a private room."

"Thank you."

He hunched down, close to eye level. "Richard has a long road of recovery ahead of him, Katy. He is going to need you more than he has ever needed you before. You have to take care of yourself." He paused, looking at Laura, who tilted her chin imperceptibly. "We will take the girls to our house and look after them tomorrow. I spoke with Mrs. Thomas and arranged for her to help. We'll figure out a schedule, but the girls need to see you as well. You are important too."

I had no idea when he had made all these plans, but being Graham, it didn't surprise me that he would be thinking ahead. He and Richard were similar in that way.

"Yes, of course. But I-I can't leave him alone—"

Graham held up his hand, interrupting me. "All I am saying is you can't spend every minute of the day here. We'll help you all we can, Katy. With the girls, making sure Richard isn't alone. Anything you need. But I have to insist—"

I pushed down the flash of anger at his words—I knew he was trying to help, but I was not leaving Richard. Not for anything or anyone—even our girls. Simply the thought of doing so caused panic to seize my chest, and the words tumbled out fast and jumbled. "I am not leaving him now. *I can't.* He needs me to be here when he wakes. I need to be with him."

"Of course not," he soothed. "You can stay here. We'll keep the girls —they've stayed with us before. Once Richard wakes up—*and he will wake up*—you can come and go as you need. We'll tell Gracie that Mommy and Daddy took a little trip and we're having a long sleep-over. You can call them so they hear your voice."

Laura nodded, interjecting softly, "The girls need you too, Katy."

I knew she was right, except it didn't sway my decision. My voice shook. "Gracie will want to talk to Daddy."

"You can distract her. When he wakes, he'll want to talk to her too."

"What if-what if…"

"Don't say it," Graham said firmly. "Don't even *think* it. He's going to wake up, and he's going to be fine."

I had to say the words out loud before they overtook every other thought in my head. "And if he's not? What if the surgery wasn't successful?"

"Will you love him any less if he can't walk? Or speak as clearly?"

"No," I replied immediately. "All I want is him to be with us. That's all that matters."

"Exactly. He'll rebuild his life." He grabbed my hands. "We're going to get through this, Katy."

I met his eyes, startled by the film of tears in them.

"We have to get through this," he added. "Your girls need you. Richard would want you to make them a priority."

I had no response to offer. I knew he was right, but for now, I had to stay.

My heart ached, desperate for the one thing it needed above all else. And that one thing was fighting for his life somewhere in this hospital. I had to be close.

"I'm staying here," I announced. "Until I know what is happening, I am staying right here."

I stood, suddenly unable to sit anymore. I began to pace, adding my own footsteps to the miles that had been trod on this floor before me.

Until they took me to Richard, this was the only way I could cope.

~

The waiting room upstairs was much quieter. Laura and Jenna left to go see the girls and get a few things for me. Mrs. Thomas insisted the girls stay overnight in their own home, stating she could be with them for a few days without issue.

"They will be happier surrounded by their own things and their routine," *she insisted when I spoke with her. "I'll be praying for Richard, Katy. For all* *of you. I'll take care of your girls. You take care of him."*

Her barely concealed distress tipped me over the edge, and I shut myself in the washroom and fought through a panic attack, begging and pleading with God for another miracle and for the strength to get through this for him. Richard got through the surgery—now I needed him to come back to me.

In whatever state he could.

Together, we would handle it. The other option was unthinkable.

Graham sat, his fingers flying over his phone, constantly checking on me. I kept pacing, grateful for the quiet in the room. At present, we were the only two people and I went around the space in a constant motion. His phone rang, and he answered it, speaking low.

He stood and cleared his throat. "I, ah, need to go check on Brad, Katy. He's awake."

"Of course," I replied, feeling badly I had forgotten about Brad in all of this. "I'll be fine, Graham."

"I won't be long. I'm sure he isn't up for much of a visit."

"Take as much time as you need. I'll be here."

He squeezed my shoulder and dropped a kiss on my forehead. "I'll be right back."

I watched him walk away and dropped into a chair, feeling exhausted. I slipped my phone from my pocket and opened my photos. Screen after screen of Richard, Gracie, and Heather flipped by. I paused at one picture, my thumb hovering over the swipe key.

I had taken it of Richard one night by the pool. The sun was setting, casting a burnished glow to the snapshot. He was looking right at me, his sharp jaw softened by the scruff I liked, his head tilted as he looked at me. His intense hazel eyes were focused on me holding my phone, a smile playing on his full lips. He held a glass of wine loosely in his hand, while he stroked his bottom lip with one long finger. Bare-chested, his skin still glistening from his swim, and his hair swept off his face, he was stunning in the muted light, his love for me evident. It was one of my favorite pictures of him.

After I took the picture, he had smirked, curling one side of his mouth higher than the other.

"Put the damn phone down, sweetheart, and get over here. The girls are asleep, and I want you on my lap."

I had acted coy. "Whatever for?"

He reached over, pulling me from my chair. "Get over here and sit that sweet ass on my knee. We'll talk about whatever pops up."

I had laughed at him until he kissed me. Deep, passionate, and filled with need. So perfect.

So Richard.

Would he ever kiss me like that again?

"Mrs. VanRyan."

I glanced up, startled.

"You can come in for a quick visit."

I scrambled to my feet and followed the nurse. She introduced herself as Carol and explained she would be Richard's night nurse. "He is right across from the desk. He won't be alone at all."

"He isn't in a room?"

She shook her head. "We're a special unit. Limited beds, with a high ratio of nurses to patients. Sort of like neonatal for adults." She smiled kindly at me. "Dr. Fletcher is one of the best. If someone I loved needed surgery, I'd want him." She stopped at the end of a bed. "Here he is."

My heart faltered at the sight of my husband. Hooked up to even more machines, he was silent and still except for the constant expansion and collapse of his chest as they pumped oxygen into him. I stepped forward, my hands fluttering, unsure and anxious.

"Can I-can I touch him?"

"Carefully, yes. Don't disturb the machines. But yes, touch him. Talk to him. Let him know you're close. I strongly believe the patient can sense when a loved one is with them."

I leaned over him, gently stroking his cheek. They had cleaned him up, the blood gone, the cuts covered or disinfected, the bruises standing out against his pallor. Richard was always so full of life, his skin healthy and vibrant. Seeing him this way was painful. I lifted one of his hands, the only thing free from monitors, needles, or patches and kissed his knuckles.

"Where is his wedding ring?" He never took it off.

"It had to be removed for surgery. There's a bag of his personal things behind the desk. I'll get it for you."

She returned in a moment and slid a plastic bag under his bed. She slipped his ring into my hand. "They had to cut it off because his hand was swollen. You'll need to have it repaired."

I looked down at the damaged ring, my heart plummeting. It was symbolic. Richard always wore it and at times was sentimental about how the circle was like his love—no beginning and no ending. Now it was broken—just like him.

I leaned close again, cupping his cheek. "I'm here, my darling. You did so well. You made it through the tough part, and I know you're tired. Sleep for a while and when you're ready, I'll be here when you wake up. We'll face the future together." A tear splashed onto my hand. "Do you hear me, Richard? Together, no matter what. Just promise me you'll wake up."

I lowered my head to the pillow and turned my face close to his.

There were none of his low wheezes, or the quiet, raspy breathing I was used to. Instead, the sound of the machines pumped and clicked.

Because he wasn't sleeping. He was fighting for his life.

"Please, my darling, wake up."

I buried my face into the pillow and wept.

8

KATY

The next couple of days passed in a monotony of repeated moments. Richard was monitored closely, his vitals checked, tests done, Dr Fletcher coming and going. I got to know the team of hardworking, dedicated nurses. I came and went, staying longer than I was supposed to, but they turned a blind eye to the fact that I stood beside Richard's bed, holding his hand and talking for hours on end. I stepped out of the way when needed, but otherwise, I was by his side.

Graham and Laura were allowed in briefly, both of them insisting on my taking a quick break. Graham had arranged a place for me to shower and change, and I called Gracie every time. Mrs. Thomas stayed with the girls when Graham and Laura were here, or Jenna stepped in if needed. It was a great comfort to know the girls were well looked after.

"When you home, Mommy?"

"Soon, baby."

"Is you and Daddy having fun?"

I had to clear my throat.

"Daddy is working, Gracie. Mommy is helping him."

"Daddy yikes that. But me miss you."

A tear ran down my cheek. "We both miss you."

"I talk to Daddy?"

"Not right now," I replied, my voice getting thicker. *"Soon. Put Mrs. Thomas on the phone, okay?"*

"Okay. I lubs you!"

"I love you too, baby girl."

Each call got a little harder. Gracie loved Richard, and he always spoke to her when he was away, so convincing her he was too busy to talk was difficult.

Time passed slowly, yet there was comfort in the dullness of it.

It meant Richard was still fighting.

Dr. Fletcher, or Alan, as he insisted on my calling him, appeared by the end of the bed, smiling kindly.

"Katy."

"Hello, Alan."

He checked Richard's chart and folded his arms over his chest, holding the tablet.

"He's stable. His vitals are holding. The swelling in his brain is going down. All good signs."

I clutched Richard's hand a little tighter.

"I'm transferring him to acute care. He'll still be monitored closely, but he'll have his own room. There is a far more comfortable chair where you can sleep instead of on the floor." He winked, having caught me napping beside Richard's bed, leaning against the rails while still clutching his hand.

"Okay," I breathed.

"We're going to wean him off the medication keeping him in the coma. It will take him a few days to wake up, and once he does, we'll know what we are dealing with. His scans are good, though, and I am hopeful."

I could barely nod, my throat constricted and tight.

He stepped forward. "If things go as I hoped, once he wakes up and heals, Katy, he has a long road ahead of him. Everything from the waist down has been affected. He'll have a great deal of muscle loss.

There will be therapy for gait training and strength. He'll need leg exercises, pool therapy, various other machines. He won't be able to do stairs, so he'll need a bedroom on ground level or an elevator."

"I understand," I managed.

"There could be other issues too."

"Other issues?"

"Psychosocial factors. Many patients experience depression, anxiety, even anger. Mood swings are common. They often require counseling, plus medication. Their entire life has changed, and they can't cope on their own, even if they have a good support system at home." He paused. "Their injuries affect not only them, but everyone around them. Nothing is the same when they wake up. It is exceedingly hard for them to grasp."

"He'll get everything he needs. I'll make sure of it."

He smiled. "I can see that, Katy. You're an amazing partner for Richard. But you have to look after yourself as well. You need to be strong physically and mentally for his recovery. No more sleeping on the floor or neglecting yourself. I want you to eat and sleep. Exercise. Go see your little girls. You aren't being selfish doing so—you are actually helping Richard."

His words made sense, even if they made me feel a little panic. I grasped at the chain around my neck that kept Richard's ring close to my heart. The crack was taped so I didn't lose it, but I couldn't bear to part with it, even for a couple of days. I would have it fixed when he woke up. "I hate leaving him."

"Of course you do. That is natural. On the ward he's being transferred to, he can have visitors. Not a lot and not all at once, but we can relax a little, and they can stay with him while you go home. He is going to be in here for a while."

He patted my shoulder, his expression kind. "You obviously have a strong bond with your husband, Katy. He's going to need that bond. He will have to rely on you in ways neither of you planned for a while. It's not going to be easy, but together, you can do it."

"Is there someone I can talk to about his needs for when he comes home? So I can get things in motion and be ready?"

"That's what I want to see—looking ahead and positive. Yes, I will have Gloria come to see you. She'll come to your house and do an assessment. You can meet with our physio team. Once a couple of these machines are gone, Colin will come by and show you some simple movements you can do on Richard to help keep his muscles from total atrophy. Colin is the head of my physio team and the best."

"All right."

He glanced at his watch. "We'll be moving Richard in a couple of hours. We'll need some time to settle him and get him stable, and a few medical items need to be taken care of that I won't get into with you. The ward is on the fourth floor, and there is a private waiting room. A nurse will come and get you when he is done. Why don't you go shower, eat, and try to relax?"

"You-you want me to leave now?"

"He's in good hands, Katy. Remember what I told you about looking after you. We have your phone number, and you're a minute away if we need you. Do this for Richard. He would want you to. Let us do what we need to do, and when you see him next, he'll be more comfortable."

I inhaled long and hard, then swallowed. I reached for my bag. "Okay."

He nodded in encouragement. "Good."

I sat, staring at the cold cup of coffee in front of me. My half-eaten sandwich was pushed aside. It tasted like dust, and I had no appetite. Despite what Alan had advised, I couldn't eat. I would try later. Alan's words kept running through my head. Richard's recovery —the difficulties we faced. The way our life together would change. Everything I knew, everything that was *us*, wouldn't exist anymore. At least not right away—in fact, perhaps never.

It depended on what happened when Richard woke up. If his mind was affected. If he was still Richard—or an altered version of the man I loved.

I rubbed a weary hand over my face, one thing certain in my mind. Whatever happened, whatever the result was, I still loved him. I would always love him, and somehow, we would find our way through all of this together.

I had texted Graham and Laura to let them know Richard was being moved and that I would send the information as soon as I had it. They responded with encouraging words and promises of being at the hospital later that day. Laura attached a picture of Gracie in the pool, splashing and having a good time. Beside her was Graham, holding Heather protectively, swishing her little feet in the water. She loved it when Richard did that with her. The delight on her face made the picture swim before my eyes as I wondered if he would ever be able to do so again.

A deep voice and a hand settling on my shoulder startled me from my thoughts.

"Katy."

I looked up, shocked.

Beside me was Maddox Riley. Co-owner of BAM and, aside from Graham, Richard's closest friend. They had struck up a relationship when BAM hired The Gavin Group as their marketing company, and it had grown and developed into a solid friendship. Maddox was tall, lean, and despite his young age, completely silver-gray. His warm blue eyes met mine, his gaze filled with worry.

I blinked, unsure he was real. I knew Graham had let them know what had happened, but I hadn't expected to see him. The surprise somehow tipped me over the edge, and with a gasp, I stood, flinging myself into his arms. I sobbed into his chest as he wrapped me up, holding me close.

"Hey, hey, shh," he soothed. "It's okay, Katy. It's going to be okay."

He didn't move or try to stop my tears. He held me and let me cry it out. When I managed to calm myself down, I pulled back and met his sympathetic gaze.

"Sorry," I sniffled.

In true Maddox fashion, he winked and wiped my cheeks. "Usually women don't cry until they've spent a little time with me. It's not often it's on first sight."

A smile pulled at my mouth. "What are you doing here?"

He sat down and tugged me into the chair beside him. He pulled some napkins from the dispenser and handed them to me.

"I've been here for two days, Katy. Graham let me know they were moving Richard and you were finally off the floor."

I blew my nose and gaped at him. "Two days? Why didn't I know?"

"Because I didn't want to interrupt or worry you. Graham has been keeping me abreast of the situation." He studied me. "Did you really think I wouldn't be here for him? For you? After what he did when I was lying unconscious in the hospital?"

I sighed, the sound long and shaky. "I haven't been thinking clearly, Maddox."

He reached out and clasped my hand. "I know. I had to come, though. As soon as we heard the news, Dee wanted to book me a ticket, but I waited a couple of days until I couldn't stay away anymore."

"Thank you."

He glanced at the table then back at me with a scowl. "You aren't taking care of yourself, Katy. You need to be strong."

A ripple of anger went through me, but once again, I pushed it down. However, it showed in my voice when I responded, the tone clipped.

"I'm trying."

He frowned.

"I know you are. But you've lost weight, and it's obvious you're not sleeping. You look like shit."

I regarded him, trying not to bristle at his bluntness.

"I imagine this is usually when the crying comes in for most women with you? Have you considered hiring yourself out for motivational talks?" I asked, hearing the snark in my voice, even though I knew he was right.

"I'm stating the facts." He stood. "If you won't look after yourself, I'll have to do it." He held out his hand. "Come with me."

Confused, I stood and accepted his hand. He pulled me along, and we took the elevator down. At the front door of the hospital, I hung back. "Where are you taking me?"

"There's a great little diner two minutes away. I've spent a lot of time there the past couple of days. You're going to eat something. We'll come back, you can see Richard, and I'm taking you to Graham's so you can see your girls and sleep."

"I'm not leaving." I shook off his hand and crossed my arms.

"Yeah, you are."

"You don't get to come in here and tell me what to do," I snapped.

My anger didn't faze him. "We can stand here and argue, but you're still coming with me. Even if I have to put you over my shoulder."

"You wouldn't dare," I hissed.

"You want to try me?" he challenged. "I'm doing this because you need to eat. You need a break from here."

"But—"

He glared down at me. "No, Katy. It will take days before he wakes up. You can't sit there and wait."

"Dee did for you," I shot back.

His expression softened at the mention of his wife.

"She did, except she didn't have two little girls who need to see their mommy. And she told me how good it felt when Richard gave her a break and she could decompress for a while and clear her head. I'm returning the favor, so stop disagreeing and come with me. The longer you argue, the longer you're gone."

I knew he was right and my anger waned, but still, I hesitated.

"Once we eat, you can check on him, and Graham will pick you up and take you to their place. You can be with the girls for a while, and I'll stay with Richard. Now he is out of ICU, the rules are a little easier. We'll make a schedule, and you are getting out of here. Richard would be furious if he saw you and knew I didn't step in. So be quiet and come eat a damn bowl of soup." He speared a hand through his hair. "I don't want Richard's main priority to be kicking my ass for not looking after his wife when he wakes up, all right?"

I gave in, seeing how upset he was. "All right."

He grabbed my hand again. "Let's go."

❧

The soup was delicious. Maddox watched me eat, insisting on a grilled cheese sandwich with the soup. He inhaled two bowls as I slowly made my way through my meal, knowing he would be upset if I didn't eat.

His presence was comforting. He knew Richard so well. Despite the miles between them, they spoke almost daily, texted all the time, and had video chats with each other. Gracie often got in on the action —she loved "Unca Mattog" as she called him. His nickname "Mad Dog" was too difficult to say with her lisp, and he loved her spin on it.

"Have you seen the girls?"

He nodded. "This morning. Who do you think took the picture of Graham with Heather in the pool?"

I had to smile. "I didn't think of that. Laura was in the pool with Gracie. I guess I assumed Jenna was there."

"No, I went to visit. I was there when you texted Graham and gave him the news. I came straight here. I saw Carol at the desk, and she told me you were down here."

I was dumbfounded. "You know Carol?"

He smirked. "I know them all, Katy. I asked them not to say I was around because I didn't want to tear you from Richard. But I've been close. They let me peek in on occasion."

Tears threatened again at his words. I clasped his hand and squeezed, incapable of words. What could I say that would be adequate? Thank you wasn't enough, although I knew Maddox didn't want thanks. He was here because of the strength of his relationship with Richard.

"Where have you been otherwise?"

"Here for the most part. I work, eat, go check on you, come back, work some more. Eat. I think I've gained five pounds. Their pie is stellar. In fact, you need a piece."

I opened my mouth to argue, but his look silenced me. He waved to the waitress and ordered us coffee and pie, waited until they arrived, and lifted his cup.

"Tell me what the doctor said."

9

KATY

As he promised, Maddox didn't keep me from the hospital for long. We returned as soon as I got a message saying Richard had been moved. Maddox followed me into his new room, a silent companion, there to support me.

I went directly to the side of the bed. There were still machines whirring and beeping away, but there were fewer of them. Richard had obviously been given a sponge bath, his hair damp around his ears where they had wiped with the wet cloth. The room was large and bright with two comfortable-looking chairs and even a small sofa. The usual kind of hospital bathroom was in the corner, and the walls the same green, but it was private and had a window that looked over the street.

I cupped Richard's cheek. "Hello, my darling. I was gone for a while, but I'm back. You look so much better. And look who I found!"

Maddox stood at the end of the bed, his hands wrapped around the metal frame.

"Hey, Richard," he stated easily, although I saw the stress around his eyes. "Don't be jealous, but I took your pretty wife for lunch. I thought she needed the break. You're a little boring these days. I think you need to wake up and talk." He moved closer and patted Richard's leg. "Honestly, Richard, I get hit by a car and end up in a coma, so you have to outdo me? Your car flipped four times and took out a bunch of signs, causing total havoc and congestion. Talk about attention-grabber. Yeesh. I would have come for a visit if you asked. No need for all the dramatics."

I didn't hide my grin. I knew that was how they were with each other. Constant teasing and back-and-forth was their way of showing they cared. The fact that Maddox was here said it all—I knew how much it would mean to Richard.

"So, listen, buddy, here's the plan. You and I are gonna hang together while Katy goes and sees your girls and gets a little sleep. Any objections?" He paused as if waiting for a response. "Good. I thought so. We can catch up and banter around a few campaign ideas I had. You're gonna love them. Might even learn a thing or two. At least I'll be able to speak my mind—you won't be too busy telling me to shut up to listen to my brilliance."

He met my gaze with a wink.

"Graham will be here soon. Go with him, Katy. I'll be with Richard, then Jenna is going to take a turn. Richard will *love* that."

I couldn't help the smile that curled my lips. Jenna and Richard were like siblings, constantly squabbling. She talked a great deal and called him on his shit, and he pretended to only put up with her, when in fact, he adored her—most of the time.

"I'll come to get you this evening. You can stay with him tonight, and by tomorrow, we'll have a schedule set up."

Before I could protest, he held up his hand. "You have to get the house ready for him coming home, Katy. You'll have meetings and appointments to handle. Details. Your girls need you. Stop being difficult. Let us help."

"I-I don't know if I can do it all," I confessed.

"You will," he insisted. "I'm not leaving until he's awake. I'll help you with it all. We all will. Let us do what we know Richard would want us to do. Please."

"All right," I relented. "Thank you."

"Thank me by going and getting some sleep. Cuddle your girls.

Bring Richard some Gracie artwork to hang on these walls. That, I know he would really love."

The thought of seeing the girls tugged at my chest. Maddox was right. I had to do this. It could be days before Richard woke, and it wouldn't be instantaneous when he did.

I bent low and kissed Richard's cheek. "I'm going to see our girls. I'll be back soon. Don't give Maddox a hard time."

Maddox hugged me, shooing me out the door. He returned to Richard's side. "You heard her. Now about those campaigns you sent me. I want to change the colors. I was thinking fuchsia and orange would be a striking combination." He winked at me.

I was smiling as I went to the elevator.

Richard was in good hands with his friend.

My smile slipped as I thought about the girls. Gracie would want to know where Daddy was. I had to tell her—at least as close to the truth as I could.

I still had to figure out how.

~

Graham brought me up to speed while he drove me to his house, assuring me that Gracie knew Daddy wasn't with me.

"I have to tell her something, Graham."

"Yes, you do. But this will give you a few moments to settle before you do. Laura is holding off on Heather's bottle. She thought you might like that time with her."

"Thank you."

He cleared his throat. "Ah, Katy, Brad is at the house for a few days. Laura's sister, Barb, is there as well."

"All right. I'll try not to bother him. How is he doing?"

"He's recovering. I need to tell you he is very worried about you being there."

"Why?"

"He thinks you will hold him responsible for the accident. That it's his fault Richard is in the hospital. God knows the boy is heaping guilt on himself every day."

I gasped and turned in my seat to face him fully. "The man driving was drunk, Graham. He was speeding and blew through the red light." We had found out he had hit three other cars—glancing off the back bumpers and sideswiping them, his speed increasing before plowing into the side of Brad's vehicle. "How on earth is that Brad's fault?"

"He has somehow decided he should have reacted faster. If he had sped up or slowed down, the car would have been hit in a different place, and perhaps Richard wouldn't have been so severely injured."

"I'll talk to him, Graham. I don't hold him responsible. That poor boy."

He sighed. "Thanks, Katy. We'd all appreciate it. Maybe if he heard it from you, he could stop this needless blame on himself."

"I will. As soon as I see my girls."

He turned the car into their driveway. "I'm sure they're waiting."

Gracie was out the door as soon as the car stopped. I was smothered in Gracie hugs and kisses the moment I stepped out of the vehicle, catching her in my arms. She giggled and talked a mile a minute, the whole time patting my cheek, dropping little smooches on my mouth, cheeks, and nose and exclaiming in delight over the stuffed lamb I had seen in the gift shop and brought to her.

I carried her inside, setting her on her feet so she could show Laura her lamb, and I took Heather from Laura's waiting arms. The feel of my baby snuggled into my chest made tears sting my eyes, and I had to bow my head to hide them from Gracie. Still a baby herself, she was still too perceptive not to notice.

"Why you cry, Mommy?"

"I missed you," I sniffed.

She looked confused. "I was wight hewe."

I forced a smile, brushing away the wetness under my eyes. "I know. How silly of Mommy."

Laura cupped my cheek affectionately. "I have her bottle ready. Go upstairs with your girls, and I'll bring it. You have a little time with them."

"Thank you," I murmured, not trusting myself to say much else right now. My emotions were too raw. Laura, being Laura, understood.

"Of course, dear girl."

Upstairs, I settled in the nursery they had set up for all their grandkids. There always seemed to be a baby on the way or here, Laura would often say. I slipped the nipple into Heather's mouth, stroking her wispy hair and humming softly.

Gracie was busy on the rug in front of me introducing "Lambie" to all his new friends. She talked and asked questions as I fed Heather, burped, and changed her, then sat back in the rocker, holding her as she fell asleep. The soothing routine calmed me, and when Gracie looked up at me, the inevitable question falling from her lips, I was ready.

"When Daddy home?"

I stood and placed Heather into the crib, stroking her back. I sat down, patting my lap. "Come sit with Mommy."

She clambered up, peering up at me with such a serious expression, the resemblance to Richard was uncanny.

"Gracie, baby, Daddy won't be home for a while."

"Why come?"

I drew in a deep breath. "Daddy got hurt, and he has to be in the hospital for a while."

Tears filled her wide eyes. "Daddy hurt? Like a boo-boo? I tiss it betta, then he come home."

"I bet that would help a lot, but Daddy needs more than kisses. He has to sleep a lot and be quiet."

"But I miss him!" Her voice rose in a plaintive wail.

I wrapped her in my arms. "He misses you too, baby girl. He'll be home as soon as he can." I paused. "When he does, he will need lots of help to get him big and strong again. Could you help him with that?"

"Yes," she sniffled. "I wants him home now."

"Me too, but he has to stay. The doctor says so. Remember when you had a cough and the doctor said you had to stay in bed? You didn't like it, but you were a good girl and did it so you got better. Daddy has to do what the doctor says too."

"Oh," she huffed.

"He needs some pictures for his walls. Maybe we could color some, so when he wakes up he can see them. You know how much Daddy likes your pictures." Richard always referred to them as his Picassos. Scribbles of color on paper, really. Except to him they were treasures —especially when she managed a crude X in the corner for him.

"Otay." She wiped her nose with her sleeve, and I let it go. This wasn't the time for a lesson on manners.

"As soon as he isn't so sleepy, I can take you to see him," I promised.

"Soon?" she asked, her expression and the furrow between her brows so like Richard, my breath caught, and I had to pause before I replied.

"I hope so, baby girl. I hope so."

~

Gracie fell asleep on top of me. She had burst into tears again, and I held her tight, shushing and cooing at her, assuring her all was okay, and praying internally I wasn't lying to her, until she fell into an exhausted sleep. I tucked her into the bed in the room and stepped into the hall.

Brad was coming out of a door opposite and froze when he saw me. I had only met him once, but I saw the toll this had taken on him. His eyes were sunken, his hair flat, and there was a pallor to his skin. Like Richard, he was bruised, with cuts on his face and arms. A heavy cast covered his arm, and he was bent over from the pain no doubt caused by his ribs. His eyes darted everywhere, unable to meet mine.

I stepped closer. "Brad, how are you feeling?"

"Fine, Mrs. VanRyan. I'm fine." His reply was clipped, his voice belying the sharpness of his response. He was holding back tears. My heart went out to the young man who stood before me, lost and broken.

I stepped closer and laid a hand on his arm. "It's Katy. And I think you're fibbing to me."

"Wh-what?"

"You're not fine, and you're holding yourself accountable for something you couldn't control. Brad, the accident wasn't your fault."

He stared at my hand on his arm. "I was driving."

"*Your* car," I said. "You were driving your car and obeying the laws of the road. You weren't the one who got drunk, blew through a red light and hurt Richard."

He lifted his tormented eyes to mine. "You-you don't blame me?"

"No, and you need to stop blaming yourself. The man responsible for this is whom I hold accountable. Graham told me he died from his injuries, and now his family has to suffer with the result of his choices. We all do—you included. But you are *not* to blame, and I need you to stop beating yourself up."

His shoulders slumped, his head falling to his chest. Sobs ripped from his throat, and I gently wrapped my arms around him. He wept, his good arm gripping my waist. I let him cry, pure rage flooding my system—not trying to tamp down my feelings this time. I was furious at a stranger who made the foolish decision to drink away his disappointment at losing his job. Who downed a bottle of liquor in his car, then decided to head home in a drunken haze, and turned the lives of innocent people upside down. I was angry for his family, for the pain Brad felt, for the tears my daughter shed, and for myself.

Because his selfish act hadn't ended yet. I had no idea what the future held for Richard. If he would wake up. If he would walk again.

If he would come back to me.

I cursed the man who caused this as I held the young man so desperate to take the blame. Brad's tears soaked my shoulder, and he shook violently as he sobbed.

And I wept with him.

10

KATY

My anger didn't abate. It grew.

For six days, it simmered and twisted in my gut. Six days as I waited by my husband's bed for him to wake up. To open his hazel eyes and look at me. Smile. Frown. Groan. Anything.

The medical staff told me to be patient. To remain positive.

Both emotions were slowly draining from me.

For six days, he remained trapped in a world beyond me. Where I couldn't reach him. His chest fell and rose with his breathing. The full oxygen mask had been replaced by cannulas, his breathing tube gone. Thick stubble grew on his face, hiding some of the cuts. His bruises were changing, fading from black and blue to yellow and purple. His expression was peaceful, his body unmoving and unresponsive.

When we were alone, I wept, begging and pleading with him to wake up. When other people were around, I remained calm, locking down my emotions, putting on a strong, brave, positive face, saying he would wake soon. Be with us.

Still, he slept.

Inside, I despaired.

And burned.

~

"Mommy, I want Daddy!" Gracie demanded, her voice loud and whiny as I attempted to dress her.

"Daddy is sleeping," I retorted automatically. "Stay still, Gracie. Mommy can't get your pants on if you keep squirming."

"Wake him up!" she shrieked, thrashing her legs. "I wants him!"

I pulled her upright. "I can't!" I shrieked back. "Mommy can't! Stop asking me to do things I can't do!"

Her eyes widened, tears flooding them.

Instantly chagrined, I pulled her into my arms. "Mommy is sorry, Gracie. I didn't mean to yell."

She sobbed, her tears almost constant, it seemed, while I was around. She did better when she was with Laura or Mrs. Thomas. Maddox made her giggle. Graham made her smile. But it was as if she picked up on my despondency and anger and acted out when I came to see her.

Laura stepped into the room, smiling sadly in understanding.

"I can get her dressed."

"I'll do it," I snapped. "I'm perfectly capable of dressing my own daughter."

Laura's expression faltered, but her tone remained calm. "Of course." She slipped from the room before I could apologize.

I carried Gracie to the rocking chair and stroked her hair. "I'm sorry, baby."

She sniffled.

Guilt ate away at me. I tried hard to be strong, but it seemed I was failing completely. I was snapping at everyone. Resenting their constant interference. Telling me when to leave, when to eat, how to feel. Part of me knew they were all trying to help, except my patience was reaching its limits.

I didn't want to leave the hospital to sleep. I wasn't hungry, and I hated being forced to eat. I didn't care that there were people willing to forgo their own sleep and life to sit beside Richard so he wasn't alone. I wanted to be there when he woke up. I needed to be there.

Why couldn't they understand when I was away from him, I couldn't relax? No sleep came to me in those few hours I was gone. I threw up anything I tried to eat, my body rejecting even the lightest of meals.

I knew how hard they were all trying. That this small group of people, Graham, Laura, Jenna, Maddox, and even Brad, were all doing everything they could to help me. They had a schedule so I could take breaks, go for a walk, eat, shower, sleep. See my girls. They all were positive and helpful, ignoring my small outbursts and smiling in understanding.

I resented them all and hated myself for it, so I let the anger simmer inside, holding back the ugliness as much as I could, ashamed and shocked at my reaction.

I lifted Gracie's chin. "Sorry, baby. Mommy is tired."

She stared at me, her eyes sad. "Otay, Mommy. I go play?"

I slid her off my knee, shame burning in me for upsetting my child. "Yeah, baby. Jenna is going to take you and Heather to the park."

That made her happy. She loved the park. "Otay!" she repeated, this time in excitement.

She scooped up a couple of stuffed animals and ran for the door, her sadness forgotten.

I watched her go, wishing it were that easy for me.

I stroked Richard's cheek, scowling at the roughness of his skin. I reached for the tube of cream, gently rubbing it into his face.

I glanced at Maddox, impatience flooding my tone. "If you're going to force me to leave, the least you can do is make sure Richard is being looked after."

He was silent.

I picked up the lip balm and swiped it over Richard's lips, wiping away a little excess with my thumb.

"His lips are dry. I don't want them bleeding when he wakes up."

"I put some on a couple of hours ago, Katy," he stated mildly. "And

I don't force you to leave. You agreed it was best not to exhaust your-self. Although," he muttered, "I'm not sure it's doing anyone much good."

"What?" I snapped.

"Nothing." He sat back. "I heard Gracie asking for Richard again this morning."

"She asks for him every day. On every call, every time I go see her. It's the first thing she asks for."

"Maybe you should give her what she wants."

I gaped at him. "You want me to bring my toddler to see her father lying in a coma? Do you know what that would do to her to see him unresponsive?"

He shrugged. "Maybe if she saw him, and knew he was alive, she would settle. She would know you aren't lying and that he is really asleep." He shrugged. "Maybe he would hear her voice and respond."

"No."

"I think—"

I cut him off. "I don't care what you think, Maddox. The answer is no. It would be too traumatic for her."

He set aside his laptop and stood. "More traumatic than seeing her mother wasting away? To have her little life blown apart and not understand what is happening?"

My heart plummeted. "You're exaggerating."

"No, I'm not. You're not there at night when she sobs in her sleep, Katy. Crying out for her mommy and daddy. Weeps in my arms and can't settle until we walk with her while she cries herself to sleep. You're not there when Heather can't relax and fusses for hours on end, needing you."

I was stunned by his words.

"I think if Gracie saw him, it would help, not hurt. And I think you need to sort your priorities."

The anger, the bitterness I had been swallowing down exploded, and I lost it.

"*My priorities?* Stop telling me what to do!" I screamed, all rational thought gone. "I am sick of being told what to do and where to go! Leave me alone!"

"No."

I crossed the room and pushed at his chest. "I don't want to go see the girls." I pushed again. "I don't want to bring Gracie here. I'm tired of eating when I don't want to. I'm tired of taking your goddamn orders!"

He remained in place, his feet firmly planted on the linoleum. "Too bad."

"Fuck you, Maddox Riley! I'm not leaving this hospital again until my husband wakes up!"

"Yell all you want."

"Get out," I hissed. "Get out, go home, and leave us alone."

"Not happening."

I pummeled his chest, my fists hitting him in useless blows that did nothing except make me angrier.

He was unmovable.

"I want everyone gone! All of you!"

He shook his head.

"Screw your schedules! Your sympathy and your looks of pity! I don't want any of it," I snarled. "I don't want any of you here."

"Too bad," he repeated.

"I'm getting you removed—you won't be allowed in here," I seethed and started to pace. "Richard's going to kick your ass when he wakes up. He'll be furious that you upset me and about the way you have treated me!"

He crossed his arms. "Is that right?"

"Yes."

"I beg to differ. He'd be glad we stepped in and made sure his kids had at least one surviving parent."

His words stopped me short.

"What did you just say?"

"You're going through all the motions, Katy, but you've shut down. You're not with us. And without you, Richard doesn't stand a chance."

Flashes of pain, like small bombs, went off in my chest.

"He needs you. Your kids need you. Hell, I need you. We need your love and patience. We need your strength. Where are you, Katy?"

"I'm right here!" I screamed.

"You're hiding," he snapped, stepping forward and gripping my arms. "For fuck's sake, let it out, Katy. Just say it!"

I wrapped my hands around his biceps, desperate for his support to keep me upright. Tremors took hold of me, racing up and down my spine, making my entire body quake.

"I'm terrified," I admitted, the words ripping from my throat. "More frightened than I have ever been in my entire life," I whimpered. "I can't do this without him. I don't want to do this without him."

"I know." He shocked me with his response. He shocked me even more by allowing me to see his tears. "I'm scared too, Katy."

The sight of his own pain was the thing that sent me over the edge. I broke. My knees gave out, Maddox catching me before I hit the floor. I began to sob. Loud, long wails of pain, tormented anger, and terrified thoughts poured out of me as I wept and raged against his chest. Everything I had been holding in came out as Maddox embraced me tightly, letting me fall apart while he held me together.

I uttered all my thoughts out loud. Some I shouted, while others were a mere whisper in the air.

How could that asshole be so careless and ruin our lives? I wanted him to be alive so he knew the destruction he caused. So he saw the consequences of his actions and had to live with that regret. I hated him more than I had ever hated another human being in my life.

The guilt of leaving Richard ate at me every time I walked away. The guilt of not being with our girls gnawed at me. The impatience I had shown Gracie earlier today shamed me. I knew I was ignoring their needs. However, my need to be with him overrode it all. I was torn every minute of every day, and I didn't know what to do with that awful feeling.

What if Richard never woke up? What if he did and wasn't Richard anymore?

I wasn't strong enough.

How could I cope without Richard?

How could I live without him?

I needed him back.

I needed his arms around me, his voice in my ear telling me he loved me.

What if our lives never went back to the way they were before the accident? Would we be able to find our way?

And finally...

I didn't want Maddox to go. I didn't want anyone to go, but...

"You need more control," he finished for me, with a sigh. "Sorry, Katy. In trying to help, we've been bulldozing you."

I eased back, looking at him with watery eyes. "I should have said something. I didn't—I couldn't..."

"Or you'd explode?" Smiling sadly, he wiped a finger under my eye, trying to lighten the tension. "Good thing that didn't happen."

Fresh tears filled my eyes. "I'm sorry. I shouldn't have said those things."

"No. Don't be sorry. We've been waiting for this. You needed to let it out, so I goaded you, Katy. You've been too stoic, too strong, and it was killing you. You were shutting down on all of us."

"I feel so angry."

"You have every right to be angry. Don't give up hope, Katy. Above everything else, Richard needs that. He's going to need all your love and strength when he wakes up. Because he will."

I glanced over to the bed where my husband was still locked in his own world.

"I miss him so much. I need him too."

"I know."

The door opened, and Laura poked her head in, her eyes wide, looking upset. "Are you, ah, all right in here?"

I nodded, more traitorous tears coursing down my face.

"I'm sorry," I whispered.

She came in, holding out her arms. I went into them, my tears soaking into her shoulder.

"Let it out, Katy," she murmured. "We have you. And no matter what happens, that isn't going to change."

So, I cried, releasing the anger and accepting the love and pain I had been trying to hide from.

I wept for Richard, Gracie, and Heather.

And mostly, I wept for myself.

~

G racie clutched my hand tight as I bent low to talk to her. "Remember what I said, okay? Daddy is only asleep."

She bobbed her head. "He knows I dere."

"Yes."

"How, Mommy?"

Maddox crouched beside me. "Like in dreams, Gracie. He'll know you're there and he can hear you, but with the medicine he takes, he can't talk back right now. He'll remember when he wakes up soon."

Her little brow furrowed, she twisted her lips, then nodded. "I leave him my Lambie. He know dat I dere."

Maddox ruffled her hair. "Good plan. He probably needs something to cuddle. I'll take a picture and show him when he wakes up." He stood, his lips quirking.

"You are so bad," I muttered.

"I am paying him back for the Oscar the Grouch stunt when I was recovering. Tit for tat, Katy."

Richard would expect no less.

I hesitated pushing open the door to Richard's room. I had discussed this with Laura and Graham as well as Richard's doctor, who made all the arrangements since children Gracie's age weren't often allowed on this ward. Although he agreed that seeing Richard might help settle her, and help Richard, I was still worried.

"It's an unusual request. Aside from the bruises and cuts, he won't frighten her," Alan had mused. *"He is peaceful and calm. If she understands he is asleep, I agree, perhaps she would like to see him. Maybe her voice will trigger something inside Richard."*

What if it made it worse?

Maddox's hand covered mine. "It's gonna be fine, Katy. I promise."

We walked in, and Laura and Graham stood. Laura closed the book she had been reading to Richard. Gracie stopped, her grip on my hand tightening as she looked at Richard. Maddox bent down.

"Want me to take you to Daddy?"

Still staring at Richard, she held out her arms and allowed him to pick her up and carry her to the edge of Richard's bed. I followed close, my heart beating so fast, I was sure it would fly from my chest. She leaned down, and Maddox arranged her beside Richard. She touched his face, frowning.

"Boo-boo."

"Yes," I said. "Daddy has lots of boo-boos, but they're getting better. They don't hurt him," I added. "Remember when you fell and skinned your knee? It didn't hurt after Mommy fixed it and kissed it better."

"I tiss?"

"Okay, be gentle like I told you."

Maddox helped her kneel beside him. She kissed Richard's cheeks, chin, and lips, then she touched the cannulas. "What dis?"

"That's so Daddy doesn't snore," Maddox said with a grin.

"Oh." She giggled, the sound odd but welcome in the room.

He winked at me, and I relaxed. He was helping make this much easier than I expected.

"Daddy?" Gracie whispered. "I hewe."

I had to blink several times as she laid her head beside his and started to talk in her sweet little voice. She told him about Lambie and staying at Graham's. About playing with Unca Mattog. How Heather was crawling everywhere.

"She no yike bottle, Daddy. Thippy cup," she informed him. "She big gurl. Yike me."

She told him about the zoo, time with Jenna, and her new friend "Blad."

"He funny. I yaff so hard, I spill my milk. He clean it up and not say nuffin," she confessed, keeping her voice low and solely for him.

I relaxed watching Gracie. It was as if we were at home. The main difference was that Richard was silent, not egging her on the way he usually did. He loved listening to her talk and encouraged her all the time, having full conversations with her daily. He was proud of how smart she was and spent as much time reading or teaching her things as he could. Not yet three, her vocabulary was more advanced than most children her age and I was certain it had a lot to do with Richard and his constant interaction with her.

I was grateful for the way Maddox stayed close, appearing as engrossed in her stories as Richard would have been. He didn't interrupt, allowing Gracie to fill Richard in on everything he had been missing. She began to sing—nonsensical words she strung together that Richard was always able to decipher, to a tune she made up as she went. Most of the time, she was bent over his face, humming close to his mouth as if that made it better for him to hear her. It was sweet and sad all at the same time, and more than once, I saw Laura brush a tear from her eyes.

Finally, Gracie looked up. "Daddy tired. He not smiling now."

Something in my chest quivered. "What, baby?"

She tapped his mouth. "He not smile now."

I stepped closer, exchanging glances with Maddox. Laura and Graham looked between us.

"Daddy smiled at you?"

Gracie bobbed her head enthusiastically. "He yike my songs. He smile when I tiss him."

I tried to calm my rapidly beating heart. "Of course he did. Daddy loves you."

She tucked her lamb in the crook of his neck. "I lubs him. I tome back yater afta Daddy has nap."

Graham cleared his throat. "We'll take Gracie home."

I couldn't tear my eyes from Richard's face. Had he smiled? Was he waking? Did he know I was there?

Gracie held out her arms, and I scooped her up, holding her tight. She bent down and kissed Richard again, and I watched closely, holding my breath. There was no movement or flicker on his face, and I tried not to be too disappointed. In her little world, Daddy would smile at her, so she thought he had. I had to stop getting my hopes up.

I walked Gracie, Laura, and Graham to the elevator, releasing my daughter to Laura's waiting arms.

"We'll call you," she promised and squeezed my arm. "It will happen."

I blew kisses to Gracie, waiting until the elevator door closed. I was glad I had let her see him. She accepted the fact that he was sleeping easily and as Maddox said, seemed calmer now that she had seen him with her own eyes.

I walked back into the room, meeting Maddox's excited eyes.

"He blinked, Katy. I swear to God, Richard blinked."

11

KATY

The next three days were filled with tension and anticipation. There were small signs Richard was waking up. The flutter of his eyelids—as quick as a hummingbird's wings—so fast you would miss it if you weren't looking. The tremor in a finger. The twitch of his arm. A quiet sound deep in his throat—something between a sigh and a groan.

Each action made me stiffen with anxiety and yearn with hope. Ache with the need for the next sign. I didn't leave his side, even sleeping with my fingers interlocked with his. I rushed to the bathroom when needed, swallowed the food that appeared, and raced through the fastest showers I ever had in my life, returning with wet hair and the same determination in my heart.

I read to him. Talked endlessly. Played recordings of Gracie singing and nattering away that Laura sent me. I stretched and bent his limbs the way Colin had shown me—easy movements to help his muscles stay active. I tried desperately not to get upset at the dead weight his legs felt like in my grip. Alan had assured me it would be the case as his spine healed. Instead, I tried to send positive energy into his daily routines, wanting to do anything I could to help.

No one—not even Maddox, suggested I leave. Laura, Graham, and

Jenna came and went, bringing support, hugs, and supplies. They spoke with Richard, checked on me, and left, allowing us the privacy I needed right now.

Maddox was never far away. Working on his laptop, speaking on his phone, taking long walks so I could be alone with Richard. I didn't hold back now. I told him how much I needed him. How I missed him. Begged him to open his eyes. Cried when I needed to. I held his hand, stroked his face, and talked about the future. Our future.

I turned to Maddox late one evening.

"You have to go home."

"Soon."

"Maddox, you can't stay here indefinitely. You have a job. Responsibilities."

"I do my job daily. Bent and Aiden can reach me in a second if they have to. Dee is as adamant about me being here as I am. I have a few more days, Katy." He raised his voice, calling out, "Cooperate, Richard. Open your damn eyes."

I sighed as I stroked Richard's palm. "You heard him, my darling. Open your eyes."

His fingers twitched. Spasmed and tightened around mine. Maddox heard my swift intake of breath and was by my side in a second.

"Richard," he commanded. "Open up, buddy. Just fucking come back."

Richard's eyes fluttered, his eyelids quivering, opening slowly, a glimpse of hazel peeking out at us, only to drift back shut.

"No, my darling," I begged. "*Please, Richard.*" A sob caught in my throat. "I'm here. *Please.*"

His mouth pulled down into a grimace. The tip of his tongue appeared, and he swallowed.

His eyes flickered back open, confused and blank.

And he groaned.

∿

RICHARD

C onsciousness came and went slowly. Gradually.
It brought with it flickers of light.

Muffled sounds.

Pain. So much pain, my body screamed in agony.

Pain won out, and I let the darkness take me away again.

In the darkness, sounds broke through.

Loud voices that made me wince.

The sound of crying that somehow made me want to fight against the pain and help the person sobbing, but darkness overcame me.

There was a sweet little voice singing. A voice I knew. A voice *I loved*. A voice that made me smile, and I felt my lips curl involuntarily at the light pressure on them before I slipped away again.

At times, there was a deeper voice that cajoled and teased. Familiar, yet distant. Other comforting sounds and voices that broke through at times but couldn't hold me. I felt touches, smelled fragrances, but the exhaustion would set in, and I would drift.

However, there was one constant voice—feminine and sweet. One filled with agony that pleaded with me to fight. To open my eyes. The sound of her anguish made me push back against the darkness and try. *For her.* No matter how hard I fought however, pain and darkness won, and I was gone.

Trapped somewhere I didn't know and couldn't break from. Names and faces circled, but I couldn't stop them. Images swam around, yet no matter how hard I tried, I couldn't make them come into focus—to concentrate on who they belonged to. Suspended between light and dark, at war inside my head, I found peace when I heard the sweet voice, not able to comprehend the words, but feeling the love soaked into them.

I needed to get back to that voice.

It was my lifeline.

Darkness receded, and I felt the pain return. It rushed into me, lighting my nerves and pushing me closer to consciousness than before.

"Cooperate, Richard. Open your damn eyes." I heard, the timbre of a male voice sinking into my bewildered mind.

There was a soothing touch on my palm, and the feminine voice that called to me often, spoke.

"You heard him, my darling. Open your eyes."

I tried, except my eyes were heavy, still too tired to cooperate. I struggled to capture that touch, desperate to grip the warm fingers with mine. I sensed movement. Desperation.

"Richard," the familiar, deep voice commanded. "Open up, buddy. Just fucking come back."

I tried again, managing to open my eyes, but the sudden light was piercing, and my eyelids fell back down.

"No, my darling," the loving voice begged, sobbing. *"Please, Richard. I'm here. Please."*

I couldn't deny the pull. The need to find the loving voice. With every last ounce of energy I had, I opened my eyes.

I grimaced with the effort. Attempted to speak, but my mouth was dry and my voice nonexistent. A low groan slipped from my throat.

"Turn down the light." That sweet voice caught my attention, and I struggled to focus on it.

The light stopped hurting, and slowly, the blurry image began to clear.

Dark hair, ivory skin, and the bluest eyes I had ever seen met my frantic gaze. A small, warm hand cupped my cheek. Love, so intense and real, burned into my befuddled mind, bringing with it one word with clarifying intensity.

Katy.

KATY

R ichard said my name. Rough, hesitant, but it was my name. He looked at me, his eyes trying to focus as he blinked and stared.

His gaze bounced from me to Maddox, who was smiling so hard, his eyes were small slits in his face.

"Welcome back, Richard."

Richard's gaze swung back to mine.

"We need the doctor," I said, unable to take my eyes off him.

Maddox spun on his heel. "On it."

I leaned closer, not bothering to wipe the tears running down my face. "Hello, my darling. I know you're confused, but everything is okay. I'm right here."

"Wh-where?"

"You're in the hospital."

He furrowed his brow, his eyes drifting closed once again.

"You were in an accident."

He opened his eyes. I watched him struggle to lift his hand, and I helped guide it to my face. His fingers jerked on my skin.

"No tears," he uttered, the words low and jagged. "I don't like it... when you cry."

That simple statement it took him such effort to say made me cry harder.

He frowned. "K-Katy?"

"Yes," I sobbed. "I'm Katy."

He closed his eyes with a sigh. "I...found you."

I pressed my hand harder, brushing my lips over his cheeks. "I've been waiting, Richard. I missed you *so* much."

"Sorry," he mumbled.

Alan walked in, Maddox following him, two nurses on his heels.

"Look who's woken up," Alan exclaimed.

Richard looked confused, and I felt his anxiety.

"This is your doctor," I explained.

Alan approached the bed. "I'm Dr. Fletcher, Richard. We've been waiting for you. I need to examine you, if you're okay with that?"

Richard's head bobbed, a flicker of pain crossing his face.

Alan met my worried gaze. "It's normal," he stated. "His body is waking up. I need you to step from the room for a moment, Katy."

Richard's eyes flared with panic, his hand gripping mine as hard as he could.

I wanted to stay, but I knew the hospital had strict policies regarding patient care. "I'll be right outside," I soothed. "As soon as the doctor is finished, I'll be back."

"I'll make sure she is," Maddox added. "I'll be right with her."

"Mad Dog," Richard mumbled. "Okay."

Maddox's smile was wide.

"You got it, Richard."

I felt Richard's gaze follow me out of the room. I hated releasing his hand. Hated walking away, even though I knew he was in good hands. One thought kept echoing in my head.

What if he slips away again?

Maddox grabbed me in a hard hug. "I know what you're thinking, Katy. Not gonna happen. He's awake, and he's gonna stay awake."

Tears spilled down my cheeks. Relief filled me as I clung to his words. Richard was awake. Although we still had a long road ahead of us, he was alive, and we would face it together.

Maddox held me tight. "It's okay, Katy. Let it out."

I cried for a few moments, letting the anxiety drain out with my tears. Maddox released me and handed me some tissues he grabbed from a box on the table in the lounge.

"You want to call Graham?" he asked. "Or should I do it before I call Bent?"

"You call him. I need a moment, I think."

He gripped my shoulders and dropped a kiss on my head. "One step, one day at a time, Katy. Concentrate on this moment. I'll make some calls, and by the time I come back, I'm sure you'll be in with him. I'll give you some time."

I beamed at him. "Call your wife and tell her you'll be home soon."

He returned my smile with one of his own, his eyes glassy with emotion. "She'll be doubly happy."

He turned and walked away, his phone pressed to his ear.

I sat down and offered up a prayer of thanks, asking for the strength I would need for the next step in Richard's recovery.

~

RICHARD

It was too much. It was all too fucking much. I was confused, in pain, and I didn't know what the hell I was doing in a hospital surrounded by machines, with needles in my arm, and some annoying plastic tubes shoved up my nose. I watched Katy leave, my anxiety mounting as the door shut behind her, leaving me with these strangers.

With an angry jerk, I yanked at the tubes pumping oxygen into my body. I was shocked at how ineffectual my action seemed. Add to the fact that the simple motion caused a spasm of pain to rip through my torso which took my breath away and enhanced my tension.

"Now, now, Mr. VanRyan. Relax. Everything is okay," a nurse soothed, bringing my arm down to my side. "I'm Carol, the nurse to my left is Hillary, and as he said, this is Dr. Fletcher. We're here to help."

"Katy," I managed to get out between struggling breaths.

"She'll be right back," Dr. Fletcher assured me. "I need to do a few tests, then she'll be right back. All right?"

It appeared I had no choice in the matter. The nurses clucked and fussed as the doctor checked my chart. They patted my arms, straightened my pillows, promising water and the return of my wife as soon as possible. I managed to calm down, bringing my breathing under control. Still, I glared at him.

He ignored me, instead asking me some questions, not reacting to any of my responses. I was able to tell him my name and the year without hesitation. My wife's name, and those of our children. I struggled a little with birthdates and what the actual date was today, but I gave it my best shot.

"July, maybe? The fifteenth?"

He didn't agree or disagree.

He gave me five things to remember, then asked some more questions. I found it difficult to focus on his words, asking him to repeat his questions at times, and finding myself floundering to get the words out. They were there, in my head, yet somehow speaking them was problematic. It was upsetting since words were my lifeline.

I tapped my head. "What is going on? Why...why am I here?"

He didn't respond to my queries. "What is the last thing you remember?"

I tried desperately to recall.

I remembered Gracie laughing, Heather eating, and Katy smiling. Something about a park? Fractured images swam through my aching head.

"No, a zoo," I said out loud.

"Pardon?"

"I was having...breakfast with...my family. I said I would take them...to the zoo...on the weekend."

I paused, shocked at how long it took me to get those simple words out. My voice sounded raspy and my words halted. Panic began to bleed into my chest.

The doctor nodded, not seeming to notice my hesitant speech.

"Good. Anything else?"

I shut my eyes, trying to clear my foggy mind. "Nothing clear. My head hurt? Did I have a stroke?"

He drew in a long breath. "No. You were in a car accident, Richard. A serious one. You suffered a traumatic blow to your head. You've been unconscious for several days. The fact that you can recall some details is a good sign."

I had no memory of what he was saying. A car accident? Did I hurt someone?

"Why am I talking...so slow? Why is my head fuzzy?"

"You're still healing."

"It will get better?" I asked, trying to fight down the returning panic.

"We'll have to see how you progress." He stepped forward. "I need to check your vitals and do a few other things, then we'll get Katy back in."

He proceeded with his tests, asking me to list the five things he asked me to remember.

I couldn't recall even one.

"What is your pain level at?" he inquired as he shone his light in my eyes, making the pain throb more.

"In my head…a nine, my chest and arms…an eight. The rest of me is… good. No pain…" My voice trailed off. There was no pain in my lower extremities. My lower back ached, and then there was nothing but the oddest sensation. As if my legs were detached from the rest of me. I rubbed my thigh, feeling a small awareness, but that was it. I tried to move my legs, yet nothing happened. In my panic, I pushed at the nurse beside me, slapping at my leg.

I could feel something, yet I couldn't move.

My breathing picked up, becoming fast and hard. The pain inside my head turned into sharp claws tearing at my mind.

"Why-why can't I move my legs?"

Dr. Fletcher leaned close. "Calm down, Richard. You suffered a thoracolumbar spine injury in the accident. We had to do emergency surgery to reduce the bleeding into the spinal canal. You're still healing."

His words made no sense in my panicked state. Surgery? *On my spine?*

"My legs," I insisted. "Why…can't I feel…my legs?"

"This is quite normal given what you have been through. Recovery takes time."

"What are you saying?" I managed to get out. "This is…" I searched for the word but couldn't find it. Why the hell couldn't I find the word?

"Your spinal cord was compressed," he explained. "The result of that compression is paralysis."

The word pinned me to the mattress, all my efforts at movement ceasing. It echoed in my head, screaming over and again.

Paralysis.

I was paralyzed.

I didn't recognize my own voice. An anguished sound escaped my throat.

"Katy. I need Katy."

12

KATY

I was already rushing toward the door when Carol opened it, looking for me. I heard the sound Richard made, even through the walls, and I knew he needed me.

Screw protocol.

I hurried to his bedside. He was almost panting in his panic, a sheen of sweat on his forehead. His hands were wrapped tight around the bed rails, and the stark fear in his eyes made my heart ache.

I brushed my hand over his forehead, leaning in as close as I could. "Shh, Richard, I'm here, my darling. I'm here."

My touch seemed to calm him. I ran my hand down his arm, loosening his grip from the metal. I intertwined our fingers, lifting his hand to my mouth. "Right here," I repeated, hating seeing him so unsettled, so vulnerable. So unlike the Richard I knew.

Alan stood on the other side of his bed. "Listen to your wife, Richard. Breathe with her and try to relax. I'll explain more when you're ready."

I pressed his hand to my chest and breathed long and slow. He struggled to calm down, finally relaxing, the panic ebbing from his eyes, although the devastation he was feeling written was across his face.

Carol handed me some ice chips, and I slipped one into his mouth. He closed his eyes with a long sigh. I could only imagine how good the cold felt in his mouth or how thirsty he was.

"He can have some water soon," she promised.

"Richard," Alan said. "Are you ready to listen?"

Richard opened his eyes. "I'm paralyzed." He said the words slowly, a slight drag to his speech.

"This is to be expected with the trauma you experienced. We hope with time and work, you will regain the use of your legs."

"And I can't...talk good."

Hearing his stumbling speech filled me with dread, but Alan hastened to assure him.

"I'm sure that will improve. You just woke up, Richard. There were moments we weren't sure that would occur. You were severely injured—this isn't going to happen instantly." He smiled wryly. "This isn't a TV drama. It will take time and effort." He finished typing on the tablet, making notes and comments, then slid it under his arm.

"We'll do another CT scan and some other follow-up tests. You'll see a speech pathologist if needed. Once you've recovered a little more, you'll be moved to the rehab ward. You'll have a strict routine to get your strength back. "

"I'll walk?"

Alan folded his arms. "That is my hope. But we need to do the tests and see how you respond."

"When can I—" Richard swallowed "—go home?"

"Not for a while. It depends what the tests show and how you respond. On the effort you put into your recovery. Let's take this one step, one day, at a time." He smiled at me. "I think your wife will be a great help to you."

Richard's hand tightened on mine, but he remained silent.

Alan stepped back. "I'm going to let the nurses get you settled. They'll clean you up and get you some water. If you're hungry, you can try something light later. And we'll get you off the IVs and oxygen as soon as possible." He laid a hand on Richard's arm. "Patience,

Richard. This won't happen overnight or even this week. Spines are tricky and heal in their own time. Your head needs a chance to catch up. Each one is different. Once we have some results, I will sit with you and discuss all the options and plans. All right?"

Richard barely acknowledged him. Alan met my gaze with an understanding nod and left the room. I stepped back to let Carol and Hillary do what they needed to do. I stood at the end of the bed with Richard's gaze locked on me as they worked, talking to him in quiet voices. Without thinking, I rubbed his feet, and the look of despair on his face when he realized I was touching him and he couldn't feel it rocked me to the core. But I didn't stop. I had to show him it didn't matter. He was here. His legs, working or not, didn't matter.

He did.

～

The room buzzed all day. Maddox came and went, talking to Richard in a low voice. Graham and Laura arrived, both encouraging and thrilled to see Richard awake. Nurses were in and out, tests performed, and Alan checked him again, promising results in the morning.

Richard's eyes tracked me everywhere. He was distracted and quiet, letting others do the talking. He was tired and napped, his eyes shutting at times, although he tried to fight it. He would wake, startled, calling my name. I stayed close, soothing him, seeing his turmoil and worry.

Finally, the quiet of the evening arrived, and I was alone with him. One of the nurses brought me a basin of warm water and some cloths, and I gave him a sponge bath. He sighed as I ran the cloth over his arms and chest. They capped his IV, with the promise that if he continued to progress, it would be removed. He wasn't happy about the catheter or some of the other equipment, but he studiously ignored it all as I cleaned his skin.

"Feels nice," he muttered, watching me.

"Good." I glanced at his dinner tray. "You didn't eat much."

He lifted his shoulder dismissively.

"I can get you something—order anything you'd like."

"Not hungry."

He needed to eat, and I decided not to push it for now. "Maybe tomorrow."

He grunted but didn't say anything else. I had noticed he kept all his answers to a minimum with everyone. I got a fresh cloth and wiped at his face and neck. "You've got quite the beard. Maybe I can shave you tomorrow." I tweaked it playfully, wanting to see a smile. Even the curl of his mouth would be good. "Gracie won't like it." She always hated it when Richard's scruff got longer. She insisted it scratched when he kissed her.

"I heard her."

I stopped and looked at him. "What?"

"Gracie. I heard her singing."

"Yes. She was here. She talked to you and sang. She told me you smiled."

He was silent as I wiped him dry and tugged up the gown over his shoulders. I emptied the bowl and sat beside him.

He held up his hand. "My ring?"

I pulled the chain from my neck. "They had to cut it off. I've been keeping it safe."

"I want it."

"I'll have it fixed."

"Tomorrow."

His insistence was touching. "Yes. Tomorrow."

I linked our hands together, sitting close to the side of the bed. "What else do you remember?" I asked.

"I heard you talking. Asking me…to come back."

I nodded, encouraging him to talk. It was getting smoother, the hesitation between his words shorter.

"And crying." He frowned. "I didn't like that."

I drew in a shaky breath. "I was scared I was losing you, Richard. Terrified that you wouldn't come back to us."

He was silent, staring down at his legs. "You want me—even like this?"

"Like what?"

He rubbed his thigh. "Useless."

"You are *not* useless. You were in an accident and had surgery. You have to recover."

He met my gaze, his eyes filled with anguish. "And if I don't, Katy? What if—" he swallowed "—what if I can't walk again?"

"We'll figure it out, Richard. Together. As long as you're here with us, that's all that matters. It's you I love. Your heart. Your spirit. Your presence. Not your legs."

"I don't know if I can do it."

I frowned, confused. "Learn to walk again? It's too soon to be deciding that, isn't it? You only woke up this afternoon. Give yourself a chance."

He exhaled, his eyes drifting closed. "That's not...what I mean."

A small frisson of panic hit my chest. "What do you mean, Richard?"

He didn't open his eyes. "Be less of a man than I was. What if I don't fully recover?"

I knew how Richard's mind worked. I understood he was focused on the worst-case scenario and needed to reassure him. I stood, the chair scraping across the floor as I pushed it back in anger. Richard's eyes flew open, his gaze startled. I leaned over him.

"Listen to me, Richard VanRyan. Whether you're walking on two feet, with canes to help you, or in a wheelchair, I don't give a damn. You'll be here with me. Helping raise our daughters. By my side. You can still work. Be a father. My husband. There'll be adjustments and changes to our life, but *you'll still be here.*" I paused, sucking in a much-needed breath. "Your legs don't determine your worth as a man. Your heart does. You proved that once before when you changed and became the man I loved. This time, you won't do it alone. I am right here, and I'm not going anywhere. Do you understand me? Neither are you. We are going to figure this out together." By the time I finished my diatribe, tears were running down my face.

Richard's eyes met mine, seeing the determination in them. "I'm scared," he admitted.

I lifted his hand and kissed the knuckles, then brought it to my cheek. "So am I, my darling. But not as scared as the thought of facing my future without you. I need you. Your girls need you."

"I need *you*," he replied, his voice shaking with emotion. "I love you, Katy VanRyan."

"I love you." I bent down and brushed my lips across his. "Nothing will change that fact, Richard. *Nothing.*"

He held on to my neck like a lifeline, a tear slipping down his face. It was rare I ever saw that sort of raw emotion from him. "I'm going to hold you to that."

"You do that."

I kissed him again and held him close until he relaxed. Brushing his face, he indicated the side of the bed. "Sit beside me, please."

I perched on the mattress and held his hand. He was quiet, and I let him think. That was how he did things. He thought them through, then he acted.

"When can I see Gracie and Heather?"

I smiled. "I'll have Laura and Graham bring them tomorrow."

R ichard looked determined the next morning, despite not sleeping well. He kept waking, confused and worried. Even after I would get him settled, I felt the tension and concern radiating from him. He kept his eyes shut, but I knew he was pretending. I knew him well enough to know his mind would be racing, sorting and filing away all the information he had and figuring out how to deal with it. I wanted him to talk to me, yet I also knew that he needed to do this. It was how Richard coped.

He picked at his breakfast, made faces at the oatmeal and juice, and he pushed away the tray.

"What time are the girls coming?"

"Heather has a little cold, so she's staying home. Gracie will be here in about an hour. You have to see the doctor and the physio people this afternoon. I don't want you to get tired out."

"Don't baby me, Katy. My legs aren't working, but I don't need to be mollycoddled."

His tone of voice was sharp, and I frowned. "I'm not worried about your legs, Richard. You just woke up from a coma. You have to take care of yourself."

He blew out a breath. "Right. Sorry."

I lifted his tray. "Okay."

He reached out, laying his hand on my arm. "Katy, sweetheart. I am sorry. Really."

"I know. You would feel better if you ate something. I'd feel better if you ate something."

"Have you tasted what they call food here?"

"How about I have Maddox pick you up something?"

"I'd like a bagel."

"I can arrange that."

"And some decent coffee."

"On it."

"And a shower."

"That, we'll have to talk to the doctor about."

He agreed. "I have a lot to talk to him about."

I liked seeing the purpose on his face and hearing it in his voice. He needed that to tackle what was ahead of him.

"Okay. I'll go call Maddox."

~

Gracie raced into Richard's room, excited and eager.

"Daddy!"

She stopped by his bed, lifting her arms. He grimaced as he struggled to reach for her, unable to do so with his injuries. Maddox bent and lifted her beside Richard.

"Careful, Gracie. Daddy still has lots of boo-boos."

Neither of them listened. Gracie crawled over Richard, getting as near as she could, and despite the grimace of pain that crossed his face, he held her close. I had to turn my head to stop from crying at watching the sweet moment. Gracie laid across him, talking directly into his face, her little hand patting him everywhere as if to make sure he was real. Tears leaked from the corners of his eyes as she babbled, her words coming so fast I couldn't make them out.

Maddox had to turn away. Laura cried unabashedly. Graham blinked, then muttered something about having to return to the office. He kissed Laura's head and left the room.

When Richard grimaced again, I leaned over and rubbed Gracie's back. "Daddy needs you to sit up, okay?"

"Not go yet!"

"No," I soothed. "You can stay for a while. Sit up beside Daddy."

She squirmed as I arranged her beside him, and he wrapped his arm around her and let her talk, a smile on his face as he listened and caught up with his girl. He became tired quickly, his eyes drifting shut, then snapping open when she would pat his cheek.

I moved to the edge of the bed. "Daddy needs to have a nap."

She looked at him, her brow furrowing. Her chin began to quiver. "He go to sweep again? For long time?"

Richard's breath caught, and I hastened to reassure her. "No, he's just a little tired, baby girl."

He stroked her cheek with his index finger. "Daddy needs to get better so he can come home."

His speech was getting better, and although still slow, it was improving. It was a good sign.

She almost vibrated with excitement. "Soon?"

His voice was weary. "As soon as I can."

She pressed kisses to his cheeks and nose. "Otay. I tome back."

He smiled, already drifting. Maddox lifted her down and turned to Laura. "Come on, I'll walk you to your car."

At the door, Gracie turned. "We play when you tome home, Daddy! I wants to swim wif you!"

Her words hung in the air. Richard's expression became morose and withdrawn. I brushed the hair off his forehead.

"You will, Richard. With time, you will."

He didn't respond. Any lingering happiness faded, and the light dimmed from his eyes. He turned his head, rejecting my touch.

13

KATY

Maddox came out of Richard's room, his suitcase in hand. He had been a tower of strength for me, and I was going to miss him. But he had a wife that missed him, a job that had been pushed aside too long on our behalf, and a life he needed to return to.

He dropped his case and swept me in for a hug. "If you need me, I'm a call away. I can be here in a day."

"Thank you for everything," I murmured, the words somehow inadequate.

He pulled back. "It's not going to be easy, Katy. Be strong." He glanced at Richard's closed door, a faint scowl on his face. "He's holding himself in."

"I know." I had seen a subtle change in Richard the past few days. He spoke less, snapped more, and barely acknowledged the future. I watched him with the therapists. The determination I had seen the first day he woke was dimming. I encouraged him—everyone did— reminding him it would take time and patience, and although he nodded, I worried he didn't believe us. If he gave up, he had no chance of recovering.

"I'll check in on him. And you." He pressed a kiss to my head. "And the munchkins. Kiss them every day for me, yeah?"

I was unable to speak. He cleared his throat and, after another hug, walked to the elevator.

I watched him leave, knowing how much of a difference his absence would make in our life.

My phone rang, and I hurried to the waiting room to take the call. Attending to Richard, trying to arrange changes to the house, and make sure I saw the girls kept me busy and exhausted. Richard became agitated and upset when I wasn't there, barking at the staff and causing problems. The girls were now with Mrs. Thomas since her husband was away on his annual golf trip and she insisted she was too lonely rattling around her empty house. I went there every day to check on the work being done at our place, see the girls, and spend time with them to give Mrs. Thomas a break. She laughed when I told her, saying that the girls had so many visitors, she was lucky to see them at all.

I listened to the information the contractor was giving me, not caring about the cost, only having it done and ready before Richard came home. Fifty thousand dollars meant nothing if Richard could get upstairs. I had thought about turning the family room into a bedroom for us, but Laura had suggested it might send Richard the wrong message.

"Moving your bedroom to the main floor says permanence, Katy."

I had sighed and leaned my head on my hand. "And an elevator doesn't?"

She shook her head. "It can be useful. Think if you ever broke your leg and had to get up all those stairs to the bedroom. Or when Graham and I get old and spend the night. We're not getting any younger, you know." She winked.

I looked at the plans. We'd lose a large closet on each floor, but the contractor had also pointed out a good place to add more storage on each level. It seemed the best solution and the space was perfect.

"I can secure the permits needed and start as soon as they're clear, Mrs. VanRyan. I need to order the elevator today." Mr. Brown's voice interrupted my musings.

"Of course. If you can bring the paperwork to the hospital, I can sign it and get your deposit."

"I'll see you later."

I hung up and sat staring out the window. Richard was short with me today, often ignoring my questions and being snippy with the nurses and physio people. He hated everything about the hospital and the reason he was here. I couldn't blame him for wanting to be home; however, I didn't like it when he spoke to people rudely—not that any of the staff seemed to be bothered. Still, it bothered me, stirring memories of the Richard I first knew and loathed.

With a sigh, I stood and brushed some lint off my pants. I pulled on the waistband with a grimace. They were getting looser. My appetite was still off, and I wasn't sleeping well. But at the moment, my concentration was on Richard, not me. I pushed my hair off my shoulders and returned to Richard's room. I heard his raised voice, and I hurried inside, wondering what problem had occurred while I had stepped out.

He was arguing with a woman I had never seen until this moment. She was regarding him patiently, a clipboard in hand, not interrupting him as he ranted.

"What's going on?" I asked.

"This *lady*," he choked, "tells me she is going to give me a shower. I told her I don't fucking think so."

"Language," I admonished. He had started cursing more since he woke up, and I wondered if it was another subtle change to his personality. His anger flared fast and he started swearing. Again, it reminded me of the man he had been, and I didn't like it.

The woman cleared her throat and introduced herself. "I'm Doris, one of the day nurses. I've been on holidays, so I have yet to have had the pleasure of meeting you both." Her eyes twinkled. "What I told your husband was I was going to help him get to a shower. I didn't plan on getting naked with him." She winked. "Not that I would complain."

I covered my mouth, trying not to giggle. Richard looked so scandalized, I couldn't help it. Fighting back my amusement, I patted his hand.

"You've been begging for a proper shower, Richard. And a shave." He was off all of the equipment now, free from IVs and oxygen.

"In private," he snarled. "I'm not flashing the goods to some stranger."

This time, it was Doris who laughed. "Mr. VanRyan, goods like yours, as you so delightfully refer to them, have been flashed on the ward a great deal. You have nothing I haven't seen before, young man. So, you have two choices. Sit there and bitch about me seeing your naked ass for a moment, or let me help you get into the shower. Then I will leave you in your wife's capable hands."

He crossed his arms. "Are you aware I can't walk?"

She met his surly gaze. "Are you aware we have a machine that will lift you from that bed and seat you safely in the shower?"

"No," he muttered.

She set down her clipboard. "And obviously, you are not aware I'm a trained professional. No matter how spectacular 'the goods' are, they are nothing but anatomy to me. I have dealt with hundreds of men and their egos. So, when you decide, let me know."

I stopped her before she could walk out. "He wants the shower." I glared at him. "Right, Richard?"

I could tell he wanted to say no to spite her, but looking at my narrowed eyes, he huffed a breath. "Yes."

Doris picked up her clipboard. "Yes…" Her voice trailed off.

Richard practically snarled out his response. "Please."

Doris smiled. "I'll get things ready. I'll have a waterproof bandage for your incision and I'll explain the way you'll be transferred and how to sit properly."

She left and he glared at me. "I hate this."

"So you've mentioned," I stated mildly, looking through his toiletry bag that Maddox had brought him one day along with a few shirts and other items.

I didn't dare show him how amused I was by his reaction to having a shower. Under different circumstances, Richard would have reacted with a grin and a wink and offered to *flash his goods.* He would have had Doris eating out of the palm of his hand. The entire staff, actually.

The difficult, humorless man in front of me felt like a stranger at times.

"Where were you?" he demanded. "How long does it take to say goodbye to Maddox? Giving him extra thanks for all his *help*?"

I paused in my search. "What does that mean?"

He crossed his arms. "You were gone a long time."

"It sounds as if you're saying a lot more than that."

He narrowed his eyes. "Your lips are red."

I had been chewing on them again, my anxiety peaking. I was trying to hide it, but he was making me angry.

"I'm under a little pressure here, Richard. I was biting them."

He raised an eyebrow, looking skeptical. "As long as it was *you* doing the biting."

I gaped at him, his unspoken implication insulting. Before I could reply, he started over again. It happened a lot these days. He'd get a thought in his head and expound on it endlessly.

"You took longer than I expected."

"I got a phone call, and I took it in the lounge. The reception is better."

"Who was it?"

I frowned. "A contractor I'm dealing with."

"So secretive these days, Katy."

I closed my eyes and counted to ten. "I'm not hiding anything, Richard. We need to have some temporary changes made to the house for when you come home. I was discussing one of those changes with a contractor." I drew in a steadying breath. "If you are insinuating something, say it."

"I'm saying you were gone a long time."

I was done.

"You are insulting both me and Maddox. He's your best friend. I'm your wife. He was a huge support to me while you were in a coma." My voice shook with repressed anger. "You should be ashamed of yourself."

His gaze dropped, and his shoulders slumped.

"I can't believe you would even think—"

He scrubbed his face. "I didn't. I'm sorry. I was being an ass. I get frustrated with everyone making plans and not being part of them."

"I was going to discuss it with you when I came back. However, you were berating a nurse and throwing out attitude, so that took precedence."

"I'm sorry, Katy."

I shook my head. "We're all doing our best for you, Richard. I'm hurt you would even think something so terrible."

I turned and he reached out, grabbing my arm. "Katy, baby, please."

I shook off his grip. "I know you're upset. But even thinking that..."

He pulled on my arm, dragging me close. He lifted my hand to his mouth, kissing my knuckles, his expression contrite.

"I thought you were going to die," I whispered, tears streaming down my face. "I thought I had lost you, and I didn't know how I was going to cope. How could you think that of me? Of Maddox? After everything he did for you? For our family?"

"I didn't mean it."

I lifted my gaze to his face. "Then why did you say it?"

"I have a lot of anger, and I can't seem to control it. I lash out without thought," he admitted, his voice low. "I know you would never... That Maddox... *Fuck*. I'm such an asshole. Katy, baby, please forgive me. I'll do better, I promise I will."

Doris walked in, pushing a machine.

"Okay, Mr. VanRyan, let's get you cleaned up. Maybe that will help brighten your outlook."

I shook off his hold, still shocked at his inference.

"Maybe it will."

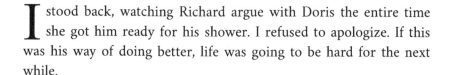

I stood back, watching Richard argue with Doris the entire time she got him ready for his shower. I refused to apologize. If this was his way of doing better, life was going to be hard for the next while.

121

In the private bathroom, Doris lowered Richard into the enclosed bath chair.

"Are you sure you can do this?" she asked me. "I can get in a male orderly if you prefer."

Richard hated strangers touching him, which was one reason he was being such a difficult patient. "No, I'll be fine."

"All right, I'll leave you to it. Hit the call button when you're ready, and we'll get him settled back into his room."

She pulled the curtain closed, giving us privacy. I undressed, then slipped Richard's gown from his shoulders, turning on the water and making sure it was warm. I adjusted the seat for him and let the water rain down on his head. He slumped forward, all the tension leaving his body. My anger slipped away at his posture, and I ran my hand over his shoulders. He grabbed it and kissed the palm in a silent apology. I bent down and met his tortured gaze.

"I'm sorry," he begged. "I didn't mean it."

"You hurt me."

"Forgive me. I'll try harder. I will, Katy. I promise."

His gaze was tormented, his words sincere. I exhaled.

"Try very hard."

"I will."

"I know."

He cupped my face and kissed me. It was soft and gentle, filled with regret and trepidation. I kissed him back, straightened up and reached for the shampoo. I stood in front of him, washing his hair. He wrapped his hands around my hips, his long fingers pressing into my skin. Although I was still upset, I felt the familiar shiver as he touched me. He kissed my stomach, and my muscles clenched.

I wondered if he felt my shiver and was feeling the need to explore. I longed to feel his touch again, and I was ready for whatever he wanted to try, even if we had to go slowly due to his healing ribs and restricted mobility. Richard had always been a fan of sex in the shower, the pool, or the hot tub. Even if we got caught in the rain.

"I love seeing your skin wet, Katy," he confessed to me once, *his lips*

grazing across my throat as his tongue lapped at the water on my neck. "It turns me on more than I can express."

I rinsed his hair, picked up the soap, and smoothed it over his skin, massaging it into lathers of foam. Up and down his arms. I stroked my fingers around his neck and shoulders, sliding the soap on his wet skin, being careful around his incision area, wincing at the bruised flesh. I glided my hands to his upper back, pressing and kneading on his tight muscles. He made a low sound in his throat, and as I peeked over his shoulder, I watched his cock stir and lengthen. My fingers tightened on the soap.

I knew he had spoken to the doctor about sex. Alan had assured Richard he was capable of erections and intercourse, although things might feel different now. He told Richard we would have to be creative in our positions, but when he was ready to let his body guide him as to the limits.

I stepped back in front of him, drawing my hands across his chest, sliding down, lingering on the tight muscles of his stomach. I bent to the floor, lathering his feet and working my way up his legs. As I reached the top of his thighs, he grabbed my hands, stopping my ministrations. My eyes flew upward to meet his. I was willing and waiting to try anything. Touch. Tease. Stroke. Kiss. Seek a moment of closeness we desperately needed at the moment. Get past the hurt of his words and prove to him nothing had changed between us and we would find our way.

He shook his head, taking the soap from me. His cock softened, curving against his thigh.

"I can't," he said.

I stood and rinsed him off, then turned into the spray and grabbed the shampoo, refusing to let him see my hurt.

I knew he was healing, and perhaps it had been too much, but the Richard I loved would have kept me close. Talked to me. Explained the disconnect.

I let the shower wash away the tears that burned as I admitted that, perhaps, this Richard wasn't the same person at the moment.

Silently, I cried a little harder at the sudden thought that maybe he never would be that person again.

~

"What the hell is that?" Richard hissed as the van parked in our driveway.

"A ramp for you to get into the house," I explained. "I told you I had made some adjustments."

He glowered, his hands curving around the handles of the wheelchair.

"Why don't we announce to the world I'm paralyzed?" he snapped.

"Don't be absurd. The ramp is temporary. Once you're walking, it will be removed," I said wearily. He had been arduous, fighting everything I told him was happening at the house. Finally, I stopped telling him, and Laura oversaw the work, making sure things were on track for us. How she had pulled off having it ready in such a short time frame, I didn't know, but I would be eternally grateful.

The front door opened as the van came to a halt. Mrs. Thomas appeared, holding Heather. Gracie was beside her, practically vibrating with delight at the fact that Daddy was home. I stepped out of the van and waited as the side door opened and the ramp was lowered. Richard came from the back, his lips twisted in displeasure.

For a brief moment, the frown disappeared, and he smiled at Gracie.

"Hey, baby girl."

Except she ran full tilt at him, barely stopping before she crawled up into his lap. She squirmed and wiggled, her unbridled joy evident.

Richard stopped smiling. He lifted her from his lap, setting her on her feet in front of him. "I can't wheel the chair and hold you, Gracie. Don't get on my lap."

Her face crumpled and I was quick to lift her into my arms. I shot him a glare, then kissed her cheek.

"Once Daddy is in the house, you can have a cuddle, okay?"

"Otay," she replied, her voice subdued.

Richard pushed away the hands of the attendant. "I can do it," he snarled and wheeled up the ramp on his own. I had to admire his upper body strength. Always strong, his muscles rippled as he bent and pushed. I tried not to feel the disappointment that his efforts hadn't affected his legs yet. It had only been three weeks since he had woken up. He'd had daily therapy and it would continue, but his medical team had agreed he might do better at home. Medically, there was nothing left they could do for him. The effort was now in his own hands, and the house was ready. Mentally, I hoped it was the change he needed—familiar surroundings, his family with him, and reestablishing a routine would help him focus on healing.

I tried to stifle my disappointment at his reaction to the ramp. There was so much to take in, it had no doubt jarred him. He would understand the need for all of the remodeling and adjustments once he had a chance to settle and think things over.

I knew he hated the changes, but they were necessary.

And all temporary, of course.

14

KATY

R ichard didn't appreciate any of the changes. In fact, they either annoyed him, or caused another outburst.

The repositioning of the furniture in the family room to make space for the exercise equipment was met with a glare and a down-turn of his mouth.

The lowered cabinet so he could reach the Keurig and make coffee was greeted with silence. The rearrangement of his office and the added height to his desk so he could get his wheelchair tucked under the edge earned mutterings and a glower.

Refusing to let him see my rising frustration, I opened the door to the new elevator with a flourish. "Ta-da!"

"Are you fucking kidding me with this?" he growled.

"Richard!" I gasped, indicating Gracie, who was staring at him with round eyes.

"You expect me to use that?" He kept talking, ignoring the fact that he had dropped the f-bomb in front of our daughter and was acting like a jerk.

I remained calm. "If you want to get upstairs, you will."

"This is what you've been wasting your time on? Never mind the cost," he snarled. "I bet I got taken for a ride on this little endeavor."

I gaped at him. He was worried about *money*? In all of this, that was the last thing he needed to be worried about. He had greater issues to focus on. Gracie interrupted my reply.

"I wanna go in elebator!"

"No," snarled Richard.

"Why?" she asked. "I go wif you."

I bent low to Gracie. "I have to show Daddy how it works. We'll race you up the stairs, okay? I'll even give you a head start. You can ride down after." I winked. "Then we can have the cookies we made for Daddy."

She clapped her hands, heading for the stairs. "Yay!"

I pushed Richard inside the elevator, not giving him a chance to refuse. I pushed the button hard in anger. "It's simple to use."

"Good thing since I'm simple these days," he snarled. "My brain and body don't work right anymore."

Before I could retort, the doors opened, Gracie waiting outside with a bright face.

"Me beat you!"

I forced a smile, pushing Richard out ahead of me. Gracie moved toward him, but he didn't lift her onto his lap. Instead, he patted her head and wheeled away from us.

"Let's go see what other surprises are here," he muttered.

I followed him across the hall to our room, my heart heavy.

Simple was not the word I would use right now.

Richard was fucking complicated and I wasn't sure I knew how to unravel the mystery.

I rinsed my hair, then sat under the hot water, letting it rain over my tired, aching body. The barrier-free shower and seat I had installed were met with a lukewarm reception from Richard, but I loved them. Somedays, I escaped and let the water rain over me, washing away the pain and frustration of yet another day with the new version of my husband. At least he used the shower without complaint, unlike the lift I had rented to aid him in getting in and out of bed from the wheelchair. He had lost it, swearing and muttering about his dwindling manhood, but I knew he needed it. He grew terse and angry every time I tried to help him, so I gave him the space he needed and let him figure it out on his own.

I shut off the water and opened the door, realizing I was more than just physically tired. I had never felt as torn as I did these days. Richard and his mood swings eclipsed everything in our life. His recovery, or as he saw it, lack of recovery, colored his views, his temperament, and heartbreakingly, his love for us. He refused all offers of help, even going as far as to wait until I left the room until he got dressed.

If you called sweats and T-shirts getting dressed. It was his standard uniform now.

He had always taken such pride in his appearance. His custom suits that he wore like armor in his high-stakes world. The engraved cuffs on his shirts. The perfect tie and shoes. That had been the norm.

Nothing seemed normal now.

I thought when he came home, he would try harder. That the comfort and love that surrounded him would push him toward his goal. That we would be closer.

Instead, we seemed to be further apart.

His interactions with the girls, which used to be inspiring, were now stilted and awkward. His patience was thin, and at times, he seemed disinterested. Story time, one of his favorite parts of the day that I used to have to pull him from, was reduced to a few moments a day. The first night home he tried, but after a disaster, he refused to go back into Gracie's room.

I was in Heather's room, tucking her in when the commotion started. There was a thump, and I heard Gracie shrieking and Richard's muffled cursing. I hurried across the room to find Richard on the floor, Gracie in tears, and his wheelchair tipped over. Somehow, he had gotten the scatter rug tangled into the wheel of the chair, and as he tried to untangle it, the chair tipped over. I righted the chair, pulled the twisted fabric away, and helped him get back in the seat.

He glared at me, his words burning into my skull.

"Think things through, Katy. Rugs and wheelchairs—not a good mix. Like me being here."

I couldn't get those words out of my mind.

I rolled up the rug, but the damage was done.

Story time was now a few lines he read in a monotone voice while Gracie sat on the sofa after dinner. She stopped asking to sit on his lap, but she always laid her tiny hand on his leg as he read to her. He looked down at it the first time with a strange expression on his face, then opened the book and started to read, studiously ignoring it.

At night, the small space between us stretched like a chasm neither of us was able to cross. On occasion, I would wake to find our fingers intertwined, but when he woke, he pulled away.

He was polite and distant. Every day, I watched helplessly as he pulled away from us a little more. The shadows in his eyes grew deeper, his silences longer, and his incentive minimal. He went through the motions, but it was as if he was no longer there.

Gone were his kisses and gentle caresses. If I leaned close to brush a kiss to his cheek, I felt the way he stiffened, holding himself rigid. He didn't reach for my hand or wrap his arms around me the way he had done when he first woke up in the hospital. He would pat Gracie's head or kiss her cheek, but the closeness she craved from him was denied. There were no cuddles, no shared amusement at one of their private jokes. He held Heather gingerly, cringing when she would shift, finding any excuse to give her back to me. On the occasion he would offer a kiss or a hug, it was brief, cool, and distant.

I grieved for him. His body was there, but his mind and spirit were missing.

It affected us all. Gracie was clingy and needy. Heather fussed. I had trouble sleeping and, for the first time in our marriage, was out of bed long before Richard ever moved in the mornings.

I wasn't sure how much longer we could do this for. My pleas to Richard fell on deaf ears, and I was too proud to tell Laura and Graham how bad things were.

With a sigh, I grabbed a towel and rubbed my hair briskly. I stood, flipping the wet strands over my shoulders, and met Richard's gaze in the mirror. I was surprised to see him, as he usually stayed in bed until I was out of the room and busy with the girls.

"Hi," I whispered.

He slipped his razor into the charger and ran his hand along his jaw. "I was getting scruffy."

I stepped closer and ran my finger along his chin. "Much better," I agreed and smiled, unsure of how he would react to me touching him.

He returned my smile with one of his own. It was cautious, gentle, and hinted at the playfulness I had been missing from him.

I traced the scar that ran along his forehead. "This is looking better. It gives you that bad-boy look." I winked. "You carry it well."

My breath caught as he captured my hand in his and looked at it, then lifted his eyes to mine. The swirling hazel of his irises captivated me as always. Keeping our gazes locked, he lifted my hand to his mouth and kissed the skin. He breathed my name, the sound long and sad.

"Katy."

"Richard." I echoed his sigh.

I wasn't sure who moved first, but suddenly his hand was wrapped around my neck, pulling me down to him. His mouth molded to mine in a hard press of our lips, then his tongue swept inside. Tasting, probing, sliding velvet along mine. He ravished my mouth, his touch vanishing the aching need I'd been feeling, filling me up with hope. Desire. Want.

For a moment, he was my Richard. We were us, and the world was right.

I moaned low in my throat, pushing closer. His hands slid on my wet skin, yanking me tight. I felt his growing erection press up against me.

But then he pushed me away. Gasping, shocked, and naked, I stood in front of him, my towel falling down from the sudden movement.

His chest heaved, and his hands became claws on the armrests.

"I'm sorry," he muttered. "I can't."

"Richard, please," I begged. "Let me in."

He stared, his eyes wild. He spun the chair around and was gone. He left me alone and broken.

~

RICHARD

"Gracie, stop it," I ordered. "I can't cope with you and your sister right now."

She frowned, furrowing her brow the same way Katy did when confused. Normally, I would find it adorable—today, I found it annoying. I glanced at my watch. How long was Katy going to be in the shower?

"What's cope, Daddy?" she asked, milk dripping from her spoon as she stared at me.

I stifled my groan. She was getting milk everywhere. Heather refused to eat, fussing and fretting as I tried to slip the nipple into her mouth. She squirmed and pushed at me, and I struggled to keep her in my arms. Gracie was chatting nonsense, the same way she did every morning, and usually it was endearing and I would listen to her intently, but things had changed, and I wasn't in the mood.

I was never in the mood anymore.

My body ached, my head hurt, and I was impatient. I hadn't slept well again, and all I wanted was to be alone. I needed time to think without people hovering and my thoughts always interrupted.

"It doesn't matter," I snapped.

She stared at me, her lip quivering. "Is you mad, Daddy?"

"It's are you mad, Daddy," I retorted, ignoring the voice inside telling me to stop being a dick. "Can't anyone speak properly here?"

The quiver got worse. "Did I-did I do sumfing bad?"

Katy came into the kitchen, her hair still wet from her shower. "No, baby girl, you didn't." She stroked Gracie's cheek and pulled the spoon from her hand. "You go play for a few minutes. We're going out, and we'll have a snack, okay?" She lifted Gracie from her highchair and set her on her feet, glaring at me the entire time. Gracie toddled away, her little feet thumping on the hardwood floor. She disappeared around the corner to the family room. Katy took Heather from my arms, settling her close and sliding the nipple into her mouth effortlessly.

"She'll take it from you," I grumped.

"Maybe because she can sense she isn't bothering me. Unlike the way you were half-assedly trying to feed her while correcting the grammar of our toddler and making her feel as if she'd done something wrong."

"She was getting milk everywhere and asking silly questions."

Katy stared at me, bewildered.

"Questions you used to love. And she's still a baby, Richard. Learning. Of course, she gets milk everywhere. Usually she's sitting on your lap, spilling it on you and you never think twice about it."

"Well, that isn't happening anymore, is it? Not while I'm in this chair. I can't cope with both of them while you're flitting around, Katy."

"You offered to help while I had a fast shower. Gracie was eating, and you said you would feed Heather. I was gone ten minutes. I thought—I thought maybe you were feeling a little better this morning."

"I guess you thought wrong—again."

The words, achingly familiar and hurtful, hung in the air between us. Memories of another time when I used to snap at her using the same phrase pushed on the edges of my brain.

Distress skittered across her face. However, she kept her voice steady. "What's going on, Richard?"

I ran a hand through my hair, grimacing as I realized I had milk on my fingers.

"What's going on?" I repeated, my voice getting louder. "*What's going on?*" I leaned forward. "What's going on is that I am trying to recover. I can't help with the kids, I can't clean up the messes, and I can't handle the incessant noise. I need to concentrate on me, and you aren't giving me what I need to do so!"

She reared back as if I had slapped her.

"I'm not giving you what you need? What is it that you want, Richard? Please tell me, because I'm confused."

"I want to be left alone. I'm tired of all of this." I waved my hand.

Her eyes were filled with hurt. Hurt I had caused, yet I couldn't seem to stop myself.

"All of this?" she repeated. "You're tired of our life? Our family?"

I scoffed, turning away, unable to look at her. "I'd hardly call this a life."

Behind me, there was silence. I sucked in some calming breaths and realized how horrible I sounded. I spun the chair around, but Katy was gone.

The doorbell sounded, announcing the arrival of my physiotherapist.

I would have to apologize when we were done.

~

"Try to relax, Richard. This isn't going to work if you're not relaxed," Colin advised, his voice patient as his hands worked my uncooperative limbs.

His simple words were my undoing. Everything that had gone wrong that morning—my fight with Katy, my impatience with my girls, the feeling of despair that constantly threatened—hit me.

With a snarl, I pushed away his hands and tugged myself into a sitting position.

"That's the problem, isn't it?" I snapped. "It's not working. My fucking legs are useless. *I'm useless.*"

He patted my shoulder, the gesture pissing me off even more.

"It's going to take time, Richard. You know this. We need to be patient and keep working." He indicated the table. "Lie down and let me try to help."

"No."

He blinked. "I beg your pardon?"

"I said no. I'm done."

He held up his hands. "Okay. We'll scratch today. You can relax, clear your head, and I'll come back tomorrow."

"Don't bother."

He shook his head. "You don't mean that."

I started to yell. "Yeah, I fucking do! Don't tell me how I'm feeling. I've done everything you've told me to do. I push myself every day, and I've got nothing! I'm still stuck in that fucking chair!" With another curse, I leaned and pushed over the wheelchair. "I'm done with all of this!"

He was silent, then he bent over and righted the chair. He positioned it correctly and waited patiently as I transferred myself to the chair and lowered into the seat. He stood back, crossing his arms.

"I know it seems endless, Richard. I know you feel as if nothing has changed. But it has. Your muscles are getting stronger. Your upper body strength is great. You couldn't self-transfer two weeks ago, and now you can do it with minimal effort. Your spine still needs time to heal."

"It's had weeks," I snarled.

"The damage was severe, and we knew it could take longer. *You* knew that. You also knew all the work would be on you." His gaze was intense. "Your attitude will also affect your recovery, and the last little while, you've put in the physical effort, but not the mental. If you believe you won't walk, then you won't—no matter what I do to help you."

"What about the pain? It hits me and renders me numb—why can't you get that to stop?"

He spoke slowly. "You've been checked and tested, Richard. Several times. Some pain is normal, but what you describe..." His voice trailed off. "There isn't a cause that can be found, and I agree with the doctor's assessment. It could be a phantom pain—something locked in your psyche only you can break."

I pounded my hands on the armrests. "Enough of the mental bullshit mumbo jumbo. It's not in my fucking head. I *feel* it. I *live* it. If you're not up to the challenge, I'll find someone who is. *Do your job.* Fix me."

He picked up his bag, not reacting to my anger. "I am doing my job, Richard. You're the one who isn't giving one hundred percent. I think you need to talk to someone—someone who can help you work out this anger."

I glared at him. I was getting tired of people's advice. The carefully chosen words that included *professional* and *mind over matter*. All bullshit.

"I can help heal your body, Richard. You need someone else to help heal your mind."

"Get out," I snarled.

He sighed, slinging his bag over his shoulder. "Call me when you're ready to get back to work."

"Don't hold your breath."

He shook his head. "Your stubbornness is something I had hoped would work for you. At the moment, however, it's messing with your mind. You need to figure this out. You need to find your reason, Richard."

I yanked the chair to the left, ignoring him.

He pulled the door shut behind him, leaving me with my thoughts.

The pain was driving me insane. It happened every time I was forced to move. At the start of exercises, when transferring to the bed. It was the same damn pain I recalled having before I passed out in the car. Excruciating. That was what was holding me in this chair. I was furious that no one was addressing the issue. I needed a new specialist —someone who would listen. Not some head doctor.

A few minutes later, Katy came in. She regarded me for a moment, then spoke.

"Was that completely necessary?"

"What?" I snapped.

"Telling Colin off."

"He was pissing me off. I pay him to do a job, and he isn't doing it. None of them are."

She crossed her arms, looking at me with the same thinly disguised impatience Colin had a few moments ago. It angered me further, and I narrowed my eyes at her.

"You have something to say?"

"He's right, Richard. I think you need to talk to someone."

I threw up my hands. "Great. Now you want me to talk to a shrink or something?"

"Yes. Maybe if you talked about how you're feeling instead of bottling it up inside, it would help. Maybe you could get past whatever is stopping you from moving forward."

"You think it's that simple?" I sneered.

She sighed, looking weary. "I don't think any of this is simple. I think it's so complex that we need help."

I gripped the armrests. "What would *help* is getting out of this chair. Being productive. Being a man."

Her eyebrows rose. "Is that it? You don't feel like a man? You think walking defines who you are?"

I exploded.

"What defines who I am is gone, Katy!" I yelled. "I sit in this fucking chair every day. I can't walk. I can't go for a run. I can't play with my children. I can't make love to my wife. I can't go into the office and be productive. I depend on you and strangers for everything. I'm trapped, and I fucking hate it!"

She stared at me, her expression filled with sorrow. She crossed the room and kneeled by the chair, gripping my arm.

"I know things seem dark, Richard. But this isn't going to be forever. We have to keep hoping. *You* have to keep working and pushing. If anyone can do this, you can. I know it."

I shook my head, the ugly, angry words out before I could stop them.

"So typical of you, Katy. Always trying to find the positive. See the good. Letting me walk all over you, the same way I did when you worked for me, as if in some way it would change the situation. I hated it before, and I hate it now."

Her expression changed. The woman I knew, the woman I loved, disappeared. The light in her eyes dimmed as she stepped away from me.

"You're back," she murmured.

"What the fuck are you talking about?"

"The Richard VanRyan I first knew. The man I despised. The one I thought had changed. You've come back."

I snorted, her words somehow burning me. "I never left, sweetheart. You refused to see that part of me."

Pain lanced across her face, and she wrapped her arms around her torso, hugging herself. She studied me, her expression so filled with torment, I wanted to squirm.

"Okay, Richard. I'm going to give you what you want. You want to be alone? You want quiet? You want to concentrate on yourself? It's yours."

She turned and headed to the door.

"That's right, Katy. Walk away. Run. It's what you do best, isn't it?" I sneered, unable to stop the words, even as I hated myself for saying them.

She stopped, her hand on the door. She looked over her shoulder, tears glimmering in her eyes. "I'm not running, Richard. I'm giving you what you think you want, even though it's killing me."

My chest ached at the sight of her tears. My heart screamed at me to stop her. To hold out my arms and beg her for forgiveness and tell her what I really wanted to say.

To tell her how terrified I felt.

To confess that I worried if I had to stay in the chair, her life would be miserable, and she would eventually leave me.

To tell her how diminished I felt as a man and a husband. To utter the word *failure* out loud.

I stayed quiet.

She turned the handle and walked out, pulling the door closed behind her.

I let her leave, my anger overriding all my other senses.

Ten minutes later, I heard the front door shut, and the sound of her car leaving faded away.

Silence filled the house. I got what I wanted.

A sense of loss filled my chest, and I hung my head.

What had I done?

15

KATY

I pulled up in front of Graham and Laura's house and turned off the engine. I glanced in the rearview mirror, not surprised to see Heather and Gracie asleep. After getting Gracie a treat of her favorite donut, and a cup of coffee for me, I had driven aimlessly for almost an hour, trying to collect my thoughts and calm down.

Richard's words ran through my head on an endless repeat. His actions frightened me. His impatience with our children. His cutting remarks. The way he sneered my name.

I wasn't lying when I said it was as if the old Richard had been resurrected in front of my eyes. The tone of his voice had been icy and uncaring—the same way he used to speak to me before he changed.

Or had he changed? Was he right, and I had refused to see?

I rested my head against my hands that clutched the steering wheel.

No. Richard was hurting. Scared. He fell back on his old habits and lashed out.

However, I wouldn't allow him to take out his temper on our girls. I could handle it, but they were too young to understand. It had taken me the first fifteen minutes in the car to convince Gracie that Daddy was okay and having a bad day, and she had done nothing wrong. She loved him so much and was confused. He had never talked to her the way he had earlier. And I wouldn't allow him to do so again. I had been certain his indifference would cease and he would go back to being the loving father he had always been with them.

I had been wrong.

I started at the tap on my window, and I opened the door, stepping out of the car and shutting the door quietly behind me. Laura drew me into her arms. The feel of her comforting maternal hug was too much, and I began to sob. She stroked my back in long passes, making hushing noises.

"Come with me, Katy."

"The-the girls," I hiccupped.

Graham appeared beside Laura and patted my arm. "I've got them. Jenna is on her way, and we're going to spend some time with them. Go with Laura, and I'll be along shortly. I think we need to talk."

I let Laura lead me away, knowing Gracie and Heather were in good hands. For all intents and purposes, Graham was a grandfather to the girls. Jenna was one of Gracie's favorite people, so they would be well cared for. I didn't want them to see me like this, so it was for the best.

I sipped the tea Laura brought us, the soothing scent of bergamot filling my head. She pushed a plate of toast my way, urging me to eat.

"I'm not hungry."

"You need to eat and be strong for the girls." She paused. "And for yourself—and Richard."

My cup shook in my hand at the mention of his name.

"I left him alone in the house."

"He's a grown man. I'm sure he can fend for himself."

I opened my mouth, and she waved off my protests. "I was there a few days ago, Katy. Your fridge is full of food he can help himself to if he's hungry. You've rearranged the house so he can go anywhere. If he's tired, he can take the elevator upstairs, and he's perfectly capable of getting himself in and out of his chair to the bed." She lifted her cup to her lips. "At least, in that sense, his stubbornness is paying off."

She pushed the plate my way. "Eat."

I picked up a piece of the toast and nibbled on it.

"Tell me what happened this morning."

I drew in an unsteady breath. "The old Richard—the one I despised—appeared."

She frowned. "I know he isn't himself right now—"

I shook my head, interrupting her. "No, it's more."

She covered my hand. "Tell me."

"There's a Richard you don't know—a man you never met."

"I have heard stories," she admitted.

I glanced down, tracing the edge of the table with my finger. I felt guilty saying anything against Richard. My love and loyalty ran deep.

"Katy," Graham said, entering the room and sitting down beside me. "Talk to us. Say the words and get it out. Saying it doesn't mean you love him any less. It simply means you need someone to talk to."

I broke. It all came out. Richard's anger this morning. His lack of effort and his despondent mood. Our lack of intimacy. His cutting remarks and anger. All of it. My voice shook, the tears constant as I spoke. I wiped at my cheeks when I was done, unable to meet their eyes.

"I don't know what to do," I confessed. "I don't know how to help him. I want to be there for him, but I can't let him take his anger out on the girls."

Graham and Laura exchanged a glance, then Graham spoke. "He shouldn't take his anger out on you either. You did the right thing leaving him alone for a while, Katy. He needs to think and figure out his priorities."

"His priority is to heal."

"I agree. But he can do that without being a nasty asshole," Laura inserted.

My eyebrows shot up at her words. Laura never said anything negative about anyone.

She lifted her shoulders. "I'm not blind, Katy. I agree with you—Richard hasn't been himself since he came home. I could see him regressing."

Graham nodded. "I did as well. I thought he would improve once he was home, but he seems to have gone in the opposite direction."

"Alan said this often happens with patients experiencing what Richard is going through. Depression and anger issues occur. I suggested he talk to someone, but he refused." I sighed, letting all the truth come out. "He has refused to do anything to help his progress. He goes through the motions, but his heart isn't in it."

"It's not," Graham agreed. "I tried to get him interested in working from home. I thought it would help him—take his mind off dwelling and feeling sorry for himself. Get him involved in life outside that damn chair again. He would have everything he needed, yet all he did was throw up roadblocks." He shook his head. "The Richard I know would blow up the roadblocks and wheel past them until he could jump over them. Not accept defeat and turn away." He paused, taking a sip of tea. "When I said that to him, he told me I didn't understand, and he refused to say anything else. I didn't push it. Perhaps I should have. Perhaps we all should have been pushing harder."

"I don't know how to help him. Everything I suggest is wrong, every idea he strikes down, or, even worse, shows nothing except apathy when I talk to him. Add in the anger I saw this morning and I'm worried the Richard I love is gone. Unreachable." Tears began to build in my eyes. "I don't know how to get through to him. He has always made us such a priority, but now it's as if he doesn't care anymore."

Laura covered my hand. "He does care, Katy. He's so petrified, he's lost himself."

"How do I find him?"

She leaned back, sharing a glance with Graham. "I wish I had the answer to that."

I picked up my tea, the cup shaking in my hand.

I wished I did as well.

~

RICHARD

I wheeled through the house, the quiet around me unsettling. Katy had cleaned up the kitchen, the spilled milk gone, all evidence of my family being there, gone. It felt empty—much like my heart did at the moment.

The Keurig machine was low enough I could reach it, a mug already in place for me. I knew without looking, when I opened the fridge, the cream would be in reach. Food I liked would be at eye level, easily accessible. She made every effort to ensure I had what I needed. She tried so hard to give me what she thought was necessary.

I thought of the angry words I had thrown at her. The way I had snapped at Gracie. My impatience with my helpless infant daughter who needed to be fed.

I had failed them all yet again.

They were better off without me. If I couldn't be the Richard I used to be, they would all be better off without me.

I rolled myself back down the hall, not interested in food or coffee, and stared out the window at the backyard. The water of the pool glimmered in the sunlight, beckoning. I longed to slide into the cool liquid and swim a dozen lengths, kicking and gliding through the water with no thought, and float on my back, carefree and relaxed the way I used to do after coming home from a productive day at the office.

But even that was lost to me.

I hung my head, feeling the weight of my despondency sitting heavy on my shoulders.

Everything felt lost to me.

The sound of the front door opening, and then footsteps made me lift my head.

Katy came back.

I spun the chair, expectation lifting some of the gray fog that seemed to permeate my head these days.

But it was Graham who walked in, his expression serious, a spark of anger in his eyes.

I met that anger with my own. It didn't take much to fan the flames that lurked below the surface all the time. The fact that it wasn't Katy was all it took to make it rise to the top and erase all rational thought.

"I suppose Katy ran to you with her sob story?" I snarled.

He sat down. "She came to see us, but there was no sob story." He tilted his head. "She told us what happened this morning, and of course, defended you, the way she always does."

"If you came to lecture me, spare it, Graham. I'm not in the mood."

"I came to tell you that your wife and children are safe. They'll be staying with us for a while."

I narrowed my eyes, my chest aching at his words, yet still too angry to reply.

"Katy tells me you want to be alone and concentrate on your healing."

"It would be a nice change not to be bothered all the time."

He pursed his lips, studying me. "I had no idea people caring about you bothered you so much, Richard. However, it seems there is a lot about you I didn't really know." He paused. "There was a time, not very long ago, you would have welcomed our *intrusion* in your life."

"That was before this," I hissed, slapping my legs. "Before the life I knew was taken away."

He rubbed his chin, then stood. "You have lost the use of your legs for now. I cannot imagine the implications that has had on your life or your psyche. However, I fear the loss of being mobile is nothing compared to the losses you're risking with this behavior."

I curled my fists onto the arms of the wheelchair, but I remained silent.

"You have a wife who loves you whether you can walk or not. You have two little girls who worship you. You're highly respected in your field. You have friends who care. Enough money that your world can be changed and adapted to work within the boundaries needed if you don't recover."

"Your point?" I snarled.

"Unless you change, unless you come to terms with the accident, you will lose things far greater than the ability to walk." He tilted his head. "Where is the Richard I know best—the fighter who lets nothing and no one stand in his way? Where the hell is that spirit? Why have you given up before you've even really tried?"

"I have tried," I shouted. "Nothing is working."

He shook his head. "No. You haven't tried. Stop lying to me. To yourself."

"Fuck you, Graham."

He lifted his eyebrows. "I think you're the one fucked here, Richard. You need to get your head out of your ass and back in the game. Remember what you have to lose and harness that anger into getting out of that chair." He glared at me. "Stop feeling sorry for yourself."

I snapped. "Get out."

He didn't move.

"You have no idea what you're talking about! I have tried. I have done everything I was told to do, and it hasn't fucking worked!" I shouted, slamming my hands on my thighs. "I push through the pain every time I do my exercises. I live with it, never knowing when it's going to hit and steal my strength away. I have given it everything I have, and I'm still stuck in this godforsaken chair with no answers as to why!"

He shook his head. "Katy is right. You're in denial, and you need to talk to someone. Be honest. Going through the motions isn't going to get you out of that chair."

Our gazes locked. Anger wasn't what I saw in his expression. Worry and disappointment were heavy in his eyes. Neither of which I could cope with right now. I spun my chair around, unable to look at him anymore.

"Nothing is going to get me out of this chair."

"That's exactly what is keeping you locked in there."

I rested my head on my hands, suddenly too tired to be angry anymore.

"Leave, Graham. Just leave me the hell alone."

"I'll go, but we're not done. I'm not giving up on you."

"Please look after my girls. I can't do it anymore."

He sighed, the sound echoing in the room around me.

"Yes, you can. You just need some help."

He left, the quiet click of the door shutting behind him like a gunshot in the room.

This time, the silence screamed at me.

After Graham had left, I rolled around the house aimlessly, unsure what to do with myself now that I had gotten what I asked for. Silence. I used the elevator I hated and went upstairs, sitting in the doorway of the nursery, staring at the empty crib. Across the hall, Gracie's room was an explosion of pink and white. Stuffed animals were piled high on her canopy bed. She loved it when I would stretch out on the mattress, and she would lie on my chest as I read to her. An ache began in my heart, and I had to move away from the doorway. The door to our room stood open and I wheeled in, immediately hit with Katy's soft floral scent. It was everywhere. Soaked into the very essence of the room. I stared at the bed. The adjustments she made so I could sleep there beside her at night. The lift board I loathed that helped get me onto the mattress. The special equipment in the bathroom. Everything she had done to help me.

All of which emasculated me to the point I couldn't even touch her.

She had no idea how I lay awake at night, waiting for her to fall asleep. It was the only time I could gaze at her in the dimness and let my feelings out. My fear and pain. The worry and inadequacies that filled my head. The longing I had for her. The intimacy I missed so much but was too fearful to attempt with her. Getting an erection around Katy wasn't the problem. Keeping it was. The pain would hit and obliterate everything else. I felt empty and lost. It added to my feelings of being less of a man than she deserved. Still, I couldn't live without her. The war within my head was endless. It exhausted me, leaving me listless and angry.

In the darkness, I could touch her. Stroke her hair, glide my fingers over her soft skin. Whisper my fears out loud, wishing I were brave enough to say them to her openly. We had always had the gift of communication between us, but now even that was gone.

I knew it was my fault, yet I seemed unable to reestablish it.

Angry and restless, I returned to the den, incapable of stopping the rampant thoughts in my head. The glint off my ring caught my eye and I stared at it, sliding it off my finger and holding it to the light. Katy had had it fixed—the platinum solid and new. Unlike me—I couldn't be mended. With a roar of rage, I threw it, the metal bouncing off the wall and rolling on the wooden floor. My rage burned hot and bright, and I lost it, grabbing and hurling items. Pillows, magazines, books, everything I could lay my hands on I threw as I cursed and yelled. Stormed at the unfairness of it all. Screamed at God for punishing me now for the way I used to be. Robbing me of the happiness I had found. I kept going until I drained my anger. The few things spared were my laptop and items too high for me to reach on the shelves from this goddamned chair.

And the pictures of my family. Even in my wrath, those were too precious to destroy.

Shattered, I hung my head, clenching my hands on my lap. My fingers felt strange, and panicked, I dragged myself from my chair and, using my hands to pull myself along, searched for my ring. I located it by the corner of the desk and slid it back onto my finger where it belonged.

I looked around at the destruction I had caused. The den was in shambles—a fitting image for the way my life was shaping up. And it was all my fault. I had no one to blame except myself.

Weary and spent, I dragged myself back to my chair, but I had no energy left to pull myself back up. I lay on the floor, watching the sun move across the sky and fade away, twilight descending around me, the silence deafening. Light glinted on a picture frame, the face in the picture staring down at me.

Penny.

The woman who saved my Katy from the streets and accepted me for me. She had helped me find the man inside me who could love, and she entrusted her most beloved daughter into my care. I had adored her, grieving hard when she died. It was she who brought Katy and me together. I had sworn to her I would make sure Katy was looked after and loved.

I had failed her today as well. I knew if she were here, she would shake her head in sorrow and turn away. She would be horrified at my temper and actions. Disgusted by the way I ranted at Katy and my girls.

She'd leave me on the floor where I belonged.

I shut my eyes so I didn't have to see her looking down at me.

I must have fallen into an exhausted sleep.

I startled awake, snapping up my head. The room was dark, the only light coming from those twinkling around the pool in the backyard, their glow flickering on the wide windows in my den. Another noise alerted me to the fact that I wasn't alone in the house anymore.

I remembered Katy had added a clapper to the lamp behind my desk. Luckily it had been too heavy to throw, and although I had yelled at her at the time for adding the stupid device, I was grateful for its addition. I clapped my hands, blinking at the sudden brightness, then faced the doorway and called out, hearing the hope in my voice.

"Katy?"

Footsteps headed in the direction of the den. They were far too heavy to be her footfalls, and I withheld my groan. Obviously, Graham was back. I steeled myself for his expression when he walked in and saw the destruction around me. It wasn't his face that appeared in the doorway, though.

"Maddox?" I asked, shocked to see him.

He strolled in, glancing around. "In the flesh." He stopped, looking concerned. "What the hell are you doing on the floor? Are you hurt?"

I ignored his question. "Help me up."

He pulled the wheelchair beside me and, with a grunt, hoisted me in. He wasn't gentle, but I held my tongue. I was grateful to be off the floor.

He stared at me until I couldn't take it anymore, and I broke the silence.

"What the hell are you doing here?" I narrowed my eyes. "Did Katy call you?"

He pushed a pile of debris off the chair and sat down. "Nope. Graham did."

"Well, you can turn around and go home. I'm fine."

He looked around, lifting an eyebrow at me. "I think we both know that is a bunch of BS." He leaned forward, resting his elbows on his thighs. "What are you doing, Richard?" He indicated the room with a wave of his hand. "This doesn't look fine to me."

"I took a little anger out on the room."

"From what I hear, you're taking your anger out other places."

"I had a bad day."

He snorted. "Try again."

"I've had enough lectures for the day, Maddox. I don't need to hear yours. I'll call Katy tomorrow and apologize."

"You need to do more than that. But I'm not here to lecture you or make you apologize to your wife."

"Then why are you here?" I demanded.

"Graham said you needed help. He's worried, Richard. Katy is worried. Hell, your physio guy is worried. So, I came."

"Well, you can go back home. Your wife needs you."

He laughed. "She is settled comfortably at a very luxurious hotel downtown. With her sister Cami keeping her company. She's fine."

I frowned. "If Cami is with her, then—"

A voice boomed out, confirming my suspicions.

"Holy fuck, Dickhead—what's going on with you? Katy redecorating or something?"

I turned my head and met the intense gaze of Aiden Callaghan. Another one of the co-owners of BAM, Maddox's friend, and the biggest man I had ever met. He stepped into the den, his broad shoulders filling the doorway.

"What the hell are you doing here?" I asked.

He smirked. "I'm here to whip your ass into shape. And I'm not leaving until it happens, so buckle up, buttercup. It's going to be a wild ride."

~

Despite my protests, Aiden wheeled me to the kitchen. Maddox made coffee and pulled some cold chicken from the fridge, setting it on the table.

"Eat."

"I'm not hungry."

Aiden picked up a drumstick, tearing into it. "You're gonna need your strength."

I rubbed a weary hand over my face. "Look, I appreciate your concern, but there is nothing you can do. I had a whole team, and I still can't walk, Aiden. I doubt you can make much of a difference."

He wiped his mouth and reached for another piece. "Damn, your wife can cook. Fried chicken is my favorite." He bit, chewed, and swallowed. "You're right. I can't make any difference—no one can—except you." He wiped his hands and pulled a pile of papers from the knapsack he had set on the floor. "Your physio plan at the hospital and the follow-up regimens are great. But if you're not trying, nothing is gonna work."

"First off, how the hell did you get my file, and second, how would you know? You haven't been here," I snarled.

He leaned back, not at all concerned with my anger. "Check the attitude, Richard. I'm here because Graham called and talked to Mad Dog this morning and told him what was going on. I was there, and once I heard what was happening, offered to come with Maddox. Your boss—your fucking friend—was concerned enough he arranged a private plane to fly us here. I spent the entire ride talking to him, Katy, and your physio guy. You're pissed off that I have your file? Take it up with our genius IT boy, Reid. He's as worried about you as we are. If you wanna sue me or him over it,

I'll give you Hal's number. My attorney will deal with that shit, while I deal with this. I warn you, though, Hal is a shark, and once he finds out why we did this, he'll be all over you like white on rice, and Becca will never speak to you again. And regardless, this is still gonna happen." He drew in some much-needed air. "And if you want to know why, I'll tell you. You're fucking family, Richard. And that's what we do at BAM. We look after family—even when they don't want us to."

I blinked at his tone. I had never heard Aiden talk with such a serious manner. He took my silence as permission to keep going.

"I compiled some stats for you, Richard. You're a numbers guy, and I thought it would give you some perspective. First off, your injury was severe. You were trapped in the car a long time while they waited for the jaws of life to get you out. Your spine was compressed and the blood flow constricted for an extended period of time. Your surgeon was one of the best around—you were lucky he was on call that day."

I didn't disagree. I knew Dr. Fletcher's reputation, but still, I had my doubts.

"Didn't do me much good, did it?" I snarled. "I'm still in pain and stuck in a fucking wheelchair. Useless and immobile."

"So," Aiden continued as if I hadn't spoken, "your recovery is taking longer. But, unlike you insist, it is *not* improbable. Even with the time lapse, people with severe injuries such as yours do recover and walk again. But it takes time and determination. You haven't given either a good enough shot."

"Not everyone walks," I insisted.

"No," he agreed, flipping a page. "There are approximately one percent of patients that don't recover fully. Pretty damn good odds that you can recover." He shut the file. "I've known you for a while, Richard. The only one percent *you* are ever in, is the top."

"Sometimes we don't have a choice."

He leaned forward. "In this, you do."

I slammed my hand on the table. "You think it's that easy? That I can will myself to walk and I will? I have fucking tried!"

He shook his head. "Are you listening to yourself? The first word out of your mouth for everything is no. So here it is back to you. No—you're not trying hard *enough*."

I let out a string of expletives that would make a sailor blush. "You think I want to be like this? Unable to walk? Living with this goddamn ball of fire in my back? Not able to help my kids? Do my job? Make love to my wife? I'm losing my mind over this shit!"

He held up his hands. "Wait. You're saying you haven't been, ah, *intimate* with Katy since the accident?"

"No," I admitted, looking at my lap. "We haven't had sex."

"Even with the injury you have, you should still be able to get an erection."

I huffed out a long breath. Maddox finally broke his silence. "Talk to us, Richard."

"I can't, all right? I just can't."

"Can't or won't?"

I scrubbed a hand over my face. "Katy and I... We always had amazing chemistry. I worry it won't be the same. I won't be able to—" I paused "—that it won't be good for her and she'll be disappointed. I want to, but I can't relax enough to let anything happen. And the pain kills me before I can really try..." My voice trailed off in embarrassment. "And I stop. So, no, we haven't had sex. We haven't even been close."

He studied me. "There's that word again." He crossed his leg over his knee, resting his hand on his ankle, his voice low and serious. "I think there is more to this pain than you realize, Richard—than you're willing to admit. If you can't be honest with us, at least be honest with yourself. As for the rest, your legs are the problem, not your dick. Your hands and tongue still work," Aiden informed me. "You're overthinking this. Holy shit, Richard. We need a reset in your brain."

"I need a reset in my life," I said, staring at my legs.

Aiden laid his hand on my shoulder. "That's why we're here. Maddox is gonna listen and be your friend. I'm gonna work you harder than you've ever been worked before. Unlike your physio guy, I don't care if you hurt. I'm still gonna push."

I looked at Maddox, who was watching us with narrowed eyes.

"Isn't it worth it, Richard?" he asked quietly. "Right now, you have nothing. You pushed away your family, and you're stuck in that chair. There is nowhere else but up. If you try—really try— you might be able to earn both back. Worth the effort, I think."

His words hit me. *Nowhere else but up.*

"Aiden is right," he continued. "You need to talk. Be open. Admit your fears. Overcome them. I can be your friend and support you, but to be honest, I think you're suffering from depression, and you need professional help. Aiden can guide you through the exercises, but it all comes down to you. What you want. How much you are willing to fight to get it back." He met my eyes. "You need to find that belief in yourself, Richard. You're the common denominator here. If you don't believe, nothing we do is going to work." He sighed. "You need to stop living the future you think is *going* to happen and grab the here and now and change that future. If you don't believe, you're already DOA."

I thought of the anguish I had caused Katy with my words. The look of devastation on her face when she walked away. How Gracie had recoiled from my anger this morning. The way Heather pushed against me when I tried to feed her. Katy was right. They sensed my impatience, and she had been right to take them away.

Aiden tapped his chin. "Lemme ask you a question, Richard."

"Okay."

"Can you live without your legs?"

I paused before answering. "I don't want to, but yes."

"Can you live without your family?"

There was no hesitation. "No."

"Then you know what you have to do. Find the balls and man up. Fight for all of it."

The image of Katy walking away hit me. I needed to see her come back. I needed her.

"When do we start?"

Aiden grinned. "In the morning." He clapped my shoulder and pushed the plate of chicken closer to me. "Eat, and then get some sleep, Richard. You're gonna need it."

16

RICHARD

I spent a restless night, finally dozing off at dawn. I woke up to sounds of things being moved and Aiden's booming voice downstairs directing whatever was happening below me.

I pulled myself up, glancing at the empty spot beside me. I had never slept in this room alone until last night. When Katy gave birth to each of the girls, I had stayed the night with her at the hospital, and she had never been away. I didn't like waking up without her. The sheets were cold and empty, echoing the feeling in my chest. I ran my hand over her pillow and held it to my face, inhaling deeply. I could smell her fragrance deep in the fibers, which increased my longing for her. I reached for my phone and stared at it, my fingers hovering over the screen.

I had no idea what to say to Katy. I knew I needed to apologize and to tell her what was going on, but after the way I spoke to her yesterday and the look of devastation on her face, I knew it wasn't enough. My words and actions had cut deep—not just yesterday, but since I woke up in the hospital. I had put up walls and shut down on her, effectively becoming the man she first knew. A person I swore never to become again. Even worse, I had let my children see that man. I had to make it up to them all, and I needed to show Katy I was trying. Words were fine, but actions were going to speak louder.

I set the phone aside and got ready to head downstairs and find out what was going on. The process was long and tedious, and I finally headed down, my hair wet, and my determination set. The elevator door opened, and I wheeled myself out. Voices were coming from the family room, and when I stopped in the doorway, I gaped at the changes.

The furniture was pushed aside, some of it gone. Exercise equipment replaced the sofas and tables. Aiden was talking to Colin, their heads bent over my file. The two were polar opposites. Aiden was gigantic, towering over Colin, his muscles bulging. Colin was built like a runner, lean and hard, but no doubt in top physical shape. The yin and yang of fitness. The one common denominator was their determination to get me walking. I felt a grudging sense of gratitude that I had them both on my side. At this point, I wasn't sure I deserved it.

Maddox was busy on his laptop, but he greeted me as I rolled in.

"Morning, Richard."

Colin and Aiden ceased their conversation. Aiden grinned broadly, flexing his shoulders. Colin nodded in my direction, clearly uncomfortable. I knew I had to make the first move. I rolled closer and stuck out my hand.

"Colin. Thank you for your assistance with whatever plan Aiden has drawn you into." I pulled in a long breath. "And I apologize for my behavior. It was beneath me and insulting to you."

He shook my hand, a real smile on his face. "Apology accepted. I know how difficult this has been for you, Richard." He jerked his thumb at Aiden. "The big guy here is going to do what I couldn't do. He'll be on you twenty-four seven."

Aiden chuckled darkly. "Yep."

Colin put his hand on my shoulder. "I believe you can do this, Richard. I wouldn't say it if I didn't. Still, *you* have to believe it as well."

"I know. I've been...difficult."

Aiden's merriment boomed out and Colin smirked. "That's one word," he agreed.

Aiden tapped the file in front of him. "Colin's plan is great, and I've added a few tricks of my own." He indicated some of the equipment behind him. "I'm going to work you harder than ever."

"I wish our clinic had a couple of these machines." Colin eyed them with envy. "The good they could do me..." He shook his head, letting his words trail off.

"Once I'm done, they're yours," Aiden announced, lifting his coffee cup to his mouth. "A donation from Richard."

I didn't object. "To say thank you," I added.

Colin grasped my hand and shook it hard. "That is awesome."

I glanced at Aiden. "How do I say thank you to you?"

He flashed his teeth. "I'll take it in sweat."

H e meant those words. After Colin left, Aiden and Maddox laid out my schedule. I swallowed my pride and the angry words I felt rise to my lips and accepted it. The exercise routine. The massage. The goals. The counseling. I knew it all had to happen. My priorities had to be reset, and I needed my girls back as soon as possible.

I had been such a bastard. I didn't even know if Katy could forgive me, but I knew I had to try. My entire life was at stake. Losing my family would end me, even if I had been the one to cause it.

I looked up, forcing the words from my mouth. "The goals—me walking isn't listed."

Aiden shook his head. "Nope. My goal is to make your legs strong. Reengage your muscles. Reset your focus on living your life *now*. Clear away the negative shit you've built up. Colin will be here with me every day, making sure it's done properly. He's the professional at this, not me. I'm going to push you and build your endurance and strength. That's my thing. And we're adding massage to help." He paused and took a sip of his coffee. "And you have a session every day with a counselor. Not a psychiatrist. This guy—Randy—specializes in helping people like you. He comes highly recommended."

"He'll come here?"

"Yes. He likes his clients to be comfortable."

I was certain that wasn't going to be the case, yet I knew I had to try. I couldn't open up to my own wife, so talking about my fears with a stranger seemed doubtful.

Aiden must have seen my indecision, and he offered me his perspective.

"I didn't think I needed counseling, but once I started, I realized the benefit."

I lifted my eyebrow in a silent question.

He set down his coffee. "I can say anything I want to my counselor. There's no judgment on her part. She listens and offers me ways to deal with things I'm going through, or how to lay memories to rest. I don't have to choose my words or edit my thoughts. She isn't personally involved, the way Cami would be for me, or Katy for you. She has that divide. I often share with Cami, but it comes from a different perspective, if you know what I mean. My thoughts are clearer, so I can tell her what I'm thinking, often without the pain permeating my thoughts." He studied me. "You need some help to come to terms, Richard. To find your determination and, frankly, your balls. You gotta try." His voice softened. "Remember who you're doing this for. Yourself, of course—but also, your family."

I knew what he was saying, and I let my gaze drift to the window.

"Will this make the pain worse?" I asked.

Maddox and Aiden exchanged a look. Aiden bent forward, his elbows resting on his knees.

"I went through all your reports with Colin. He told me your doctor believes the pain might be psychosomatic."

I snorted. "How can I imagine something like that?"

"The brain is a mysterious thing, Richard. The power of your own mind is limitless."

"Why would I do that, of all things? Add pain?"

He sat back, pursing his lips. "That is something only you would know. Maybe in some twisted way, you're trying to protect yourself."

I waved my hand, dismissing his words. "That's crazy."

He shook his head. "Nope, it's fact. Regardless, you're going to work through the pain, and I promise what we're going to do won't make it worse. Now, the question is, are you going to try?"

I let his words soak in, and I made my decision. I handed my phone to Maddox.

"Take some pictures for me. I want to send them to Katy."

He grinned. "Okay."

I met Aiden's stare. "Let's do this."

∽

I peered over the edge of the pool. I was desperate to get in and cool off after the workout from Aiden. He wasn't kidding when he said he was going to push me. I had worked out with him and Maddox on occasion when I was in Toronto, and I'd thought he was a high achiever then, but under his direction? He was a tyrant. He went through all the exercises I had been doing with Colin, added in some of his own, and watched me like a hawk, constantly badgering me.

"Show me some effort, Richard."

"Gracie can do better than that. Push it!"

"Go ahead, get angry, Richard. Use it and show me you meant what you said. Work!"

"Use the pain, Richard. Push past it. Think of what you are going to gain."

I had never pushed as hard for anything in my life.

"How, exactly, am I going to get in?" I queried Aiden. We had no equipment out here to aid me and my arms felt like Jell-O. I wasn't sure I could even push myself up out of the wheelchair.

"Like this," he said dryly and tipped up my wheelchair, sliding me into the deep water.

For a second, I was frozen, panic setting in fast, but a pair of hands under my arms pulled me up quickly and I broke the surface, sput-tering and cursing.

"You fucking ass!"

He grinned and Maddox chuckled as he shoved a pool noodle under my arms to keep me floating.

"You were perfectly safe. You needed the shock to wake you up. Now we're gonna do some work in here."

I groaned. "Haven't we had enough for the day? I thought this was my reward."

"Nope. Your reward is a five-minute float before we get back to work."

I let it go. The water felt too good, and I knew he was trying to piss me off. Aiden thought anger was a great motivator.

I was beginning to think he was right.

~

Leaning back against the headboard, I groaned. My body ached. Muscles I didn't know I had ached. Aiden was relentless. I pushed on my thigh, amazed at the twinge I felt as I pressed. I hadn't said anything to Aiden or Maddox, worried it was a different sort of sensation, but for the first time since waking up in the hospital, I felt a small glimmer of hope. It gave me the courage to reach out to my wife.

The pain I feared happened with every new routine, but it faded as we went along. I never knew when it would hit, but Aiden watched me closely, making notes. I had no idea what he was keeping track of, yet I knew when he was ready, he would tell me.

I dialed Katy's number, tension radiating through my body. It had been three days of silence from her. I couldn't remember the last time I had gone three days without speaking to my wife. I needed to hear her voice.

"Hello," she answered, her voice quiet and cool.

"Ah, hi. It's me. Richard," I sputtered, sounding like an idiot.

Which I was.

"I know that," she replied.

Silence stretched out between us. I had no idea what to say to my wife.

"Was there something you wanted?" she asked. "Or are you just calling to breathe heavily into the phone?"

A smile played on my lips, remembering a phone call much earlier in our relationship when she had asked the same thing. It was the first time she had been smart with me.

Was she remembering that too?

"I'm about to put Heather to bed, and Gracie is waiting." Her voice interrupted my thoughts.

"Could I talk to her?"

She paused.

"I promise not to upset her, Katy. I miss her." I sighed. "I miss all of you so much."

Her voice caught. "Here."

I heard her tell Gracie it was me.

"Daddy!" Gracie's voice was excited.

I had to swallow the sudden lump in my throat. "Hi, baby girl."

"Miss you!"

Pain lanced through my chest. "I miss you."

"You working?"

I cleared my throat. "I am. Are you having fun?"

She giggled. "Jenna take me to da zoo. I pets some goats and gots some totten tandy!"

Despite the emotional pain I was feeling, her words and lisp made me smile.

"Good. I'm glad you're having fun."

"You done soon?"

"Soon," I promised, not knowing what Katy had told her.

"I gets Mommy."

"Gracie..." How did I apologize to my baby girl and make her understand?

"Yeah?"

"I love you, and I'm sorry I yelled the other day and that I've been in a bad mood. I won't do it again."

"Dat's otay, Daddy. You have boo-boo, and it make you sad. Mommy tell me."

"Daddy won't be sad anymore, okay?"

"Otay."

"Let me talk to Mommy."

"Otay. Lubs!"

I heard her hand the phone back to Katy.

"Daddy say sowwy. He not mad now."

"Good," Katy mumbled. "You crawl in bed, and I'll come read you a story."

She spoke into the phone. "Thank you for apologizing to her. She hasn't dwelled on it, though. We've made sure she's been busy and happy." She paused. "Children tend to forget the bad stuff."

I heard her message. Gracie would forget, but she couldn't.

Had I already lost her?

"Thank you. Katy, I—" My voice caught.

"What, Richard?" I could hear the weariness in her voice. Sense her withdrawal.

I remembered what my new counselor, Randy, had advised. *"Speak, Richard. Say what you're feeling out loud. Truth is painful sometimes, but it's real. No one can read your mind, so you need to express yourself clearly."*

"I've been an ass. A total ass," I blurted. "Worse than that. A total bastard."

There was silence.

"I was scared, and I didn't know how to tell you."

"Why?" she asked softly.

"Because I was terrified to ask you if I never walked again, if you would leave me."

I heard her fast intake of air. "But I told you—"

I interrupted her. "I know. But how you see me changed, Katy. How I see myself has changed. I felt like less of a man. I was afraid to even touch you. It even bothered me to hold Gracie or Heather. I was worried I would hurt them. That they'd wiggle and slide off my lap and I couldn't catch them."

She remained silent.

"I longed to touch you. Hold you. Let you soothe me and tell me things were going to be all right."

Her voice was quiet and shaky. "Why didn't you?"

"Because if I touched you, I'd want more. And the pain was too much. The embarrassment of not being able to make love to you messed with my head. The feeling of being less and thinking that was all I would ever be now. I felt powerless and lost."

"Richard," she sighed. "You can't keep all those things from me. I'm your wife. I want to be there for you. We need to talk about these things and work them out together."

"Are we still together?"

Her voice was gentle and low. "This is a part of our journey, not the end of the road, Richard."

Her words healed a small piece of my bruised heart. "I love you so much, Katy. And I'm trying. I'm working with Aiden and talking to a counselor. I'm doing it for us."

"Do it for yourself first."

"I want my life back. Whatever form it takes. *You* are my life. The girls."

"I need you," she whispered. "For you to be there with me."

"I am, baby. I will be. Give me a few days to concentrate on this and clear my head. But I need you, Katy. I need to know you'll be there. I can't do this without you. This house is so empty without you. I'm so empty." My voice broke. "Tell me I haven't lost you."

I heard a soft sob, and I longed to be able to hold and comfort her.

"You haven't," she murmured.

"Can I call you tomorrow?"

"Any time."

"You'll give me some time, and you'll come home?"

She sighed. "Yes. I need a little time too, Richard. You frightened me the other day. Your words and actions hurt. And if we're being honest, the last while has been difficult."

"I know. I became the exact thing I swore I never would be again. The old me. I was horrible."

"Yes, you were."

"I am working on that too. Give me another chance."

"Love is filled with second chances, Richard. If I didn't think so, I wouldn't have answered the phone."

"I love you, Katy VanRyan. I'm going to prove it to you."

"I look forward to it." She paused. "Good night."

"Good night, sweetheart."

I stared at the phone after she hung up. She didn't tell me she loved me, but I heard her forgiveness in her voice. If I had that, I still had her love. I would earn it.

Maddox knocked on the door. "Everything okay?"

"Yeah."

"What's up?"

I held up the phone. "I spoke with Katy."

He perched on the end of the bed, crossing his ankles and leaning back on his hands. "How did that go?"

I shrugged. "I spoke to Gracie first. Then Katy let me apologize."

"But?"

"I need to do more. I need to win her back."

"Woo her the way you did when you were dating," Aiden advised from the doorway.

I looked at Maddox. "You never told him?"

He shook his head. "Nope. You told me in confidence, and that's where it stayed."

"Where what stayed?" Aiden demanded.

I sighed. "I blackmailed Katy into marrying me. We fell in love later. I never dated her, and I never wooed her. I've never wooed a woman in my life."

He gaped at me. "You blackmailed her?"

"Basically. I paid her."

"Holy shit, dude. You got layers."

I burst out laughing. Maddox joined in my amusement.

Aiden stroked his chin. "I didn't woo Cami much either. But I know someone who is excellent at it." He turned and left the room, calling over his shoulder. "I got a call to make."

Maddox stood. "Give her time, Richard. She knows we're here, so she's given you the space you need."

"She needs the break from me too. I hope she's getting some rest."

Maddox pursed his lips. "You know, Aiden might be onto something with the wooing thing. I have an idea. We can talk about it tomorrow. Get some rest."

I shut off the light and lay in the darkness. I reached over and pulled Katy's pillow to my chest, inhaling deeply.

"Come home soon, baby," I said into the darkness.

Sleep didn't find me easily that night.

17

RICHARD

All my days became the same. Strengthening, stretching, weights. I worked until sweat poured down my back and exhaustion set in. I was grateful to be dumped in the pool, the cool liquid surrounding me. I was weightless suspended in the water and, for that brief period, almost felt normal.

"Randy is here in an hour. I've booked you a massage after that," Aiden informed me.

"Do I really need one?"

He nodded. "I've been working you hard. You need some deep tissue work and frankly, Richard, I'd rather not do it."

I chuckled. "Me too, Aiden. You already have your hands on me enough."

He snickered, and for a few moments, I floated blissfully.

"Holy fuck, it's working." Maddox said.

"Told you."

I looked between them. "What are you talking about?"

"Look down. Your feet are moving."

I ducked my head and peered into the water. It was more of a twitch, but my feet did move.

"Holy fuck," I repeated Maddox's words. "I'm not consciously doing that."

"They're waking up." Aiden met my incredulous stare. "The muscles are reengaging."

"How?" I asked. "Why now?"

He smirked. "Because you believed, Richard."

Two hours later, I waited for the elevator. I was tired. Talking to Randy exhausted me. Delving into my emotions with someone other than Katy was difficult, yet I was starting to see the benefit. I could say anything, and there was no judgment, no reaction, because it didn't affect him. Even when I was honest with Katy, I realized I watched my words in order to make sure what I said didn't hurt her. With Randy, it didn't matter. Even when I raged, he listened calmly and offered suggestions to help or simply let the words go. It was odd; once they were out, they stopped gnawing away at me.

The massage after was a good stress reliever, and although it left me looser, she assured me I would feel it later.

I opened the door and wheeled in, thinking of Aiden's reaction when he first saw the elevator.

"Dude, this is awesome. You and Gracie must have a lot of fun riding up and down. I bet she loves it!"

I had stared at him. It never occurred to me to make it fun. To perch her on my knee and ride up and down. She loved to do that in the office when Katy would bring her to see me. I had been so mired in my own misery, I hadn't thought to try to make it easier for those around me. In fact, I snapped at Gracie when she tried to come in with me, embarrassed I would need help moving around my own house. I had made so many mistakes.

I planned on doing better.

I heard voices as I headed to the kitchen, and I wondered who was here. It was a male voice, so I knew it wasn't Katy. I kept hoping she would come. The longing I had to see her grew hourly, and although she had spoken to me last night, I was still afraid to ask her to come

165

home so I could talk to her in person. I wasn't sure what I would do if she said no.

I stopped in the doorway of the kitchen and gaped at the visitor.

"Bentley?"

The owner of BAM, my biggest client, and my friend, stood. Bentley Ridge was a brilliant businessman, stern, unflappable, and known for his rigid, standoffish ways.

Except for the people he cared about. He adored his wife, his love for her eclipsing the cold front he presented to the world. He was an amazing friend, generous, and giving to a fault.

"What are you doing here?"

He strode forward and shook my hand, then in an uncharacteristic gesture, leaned down and hugged me. It was awkward and stilted, but it meant a great deal. He clapped me on the back and stood.

"I hear you need some wooing tips."

Laughing, I shook my head. "A phone call would have sufficed."

"Nope. This was important. Besides, Emmy was missing her friends, so we came out for a couple of days. Reid will be by later. He and Becca are visiting her father."

"The whole gang is here?" I asked, torn between amazement at the fact that they would go to the trouble and appalled they were putting their lives on hold because of me. "What about Sandy?"

He shook his head. "She's holding down the fort. Her granddaughter was in town for a rare visit. Otherwise, she would have come too." He indicated the counter. "She sent some of your favorite bagels and cream cheese from the bakery you like so much."

"I appreciate it, Bent." My throat was thick again—something that seemed to be happening on a regular basis. I cleared it and spoke. "I appreciate all of this."

"You're welcome. You and Katy are—"

Aiden interrupted him. "I already covered the whole family thing, Bent."

Bentley glared at him, but Aiden shrugged. "Just saying."

I chuckled as Bentley rolled his eyes. He grinned, his expression amused. "Well, if Tree Trunk has that covered, let's get down to it. Let's make a wooing plan."

I rolled to the table and picked up the energy drink Aiden had waiting. I really wanted a beer but decided to wait and ask for that later.

"I sent flowers to her this morning. And to Gracie." Katy had sent me a picture of Gracie holding her flowers and beaming. Her text of thanks ended in two kisses and a heart. When I responded and asked for a picture of her with her flowers, I didn't like what I saw. Katy was pale, and although she was smiling, it didn't reach her eyes. I had a lot to make up for.

"Good start." Bentley sat back, stroking his chin. "Maddox and I had an idea. I did a little research on the plane. There's a great boutique hotel downtown. Five-star. Specializes in spa treatments and pampering. The chef is world-class. I think a couple of days there for all the girls would be a great idea. Laura and Jenna included. They even have in-house day care so the kids would be looked after." He explained. "They offer kid pampering too. Indoor playground and kiddie pool. Mini massages, face painting, fun food, that sort of thing." He glanced my way. "I checked—there's a two-day package, and I took the liberty of booking it starting tomorrow. I blocked an entire floor for them."

"That's a great idea."

"They can look after the girls, and we'll look after you." He winked. "I'll make sure Aiden doesn't kill you."

"Katy might prefer it if he did."

Bentley shook his head, looking thoughtful. "No. She needs some time. You both do. But she loves you."

I hoped that was still the case.

"All right, Bent. Teach me the art of wooing my wife."

He rolled up his sleeves. "Prepare to learn, Padawan."

We all laughed at his words.

L ater that night, I went into the den. We had cleaned up the wreckage I had caused the first day they were here. Aiden made me bend over in the chair, picking up papers and drawings and stacking them on the desk. I lifted items that were intact, while he and Maddox cleaned up the broken debris. Shame had rippled through me as I worked, my body exhausted from everything else Aiden had made me do, but I kept my mouth shut. I still had a lot of work to do to make the den tidy, and I didn't want Katy to see the mess I had caused.

With a sigh, I picked up a stack of papers to sort through, startling when a voice interrupted me.

"Richard."

I looked up. Becca was in the doorway, her expression unhappy.

Rebecca Holden had come to The Gavin Group on a co-op her first year in school. I recognized her talent right away and took her under my wing. She became a valued coworker to me, a friend to Katy, and an adopted auntie to my girls. I considered her part of my family, and when the contract came up with BAM and she asked to be the liaison between the two offices, I hated to see her go. I had hoped she would return, but she had fallen in love with Toronto, the office there, and more importantly, Reid Matthews, BAM's resident IT genius. I missed her in the office and having her around after hours, but she was happy and settled, and that was more important.

Except now, she was here and looking at me as if she was disappointed in me. Knowing she had seen Katy, I was certain she was upset with my behavior.

I swallowed, hating to think I had disappointed yet another person I cared for.

"Becca."

She strolled in, gazing around, and sat in the one chair that was free from clutter.

"Love what you've done with the place."

I scrubbed my face. "Yeah, not my most shining moment as an adult."

She laughed, the sound without humor. "I'd say nothing about your behavior has been very adult-ish lately."

"I'm aware."

"Are you?" she asked quietly. "Are you aware of what you've put Katy through? How devastated she is right now, Richard?" She shook her head. "I've never seen her like this. Your behavior isn't the Richard I know. What's going on?"

I folded my hands on the desk to stop the trembling. The thought of the pain I caused my Katy made me want to rage again—this time at myself. "I got lost in my head. In the what-ifs."

"The what-ifs being if you can't walk again?"

I decided to be honest. "Basically, yes. In my head, I decided I wouldn't be enough for Katy and the girls if that were the case."

She shook her head. "I don't think that's your decision to make. I know your wife. She would love you regardless."

"I didn't want that for her."

She huffed. "Again, not your decision. Katy is smart and strong. She can decide what she wants—what she feels is best for her *and* your family." She paused. "And she feels that is *you*—regardless of your mobility."

"I know." My voice caught. "She's been far more forgiving and understanding than I deserve."

"We forgive those we love, Richard. And she loves you despite the fact that you've been a total bastard."

"I miss her, Becca."

"Then work hard. Earn her forgiveness."

"I'm trying." I barked out a dry laugh. "Given my past, I have no idea why I have so many good people in my life willing to help."

She shook her head. "You don't get it, do you, Richard? It's because of your past. You changed and became a good man. By doing so, you brought the good people into your life." She scowled. "Now, stop screwing it up and acting like an asshole."

Reid Matthews sauntered in, his laptop tucked under his arm. I swore that thing was attached to him twenty-four seven.

"Hey, Dickhead."

I rolled my eyes at his nickname, which he, no doubt, picked up from Aiden, but I held my tongue. I deserved to be called much worse.

He stood behind Becca, laying his hand on her shoulder.

"You got your head out of your ass? Eye on the prize, so to speak?"

His voice was mild, although I saw the anger in his eyes. Katy had only met him a couple of times, but her maternal streak ran deep, and she had treated him like a mother would a son—something he had lacked for so long. And he, in turn, treated her with the same protectiveness. My behavior would infuriate him.

"Yep."

"You going to push?"

"Aiden is torturing me well, yes." I paused. "And being without my family is punishment enough. Even though I brought it on myself, I am suffering, Reid. I'll do whatever I need to in order to get them back."

He studied me, then sat down beside Becca. "Good. You're gonna love the changes I made to Aiden's online program where he tracks your progress. It'll give him more ways of seeing your weaknesses and making you work harder."

There was no disguising the delight in his eyes at the thought of me suffering more.

"Excellent," I stated dryly.

"You'll get your family back," Becca said quietly. "They all love you too much for that not to happen."

I met her gaze. "That's what I'm doing this for. To be the man they need."

She stretched over the desk, covering my hands. "You are, Richard. No matter what. You need to believe that in order for this to work." She paused. "They need you."

She was right. They were all right.

I glanced at the picture on my wall. My favorite one of Katy and the girls.

My family.

That was my reason.

I needed them too.

I hated to see Bentley leave. I knew he needed to be in Toronto, and with Aiden and Maddox here, his trip was a quick one. I didn't see the girls, aside from Becca. They were there for Katy, and I was glad she had the support. Reid hung around at times, making sure to tweak his program, living up to his promise of me working even harder and not letting his delight in that fact stay hidden. Still, I was going to miss him. He saw my girls and took videos of them, sharing them with me when I finished my torture sessions. Gracie playing. Heather sleeping. Katy reading to them. They helped get me through the days. Reid forgave me enough, and he downloaded them to my phone so I could watch them whenever I wanted. They were the last thing I saw before I closed my eyes at night.

When he was leaving, Bentley shook my hand and told me to keep going. He met my gaze, his expression serious.

"I know you can do this, Richard."

"Thanks." I indicated his partners with a jerk of my head. "Thanks for the loan."

"I expect to be repaid—with interest. You had better start dreaming up campaigns to knock my socks off."

"Will do."

He offered me one last piece of advice about Katy.

"Think about what she loves, and give it to her. Let her know you're thinking about her. Make her your number one priority. Never let her doubt that."

I took his words to heart.

Katy loved the spa. She sent pictures of them all enjoying the treatments, sipping champagne, even funny ones of Heather getting a baby massage and Gracie having her toes done with the girls, holding up a glass of apple juice. They made me smile, even as my heart ached.

I sent flowers to the hotel for Katy. I added a box of her preferred chocolates.

When she went back to Laura and Graham's, I sent a chef to make her favorite meal. A basket of bath products to indulge her love of soaking in the tub. I sent it with a stuffed bear, fluffy and cute with a card attached, reading:

Snuggle this until you're home.

I'll take his place when you're ready.

All my love—Your Richard.

One night, lying in our bed alone, I turned on some music. I shut my eyes and listened as the soothing voice of Neil Diamond played in the darkness. A song came on, and for some reason, the lyrics hit me as they never had before. "The Story of My Life" spoke of the depth of his love for the woman in his life and how much she meant to him. The fact that he felt he didn't exist before she came into his life and would cease to do so after she left. The song sang the words I held in my heart for Katy.

I listened to it over and again. I found the song and sent it to Katy with a voice message, hoping she was still awake and would hear what I did.

This is my song to you, sweetheart. It says what I can't. Please come back.

I waited for over an hour before she replied. Her words soothed me as only she could.

Our story isn't over, Richard. But I love the words and the thought.

The best gift of all was a picture I had found on my phone. It was a simple snap of the four of us together. We were out by the pool. My back rested against a tree, and Katy and my girls were wrapped in my arms. The happiness on her face said it all as she had lifted her arm out and snapped the picture. I had it printed and framed and sent it with a heartfelt note I composed.

My darling Katy,

This picture symbolizes everything that is good and real in my life. My family. The sweetest little girls ever to exist on this earth and the most wonderful wife a man could ask for. My children are blessed to have you as their mother, and one day I hope to be the man deserving of you again. My biggest regret isn't losing the use of my legs—it's the harsh words that sent you away from me, when I should have been honest and told you my fears.

Come back to me, Katy. Believe in me again.

I'll make it up. I promise.

Always—Richard.

Every gift was acknowledged. Each one allowed me to hear her voice, listen to her soft sigh of pleasure as she described her reaction. The taste of the meal she ate, wishing I were there to eat it with her. The scent of the lotion she rubbed into her skin, knowing how much I would have liked to do it for her. The fragrance of the flowers that perfumed the air and made her think of me.

I was as wooed by her words as she was by my offerings.

The last gift was met with silence. I waited all day for the phone to ring, yet it remained quiet. Late that night, my phone buzzed with a message, and I scanned it, the short message meaning more than any thank you could come close to.

I love us. I'm not giving up. I believe. I will always believe in you.

I love you.

Katy.

I slept better that night than I had in days.

～

Aiden wheeled me over to a set of parallel bars that hadn't been in the room the day before. Equipment arrived all the time, and other pieces disappeared as Aiden changed his plan or Colin suggested something new to try.

He locked the brakes and stood in front of me. Colin walked over and stood beside me.

"Today, you stand."

I eyed the bars. "I don't think—"

"We don't say that here," Aiden interrupted me. "We try. With everything we have. Get your ass out of that chair and stand."

I studied the bars with trepidation.

Aiden grunted impatiently. "Richard, you've made great progress. Your muscles are getting strong, the feeling is coming back, you can wiggle your toes on your own. Trust me on this. You can do it."

I looked at his serious face, then at Colin. He nodded in encouragement.

"I'm not sure I can pull myself up to the bars," I admitted.

"Okay," Colin agreed. "Baby steps."

He took one arm, and Aiden took the other. The feeling of being lifted to my feet was odd. I knew my legs were there, I could feel the pressure, yet I was like a newborn, unsteady and off-balance. I grasped the bars, holding with all my strength.

Pain hit me, a burning fist of pressure in my lower back. I gripped the bars harder, sweat breaking out on my forehead.

Colin and Aiden exchanged a look.

"Breathe through it, Richard," Aiden said. "It will go away."

I shut my eyes and concentrated. My pulse rate returned to normal, and my body eased as the pain lessened.

"Let go," I huffed out.

They released me, and I stayed up. Shaking and unsure, but I was up. On my own two feet.

"I want to walk."

"Then walk," Aiden said in a calm voice.

I concentrated, pushing with all my might. My leg slid forward, not more than a few inches, and I managed to drag the other one behind it. Sweat poured down my neck, my arms shaking, my body firing all sort of nerves and reactions at the effort. The pain fisted me again, and I grunted.

"One more," Colin encouraged. "You can do one more."

I pushed and tried, yet nothing happened. Deflated, I faltered, Aiden and Colin moving quickly to grab me before I fell. They eased me back into my wheelchair.

Aiden crouched down. "Do not get fucking discouraged. That was amazing. You took a step, Richard. Tomorrow, you'll take another. The light, dude. You're seeing the light."

I met his gaze. He was beaming. I looked back at the bars and gritted my teeth.

"I want to try again."

He stood. "Now you're talking."

~

I spent three days of torture using the bars. Pushing upon my own, grasping the metal, and forcing my feet to move. Some attempts, the pain grabbed me, other times, it was absent.

I looked awkward and awful, but I didn't care. I was finally free from that chair—even if it was only for a few moments. I pushed myself to the maximum every day. Maddox filmed my progress, letting me watch it after so I could see the improvement myself. The progress was there, but it was slow. I struggled both physically and mentally to go forward. To accept and to live in this moment and not get discouraged. That was one of the hardest things for me.

I sighed as I got dressed having finished my morning workout. Aiden and Maddox had sat down with me, and I knew what they were going to say even before they said it. They had to go home—return to their lives. Bentley needed them back in Toronto. I held up my hand before they could talk.

"I know, guys. You've given me two weeks of your time. I will forever be grateful for it." I looked at Aiden. "I'll work with Colin and on my own. I promise." I rubbed my legs. "You've given me something I didn't have before. Hope."

"You will walk, Richard."

"I know I will. However long it takes, I will get out of this chair." I pulled in a long breath. "When do you leave?"

"Day after tomorrow."

"Does, ah, Katy know you're going?"

"Yes."

I nodded. I missed her terribly. The texts and calls weren't enough, and I was desperate for her to come home. As much as having Aiden and Maddox here was great, I wanted my wife and girls back. I was determined to talk to her today. I needed her to come here so we could talk face-to-face.

My thoughts were grim as I headed to the kitchen. Maddox and Aiden were standing in the family room, looking as if they were hiding something.

"What's up?"

Aiden indicated the bars. My eyes widened at the sight of the person standing at the other end of them.

Katy.

"Hello, my darling," she greeted me.

"Katy, sweetheart—"

She held out her hand. "I was told you had something to show me." She waggled her fingers. "Come to me, Richard."

Part of me wanted to scream no. I didn't want her to see me that way—unsteady and vulnerable. However, seeing her there, so close, yet too far away to touch, I knew I had to show her that trust. To let her see me and accept me for the way I was now. Prove to her that her belief in me was warranted.

I wheeled over and pulled myself up. I held the bars so tightly, they shook under my grasp, but I was mercifully pain free. I looked at Katy, who stepped closer. "I'm right here, Richard."

I concentrated on her face. Her incredible blue eyes that watched me, filled with nothing except love. One foot went in front of the other. Slow. Dragging. But the faltering steps led me to her. Time seemed to slow down as I moved toward her, closing the gap that separated us. Finally, I stood in front of her, shaking, sweating, and broken. All my effort went into standing. I stared into her eyes, watching the tears fill them and spill over down her cheeks.

"I'm so proud of you," she whispered, cupping my cheek.

I didn't try to stop my tears. I allowed my emotions to escape, letting her know how grateful I was that she was there, how much I missed her.

I pushed my face into her hand and managed to get out one word. "Stay."

She leaned up, her mouth pressing to mine. "Yes."

That one word had the power to break down the last of my walls. Not caring who was there to witness it, I let out my pain, knowing the woman in front of me would be the one to piece me back together.

18

KATY

R ichard lifted his face from my neck, his eyes red, his cheeks damp. I had never witnessed him break down that way. The rare occasions when he cried, he still held himself in check, his pride unable to allow even me to fully see his pain.

I grabbed the tissues Aiden had dropped beside us and wiped Richard's face, cupping his cheeks.

"Hey," I whispered, looking up at him from where I crouched between his legs.

"I guess I lost the last piece of my man card with that display," he mumbled.

"I doubt it. Aiden was openly weeping before you even finished walking, and Maddox had to leave the room."

He frowned in confusion. "Why?"

"They're as proud of you as I am, Richard."

"Where are they?"

"Aiden made sure you were back in your chair, and they left. I heard the car driving away, so I assumed they left to give us some privacy."

He looked down, surprised. "I have no recollection of being moved."

I softened my voice. "You were pretty emotional."

"Katy, I have so much to say. So many things to apologize for."

I walked to the ottoman and sat down, extending my hand. "I'm listening."

Richard pulled up as close as possible and hunched over so we were at eye level.

He grabbed my hand and held it to his chest. "I don't know why you're proud of me. I was horrible to you. I yelled at our girls. I told Graham off. Never mind the attitude I've been throwing around all the time. Instead of being grateful to be alive and accept the help I needed, I acted like a bastard. Especially to you. My behavior is nothing to be proud of."

"You were in pain."

"I should have talked to you about it." He swallowed. "I was so busy being selfish and thinking about me, I forgot how this affected you and the girls. I forgot to be the husband I promised to be. To be Daddy for my girls. Instead of thinking how grateful I was to still be here with you, I concentrated on the negative." He paused, his eyes focused on our hands. "Randy says I'm struggling with depression."

I waited until he lifted his face.

"Alan said it happens often," I admitted. "I've never dealt with someone with depression. I wasn't prepared and I didn't react the way I should have. The mood swings and temper threw me off, but I understand more now." I paused. "Is, ah, Randy helping?"

"Yes." He hesitated.

"What?"

"He—all of them—think the pain I feel at times is in my head."

"What do you think?"

He shrugged. "In some ways, I understand what they are saying, yet it seems impossible to me. But they're right. It happens when I'm unsure and about to do something new. As if my body is already anticipating pain and reacting."

"That must be frightening for you."

"I don't know how to stop it."

"Maybe you have to give it time, Richard. Maybe your body and mind have to catch up with each other."

He took my hand, rubbing it absently and stayed silent for a while. I let him think.

He lifted our hands and kissed my knuckles. "Katy..." His voice was unsure.

"What is it?"

"Can you forgive me?"

I smiled at him. "I already have."

"Will you come home? Bring my girls back and come home? I promise I'll do better. But I can't do it without you. I need you here."

"I thought you'd never ask," I replied. "Every time I've come, it's been so hard to leave."

"What?" he gasped. "You've been here?"

I nodded. "I usually come when you're in the middle of a workout or in the pool. I had to see you every day for myself."

He looked upset, and I sighed.

"As hard as this was, you were right on one thing, Richard. You needed some space. And I needed some time away from you—"

He interrupted me. "I don't need that anymore—I never did. I was being a bastard. I need you home. I need my girls, and I need our life back."

Before I could answer, he leaned close. "What you saw might be as good as it gets, Katy. I might never be one hundred percent Richard. I might need canes or—"

"I told you before, and I'll tell you until you believe me. If *you* are here—if the Richard I know and love is here—then you are one hundred percent you. Your heart is what I love. Not your legs, not if you walk with a limp, a cane, or if you have to use this damn chair. *You*," I insisted. "When will you believe that?"

He stared at me dumbfounded.

"How I see you hasn't changed, Richard. You're my husband, my partner, and my best friend. How you get from point A to point B doesn't matter as long as you get there. It makes you no less of a man. How you treat me, our family, and our friends is what makes you the man I love. Please find that man and hold on to him. *He* is what I need. What we *all* need."

He smiled and leaned close, brushing his mouth on mine. "You're so fucking incredible. Has anyone ever told you how incredible you are, Mrs. VanRyan?"

I frowned. "If I'm so incredible, when am I going to get through that thick skull of yours?" I waved my hand in vexation. "If the roles were reversed, Richard, what would you do?"

"Exactly what you have been doing—fighting for you."

"When will you believe me? When will you believe in us?"

"Now. I believe that now."

"Then we start again."

I gasped as he grabbed my legs and pulled me to his lap, kissing me hard. He hadn't allowed me that close since his accident. He kissed me endlessly, holding me tightly, as if afraid I would disappear.

"I love you, Katy VanRyan," he vowed against my lips. "I won't let you down this time. I promise."

I snuggled into his arms, the feeling of being home and safe settling into my chest.

"I love you."

His breath drifted across my head.

"That's what I needed to hear."

～

Aiden's face was wreathed in smiles as he sat across from Richard and me. I had made sandwiches and coffee, and Maddox opened a box full of pastries they had picked up while out. Richard stayed as close as he could, always holding my hand or touching my arm.

"Katy, would you make me fried chicken tomorrow before we leave? Next to Dee's, it was the best I ever tasted."

I agreed quickly. It was the least I could do after all he had done for us. "Sure. I'll bring the girls home tomorrow, and we'll have a big picnic outside for supper. They'll love it."

"I don't see why they can't come home today," Richard griped.

"Because Gracie and Jenna are having a sleepover in the tent tonight. Just the two of them. Gracie is so excited, I don't want to disappoint her."

"Jenna might thank you. I can't see her sleeping on the ground."

I laughed. "They have a blowup mattress. Plus, it's Jenna. The tent is like the Taj Mahal."

"So, tomorrow—sunup—you'll be here with the girls?"

His words made me happy. The anxious, miss-my-girls man was the Richard I loved so much. His family was important to him, and to see glimpses of him returning helped to heal the hurt and worry I had been experiencing.

"We'll be home in the morning."

"Sunup is morning," he muttered, yet there was a smile playing on his full mouth. It made me want to kiss him, so I did. His hand flew up, cupping the back of my neck and holding me close. He kissed me back, hard and deep.

Aiden and Maddox both let out catcalls. I was blushing as I pulled away.

"I think, Mad Dog, we're leaving at the right time."

Maddox smirked and threw me a wink. "I agree, Tree Trunk. The perfect time."

Gracie's feet kicked in excitement as we turned down the street. I smiled at her in the rearview mirror.

"Daddy waiting!" she crowed.

I felt both excitement and trepidation as I pulled into the driveway. I wanted to come home so much, yet I was afraid of what was going to happen when we were alone.

Would Richard continue moving forward, or would our presence once again cause him to slide backward? Once he got over the initial pleasure of seeing his girls, would he again find them, and me, more of a bother? I wasn't sure I could take it if that happened.

I couldn't watch the man I love disappear into the shell he used to be.

But a small voice in my head kept telling me he wouldn't. The gifts, the notes, the calls, and texts from him were all sent by the man I loved. He had made sure I knew how sorry he was feeling and how hard he was working to come back to us. He even opened up and expressed his worries, finally letting me know the depth of his fears. Finally letting me understand what was holding him captive inside his head.

And he had made progress. Not enough to please him entirely, but Aiden and Maddox had put him back on the right track.

The question was, could he sustain it?

Either way, I had to find out. I pulled up in front of the house, Richard already outside, sitting in his wheelchair, looking anxious. Maddox and Aiden were sitting on the steps above him, both smiling.

I stepped out of the car and opened the back door, unfastening Gracie from her car seat. She was so eager that her body quivered in anticipation. I'd barely set her on her feet, and she was running. Richard was hunched low, his arms stretched out wide. He caught her, lifting her high, the way he used to, and wrapped her in his arms, holding her tight. His head was bent, and I could see her little arms clutching his neck.

I had to blink away the tears that formed at the sight of them together.

She squirmed back, talking to him, patting his face, waving at Maddox and Aiden and giggling—all at once. It was loud, chaotic, and beautiful.

"Mommy!" she called. "Daddy leaking!"

I had teased her once when I was crying, and I said I was so full of happiness that I had to leak some out or I would explode. She never forgot it. And despite her young age, she was smart enough to know the difference when I cried in sadness or "leaked" in happiness.

I nestled Heather into my arms and approached my husband, who was radiating joy. I hadn't seen that expression on his face since he'd woken up. I knelt beside him and slid Heather into his waiting arms. He pressed a kiss to her forehead, tears streaking down his face.

He'd always felt tears showed his weakness and made him less of a man. It was drummed into his head over and again as a child, and he still struggled with the concept, always hiding his emotions from most people. I thought it showed how strong he truly was when he allowed his tears to show. He had never been as handsome or as sexy as he was in that very moment. Emotional, open, and filled with love for his girls. For us. For me.

"I'm leaking too, baby girl," I murmured, wiping away my tears. "Today is a happy day."

"Yay!" She clapped her hands. "Look! Unca Mattog and Unca Aiden is leaking too!" She wiggled on Richard's lap, and I helped her down so she could go see them. They took turns tossing her in the air, her happy squeals ringing out.

I bent over and kissed Richard. He smiled up at me.

"Thank you," he whispered. "Welcome home, sweetheart."

I cupped his face and kissed him again. "Welcome back, my darling."

It was sad to see Maddox and Aiden leave, although I knew it was time. I was eternally indebted to them for what they had done for Richard. For my family. When I tried to find the words to express my thoughts, they had both waved me off.

"Family," Maddox stated fiercely, hugging me tight. "You are my family."

Aiden had lifted me off my feet with his hug. "What he said," he growled. "And if you need me, I'm right back here to kick his ass."

"Won't be necessary, Tree Trunk," Richard assured him, pulling me back to his side, his hand wrapped around mine tight. "Next time you see me, I'll be walking into BAM with some Danishes and coffee, ready to blow your mind with my next campaign."

Aiden shook his hand hard. "I'll hold you to that."

"I can't begin to express my gratitude for what you've done for me," Richard began, his voice thick.

Aiden shook his head. "I already know, so don't say it. Move forward, no matter what. That's my one piece of advice." He grinned and winked at me. "And don't be a *Richard* to your wife."

I couldn't help the giggle that escaped my lips. Richard frowned, then chuckled.

"I won't."

I handed Aiden a large container, smiling as his eyes lit up.

"Fried chicken for the trip home." I winked. "Wouldn't want you to get hangry on the plane."

He laughed, holding the container like a trophy. "Score!"

Heather was napping, but they had kissed and cuddled her before I carried her upstairs to her crib. After another round of hugs, and lots of kisses from Gracie, they slid into their car and left.

I blinked away the moisture in my eyes.

"We're very lucky to have them."

Richard nodded and swung Gracie up on his lap. "I'm lucky in many ways."

Gracie tugged on his hands. "Ride, Daddy."

He laughed low and spun his chair. "Okay, baby girl. Then Daddy has to work."

I followed them, smiling at the subtle change. After he came home from the hospital, he didn't want to be touched. By me, or the girls. He didn't like having them on his lap or anywhere near his wheelchair. Any attempt by Gracie was rebuffed. He was self-conscious and angry all the time. Now he was cautious, yet open. And he wanted to be close to all of us as much as possible. I had missed his touch greatly, and I knew Gracie had as well, so it was lovely to see them together.

In the house, the little voice on the monitor let me know Heather was now awake. Richard glanced over his shoulder. "You go, sweetheart. I got my munchkin. She can count my reps with me."

"I tount to ten, Daddy," she informed him with a frown.

He grinned down at her, kissing her cheek. "Daddy will teach you more today, okay?"

"Otay!"

I watched them wheel away, my heart full.

We were going to be okay—I was sure of it.

There simply wasn't another option.

~

Heather squirmed and squealed, flailing her arms and legs, splashing the bathwater everywhere. She loved her bath time, and I always enjoyed the relaxed moments with her. Richard was reclined in our bed, reading Gracie her bedtime story. It had been a busy day all around, and it felt as if we were finding a routine. Different than it used to be, yet still good.

I was glad to be home.

I lifted Heather out of the tub, dried her off, and got her ready for bed. I sat in the rocking chair, holding her close. She still liked a bottle at night, and although it was water, it was a time I always cherished. Her hazel eyes, so like Richard's, grew heavy, her long lashes resting on her cheeks as slumber pulled her under. I stroked her soft skin, marveling at her. I stared at her for a few moments, then stood and carefully laid her in bed, tucking a light blanket around her and making sure her favorite bunny was close.

I headed to our room and stopped in the doorway, a smile lighting my face. Richard was asleep, his head resting against the headboard, his snore low and steady. Gracie was curled up on his chest, her little arm flung over him, barely reaching midway. She was spread across the bed in her usual starfish position. The book they'd been reading was on the floor. I slipped my phone from my pocket and snapped a picture, wanting to capture the sweet memory to show Richard later. Carefully, I picked up Gracie and carried her to her room, tucking her in. I knew she had to be exhausted when she didn't stir. I kissed her and ran my hand through her wild curls and made sure the monitor was on.

Back in our room, I picked up the book and set it on the table. Richard hadn't moved. Today, I had seen how hard he pushed himself.

185

The exercises, the parallel bars, the pool. Plus, he worked with Colin and had a session with Randy. I knew how emotionally drained the sessions left him, and he had been quieter the rest of the day, but no less affectionate. After dinner, he had reached for my hand as we sipped coffee and watched the girls play. Gracie was doing a puppet show for Heather, who chortled and waved her hands, making Gracie laugh.

"Would you consider sitting in on a few sessions with me, Katy?" he asked, not meeting my eyes. "Randy thinks it would do us good to talk about some things together."

I tapped his knee, thrilled when he felt my touch and looked up. "I would like to. I was going to ask if I could."

He breathed out a sigh of relief. "Yeah?"

"Yes. I will do anything for us, Richard."

He kissed me hard, then drew back. "Thank you."

He focused his attention back on Gracie and Heather.

I touched my lips, wanting to feel his mouth on mine again.

He had held me close the night before, but nothing else. He was affectionate and sweet, yet I wanted more. I didn't want to push him, and I wasn't sure how to tell him without adding pressure. I had been planning to talk to him tonight, except he was already asleep.

I vowed I would bring it up tomorrow. Still for now, my family was asleep, and I was too keyed up to join them. I decided to take advantage of the quiet and have a bath.

Picking up the baby monitors so Richard wouldn't be disturbed, I slipped into the en suite and turned on the tap, studying the large basket of products Richard had sent me while I was at the Gavins' house. I had loved his gifts, knowing how much effort he put into choosing them and why he was doing so. I felt his love in every gesture. The basket was filled with an exquisite array of bottles of foams, oils, bath bombs, soaps, and lotions in all my favorite scents. I picked a bottle of lavender honey—Richard's favorite—and added it to the water, inhaling the soft fragrance with appreciation. I sank into the water with a sigh of happiness.

Today had been a good day, and I hoped the beginning of many of the same. I knew there would be setbacks, but I wanted to think we were stronger and could handle them together now.

I reached for the small bathtub radio Richard had given me and turned on a relaxing blend of music. The warmth of the water soothed my muscles, the scent of sweet lavender filled my head, and I allowed myself to drift.

Until I heard Richard's agonized voice call out my name. Grabbing a towel, I scrambled from the tub and rushed into our room, leaving a trail of water behind me.

He was still in bed, his hands lifted, his voice raised in panic, locked in a dream somewhere in his head.

"Katy...*no*...baby, *come back!*"

I crawled onto the bed, shaking his shoulders.

"Richard," I begged. "Wake up, my darling. It's just a dream."

His eyes sprang open, and he gripped my shoulders, clutching at my wet skin.

"Katy," he gasped.

"I'm here."

He looked around wildly. "You were walking away. You wouldn't come back," he panted. "I couldn't chase after you. My legs don't work!" He gripped me harder. "I couldn't get to you. You were leaving—"

"Shh," I comforted him. "It's all right, Richard. I'm not going anywhere. I'm right here." I pried his hand off my shoulder and pressed it to my cheek. "I'm right here."

He stared at me, blinking, panicked, and confused.

"Right here," I repeated. "I'm not going anywhere."

He swallowed, and then his mouth was on mine.

19

RICHARD

The taste and feel of my wife chased away the last lingering remnants of my dream. Katy wasn't walking away. She was right here, with me, in my arms.

Right where she should be.

I kissed her deeply, seeking out her tongue with mine, stroking hard and deep. Reclaiming her mouth. Reclaiming her. I yanked her tight to my chest, pulling off the towel she had draped around her body. I pushed down the blanket that covered me, needing to feel her. I dragged her over my lap, groaning at the feel of her weight pressing down on me. Still kissing her, I slid my hands over her silken thighs, parting them and settling her so she straddled me.

She pulled back, gasping. "Is this okay?"

"Fucking yes, it's okay." I pressed my mouth to her neck, licking up the damp, elegant column of her throat. "It's fucking perfect."

I grazed my fingers over the scar on her thigh, remembering how I discovered it. Discovered her. Fell in love with her. I was doing it all over again.

"We both have scars now," I murmured. "You're so perfect for me, Katy. And I'm such an idiot. Yours made you stronger. Mine weakened me."

She grabbed my face, holding it tight. "You stumbled, Richard, but you didn't fall. You're here with me, so *be* with me."

Her words filled my heart. Her passionate pleas stirred something entirely different.

I yanked her to my mouth again and kissed her until she begged.

"Richard," she whimpered.

"Katy," I hissed as she shifted. My cock was waking up, my erection growing as I pulled her close.

"Oh God, I *feel* you," she moaned, undulating again. "I can feel you. You want me."

"I've never stopped wanting you."

"I want you, Richard."

"You're going to have me," I promised. "But I need to take this slow."

"Are you in pain?"

I ignored the spasm I had felt, pushing it aside. It didn't matter. Nothing mattered except her. "No."

She met my eyes, her gaze hooded and dark. "I'm good with slow." She tugged on my T-shirt. "But this has to go."

I let her yank the cotton off my torso. She sat back, running her fingers up and down my arms, gliding them down my chest and across my abdomen. My muscles tightened under her touch, desire building beneath my skin like wildfire.

She looked up, catching her bottom lip in her teeth. "You are so sexy," she breathed out. "You've always been sexy, but Richard, your muscles—you're so cut now. So defined." She lifted an eyebrow. "I want to lick every inch of you."

My cock twitched at her words. I knew I had gained more definition thanks to Aiden and his regimens. I had done it to gain back my strength, but the desire that darkened Katy's eyes as she took in my harder, toned upper body was an added bonus.

I gripped her chin. That stubborn little chin with the dimple I loved to kiss—so I did. I dragged my lips to her ear. "Lick anything you want, baby. I'm yours. However you want me."

She gripped my neck and kissed me. I groaned at the feel of her mouth moving with mine. The way her fingers trailed over my skin. I hissed as her mouth descended. Sucking on my nipples the way she knew I loved, nipping at them with her teeth and making me hiss in pleasure. Brushing her lips along my abdomen, teasing the taut muscles with her tongue. She moved down my body, shimmying past my knees. She gripped the waistband of my sweats.

"Can I?"

Using my arms, I pushed my body down the mattress, so I was lying flat. With a deep breath, I was able to lift my hips enough to allow her to drag the heavy material down my legs. I refused to let her see how great an effort it was for me. I didn't want to ruin the moment.

My cock sprang free, fully erect and hard. Katy crawled closer, the look in her eyes making me shiver and forget any effort I had put forth. She wrapped her hand around my dick and tugged. I pressed my head into the pillows at the sensation of pleasure.

"More, baby. I need to feel more," I urged.

I had to swallow my shout as she wrapped her lips around my cock. I felt everything. The wet. The warmth. Her gentle suction. The way she slid her tongue along the underside of my shaft and swirled it around the head.

Every touch I knew well, except every sensation felt like the first time. My nerves tingled, my balls ached, and pleasure built and spiked.

It was everything I remembered and more. I reached down blindly and tugged at her shoulders.

"Katy, come here."

She released me, the air cold on my skin. She straddled my waist, her face close.

"I love you," I murmured.

"I love you too."

I pulled her to my mouth and kissed her. Long. Slow. Deep. The way I knew she liked. Her full breasts pressed on my chest, her nipples rubbing the coarse hairs scattered on my skin. Her back felt like satin under my fingers as I traced the bumps and curves of her spine. Her ass fit perfectly in my hands as I gripped the full cheeks and pressed her against me.

"I don't know how far this will go," I confessed. "If I can finish..."

"We'll take this as far as we can," she replied. "Just try with me."

I captured her mouth again, holding her neck and stroking the skin. Finally, she lifted her head and sat up, straddling me once more. She slid down my body, her pussy leaving a hot trail on my skin as she moved down. She hovered over me, meeting my eyes.

"Let me do the work."

Before I could reply, she sank down, taking me inside her. I felt her weight on my thighs as she settled, her head flung back in pleasure. My cock was surrounded by heat. By her. I groaned in ecstasy at the sensation. She began to move, undulating over me, one hand braced on my stomach, one buried in her hair.

"It's been so long," she mumbled. "You feel so good, Richard."

"You look so fucking amazing, riding my cock. Taking control. Use me, Katy. Fucking come all over me," I urged. "I love watching you come."

"Not without you."

"No," I shook my head. "I want you to. Ride me until you come."

Her eyes glittered and she moved faster. "I'm taking you with me."

She reached behind herself and stroked my balls. She moaned and whimpered. I was fascinated watching her. Awash in the sensations she created. Rejoicing in the fact that I could feel them. Feel her. A tremor started in my stomach, my body catching up with the visual in front of me. Tingles of anticipation rippled inside me. My cock began to swell. Katy's eyes widened.

"Yes, Richard. Yes! I feel you." She shifted, changing her position and riding me harder. "Come with me."

I grabbed her hips, guiding her. Pushing her up and pulling her back down. She sobbed my name, her back arching as her release washed through her. I watched as she lost herself in the moment. I had forgotten how beautiful she was in her release. The way her entire frame shuddered. How she bit her lip and lowered her chin as if sinking into the feeling. The breathiness of my name falling from her lips. And how it felt when her muscles fluttered, tightened around me, taking all I had—giving me so much more.

My body strained, the urge to thrust and grind against her eclipsing everything else. An orgasm hit me, obliterating everything in its path. I saw stars, the ecstasy was so great. I opened my mouth in a soundless scream, and somewhere, deep inside, I felt a flex, the pinching of muscles not used for so long now gripping, then vanishing as fast as they had engaged. A long, agonized sound escaped as my entire being surrendered. The pain, the pleasure, the sweet torture of it all.

Katy collapsed onto my chest, her breathing ragged and hard. My own chest was moving rapidly as I tried to find enough oxygen to fill it.

I wrapped her in my arms, exhausted, triumphant, and scared.

"Are you okay?" I asked.

She lifted her head, her eyes soft and content. She traced my lips with her finger. "More than okay. That-that was mind-blowing, Richard."

I kissed her fingertip. "It wasn't only my mind that blew."

She giggled, burying her face into my neck. Her breath washed over my skin, the sound of her happiness soaked into my mind.

"I guess Aiden and Colin were right," I mused. "I didn't believe them, and I was too afraid to try. Too afraid to fail, thinking I would never recover if I did." I huffed out a long breath. "What an idiot."

Katy slid off of me but cuddled close to my side and rested her head on my chest. "Why were you afraid?"

"I already felt so diminished as a man," I confessed.

"Did I make you feel that way?"

I stroked her hair, trying to find the words.

"Not intentionally, no. You did everything right, Katy. It was me and my own perception."

"Tell me."

I paused, and she glanced up, my hesitation saying more than I knew.

"Don't be afraid to talk, Richard. Say it and get it out. I promise my feelings won't be hurt."

I tugged her head back to my chest. It was easier to talk when I wasn't looking at her. "It was everything, Katy. All the things you did to make everything easier for me. The ramp, the stuff in the bathroom, the adjustment of the bed height, the contraption to help me get into it. Arranging my therapy, rides to the doctor, and the office." I sighed. "And the elevator. Especially that godforsaken, necessary elevator."

"Why do you hate it more than anything?"

"I hate what it represented. What it all represented. I didn't see them as tools to help me get better. I saw them as things mocking me and reminding me that I would never be whole again. I would never carry you up the stairs or throw you on the bed and fuck you for fun. I would never chase Gracie and Heather around the backyard or be able to have them jump into my arms in the pool because I couldn't catch them since I couldn't stand. The walk-in shower reminded me I couldn't have bath time with them." I curled a piece of her hair around my finger, rubbing the silky strand with my thumb and letting it bounce back into place. "I was so lost in my head, I couldn't see past any of it, so everything you did right, felt wrong."

She was silent for a moment. "And now?"

I slid my hand under her chin, lifting her face. I scanned her eyes looking for hurt, except I saw only concern and worry.

"Now I see how hard you tried and how little effort I put in. Except that's changed, Katy. I swear to you." I shook my head in sorrow. "I'm ashamed of the way I treated you and my girls."

She lifted her finger, tracing it over my jaw. "All they want is for you to love them, Richard. You are the most amazing daddy. They don't care if you have legs that move or you sit in a wheelchair with them on your lap. They adore you so much, and Gracie has missed you terribly."

"I missed her. And Heather changed so much in the time you were gone." I pulled her close, dragging her up my chest so we were nose-to-nose. "And you, Katy. *This*. The thought I could never make love to you again destroyed me. Every time you were close, all I could think of was I wasn't ever going to be able to love you again. It flipped something inside me to the point I couldn't even bear to touch you, even though I was dying to do so."

"I felt as if you were rejecting me," she admitted, a quiver in her voice.

"No. I was rejecting me. The man I thought I was going to be from now on. I used to lie here at night and touch you when you were asleep. Whisper my fears to you because I was too afraid to say them out loud."

Tears glimmered in her eyes. "Oh, Richard…"

I kissed her soft lips and wiped away the tears.

"When you were gone, I was empty. I thought of you all the time. I missed being able to talk to you, to touch you. Promise me you'll never leave me again. No matter what I do, or how much of an asshole I am. Slam my head in a cupboard or something until I come to my senses."

She widened her eyes. "That sounds painful."

"Not as painful as being away from you. Never again."

"Never again," she whispered.

I kissed her—gently, sweetly, and thoroughly. I lingered on her lips, having missed the feel of them for days.

With a sigh, she settled back with her head nestled into the crook of my neck. We lay close and connected. I ran my fingers up and down her arm, reveling in the feeling of the moment and having her beside me again.

"I have to go see Graham. I have a lot more groveling to do."

"Yes, you do."

"I was as horrible to him as I was to you." I huffed out a lungful of air. "I wonder if he'll forgive me this time."

"I think you'll be surprised."

"I think he'll have a few choice words for me. I, ah, I told him to go fuck himself."

"I know. Laura was going to come over and wash your mouth out with soap. I suggested Ivory soap. I told her it was the worst."

I couldn't help the bark of laughter. "And how would you know that, Katy VanRyan?"

"I have my ways."

"Thanks for suggesting it." I nudged her. "Even mad at me, you're supposed to be on my side."

"Oh, I was," she insisted, peeking up at me with a mischievous grin. "The truth is, my dad told me a story when I was young. He cursed a lot, and his mother punished him and washed his mouth with soap. He said Ivory was awful, yet he kept cursing. So the next time, his mother used Dial, and he never forgot the taste. He was very careful never to curse again." Her eyes danced. "In front of her anyway. He said it was the foulest thing he ever tasted. I was trying to spare you."

The hilarity only she could ever cause bubbled up again, and this time, I let it out. It felt good to let go. To laugh at a silly story and share that amusement with Katy. She giggled so hard, she snorted, and the two of us guffawed until we were both spent.

I pulled her close, pressing a kiss to her head.

"Thank God for you, Katy VanRyan. *Thank God you're mine.*"

She snuggled close. "Always, Richard."

It didn't take long for her to fall asleep. The sound of her even breathing and the feel of her, warm and close, relaxed me.

I shut my eyes and let sleep take me.

I stared at the phone, mentally giving myself a pep talk. As much as I dreaded this call, I knew I had to make it.

Another fence to mend, another apology to make. I sighed as I stared out the window. Gracie was running around her playset, calling to Katy, who was following Heather as she crawled through the grass. The sounds of my girls made me content. My gaze focused on my wife, her dark hair glinting red in the sun as she scooped up Heather, lifting her high. Katy's hair flowed down her back, long and soft, grazing the ground, the way it grazed my thighs last night as she rode me. I had missed the feeling of her silky hair on my thighs, and when I had confessed that to her in the dark, she had leaned up and kissed me.

"Something to strive for."

My wife always knew what to say. Because she was right. I would push for it. For all of it.

Simply thinking of last night made my cock twitch. Katy had been so beautiful in her desire, taking me to new heights with her as we soared in a blaze of passion together. Our lovemaking had been a reaffirmation of us and our commitment to each other. When I thought of how close I came to throwing that—*throwing us*—away, because of my pride and inability to express my fears, I shuddered. A lifetime without Katy and my girls wasn't a life. I would exist, but not live.

I spun my chair around and picked up my phone, punching in the numbers with more force than needed.

It rang three times before he picked up. He knew it was me, but he answered with his usual greeting.

"Graham Gavin."

"Graham, it's Richard."

I didn't know what to expect. Silence. Coldness. A dismissive reception. But I should have known better. It was Graham after all.

"Richard VanRyan. How are you?"

"Ah, good, Graham." I cleared my throat. "I'm doing well."

"That's good to hear. Katy and the girls settling back in all right?"

"Yeah, they are. We're all good. Really good."

"Excellent. Is there something I can do for you?"

It was then I heard it. The disconnect. The distance. He was being kind but reserved and was holding himself back. Hardly a surprise given how I had acted.

"I was wondering if you could spare some time to meet with me?"

"Is there an HR issue or some other business you need to talk about?"

I shut my eyes, knowing how hard I was going to have to work to fix this. Next to Katy and my girls, Graham was my closest ally. He wasn't simply a boss. He was my friend and family.

"Yes, there is an issue, Graham. My behavior. I would like to see you and apologize for it and discuss what the future holds."

For a moment, there was silence. When he spoke, his voice had lost some of the formality it held.

"Do you see a future now, Richard?"

"Yes, I do. It's amazing how clear the view can be when one pulls his head out of his ass."

Graham barked out a laugh. "So I've heard."

"Please, Graham. I need to speak with you. Face-to-face." I pulled in a long breath. "I'll come to the office if you prefer."

He was quiet, and I knew he was pondering. I could hear his fingers drumming on his desk as he contemplated how to handle me. If he would insist on me coming to him or he would allow me to apologize in the comfort of my own home.

"I will come there. I think it's best at this point," he stated. "Later this afternoon work for you?"

"Yes," I responded, grateful. "Anytime."

"I'll see you at four." He hung up.

I set down the phone and scrubbed my face. This wasn't going to be easy, yet it had to be done.

The sound of more hilarity outside brought me out of my growing unease. My goal, my one real need in life, was waiting for me out in the sun, their love assured and beckoning.

I decided to go and soak up the love that waited. I would deal with Graham this afternoon.

I spent the morning with my family, hours with Colin, then I worked out on my own, pushing myself until I was a sweating mass of shaking limbs. I used the parallel bars and walked until I couldn't hold myself up anymore. Gracie was my little shadow, following me around the room, handing me my water bottle and towel, doing her "cercises," at the same time. My pint-sized cheerleader clapped her hands, counted with me, and kept my spirits up.

She could count to fifteen now, and I knew soon enough that would go higher. She was a smart little girl, taking after her mother in that sense. Thank God.

Her reward was a trip up and down in the elevator on my knee—ten times. I'd make funny faces and noises, making her giggle and squeal, which in turn made me smile.

Aiden was right. The damn thing was fun.

I couldn't help but wonder if Katy had any elevator fantasies. I bet those could be fun too.

20

RICHARD

Graham arrived, Laura with him, shortly before four. Katy was greeting them as I rolled around the corner. We regarded one another in silence as they hugged her and Gracie, and Laura inquired about Heather. I moved the chair forward and extended my hand.

"Graham."

He shook my hand, his grip firm. Laura leaned down and brushed my cheek with her lips.

"You are looking well."

"I feel well."

Katy laid her hand on my shoulder and squeezed. Reaching up, I grasped it like a lifeline.

"I made coffee," she said.

"We bake cookies!" Gracie exclaimed, tugging on Laura's hand. "Come, Nana L, come hab cookies!"

Laura hesitated, and I smiled grimly. "I'd like a moment with Graham alone if that's okay. Maybe you can visit with the girls for a while and join us?" I sighed. "I have something I'd like to say to you as well, Laura."

She crossed her arms. "So do I."

Graham followed me to the back of the house. He stopped in the family room, looking at the equipment.

"Impressive," he said. He walked to the parallel bars, running his hand along the rails. "I understand you're able to use these."

"Yes, more every day." I exhaled, rubbing my thighs absently. "I hope one day not to need the support, but until then..." My voice trailed off.

He nodded and headed to my den. I followed him, leaving the door open behind me. He perched on the edge of my desk, crossing his arms over his chest and waiting.

I had a speech prepared. Carefully chosen words of regret and repentance. They flew out the window as I looked at him. I tugged on my cowlick in vexation.

"Fuck, this is getting to be a habit, isn't it?"

He lifted one eyebrow. "Habit?"

"Me, apologizing for some major poor-ass decision I made in my personal life that affects my business one. You having to come to me so I can grovel and ask forgiveness and hope I haven't fucked up my entire relationship with you."

He stroked his chin thoughtfully. "It's only happened one other time, Richard, and I'll say this. I'm not sure your behavior was a conscious decision. More like an off-the-cuff reaction to a shitty situation you were in."

His words somehow eased the tension in the room.

"Graham, I'm sorry."

"For?"

I ran a hand through my hair. "All of it. The words I said, the horrible way I acted, the pain I caused, and the responsibility I heaped on your shoulders."

"That's a lot of guilt to be carrying around," he stated mildly. "I think you have enough to deal with already."

I shook my head, rolling closer. "No. I deserve the guilt. You're right. I reacted. I reacted badly. I was scared, Graham. Scared and trapped in my head. I thought it was over."

"What was over?"

I waved my hands. "Everything. I was happy. So fucking happy. I had more than I ever thought I would get out of this life. My family, friends, my career—" I swallowed the thickness in my throat "—you and Laura, two people I considered my adoptive parents. I thought the accident ended it all. I couldn't be the husband I was. The father I needed to be. The man you needed in the office."

He tilted his head. "But you were still *you*, Richard. It was all any of us needed or wanted."

"I get that now. But I couldn't see it. I thought—well, I thought if my role changed, diminished, then I wasn't good to anyone and you were all better off without me."

He crossed his legs and rested one ankle across the other. His foot beat a steady rhythm on the floor as he studied me.

"As brilliant as your mind is, sometimes your thinking patterns are messed up," he stated. He held up his hand before I could respond.

"I told you what you mean to me and Laura personally. I get that you've never had people like us or your family in your life before. I also know you were scared, yet I admit I had no idea how deeply your psyche was affected."

"Basically, I'm fucked in the head, my counselor says."

He chuckled then grew serious again. "I'm glad to know you're back on the right track, Richard. Your exercise, the counseling, all of it is working. You have to trust the process."

"I do now." I sucked in a deep breath. "And once again, I have you to thank. You reached out to Maddox. You took care of my family when I couldn't. You gave me the space I needed to find my strength. This is all because of you. I know it and I am more grateful than I can express."

He inclined his head, letting me continue.

"I can't repay you, except to say thank you. To apologize and promise that I will endeavor to do better. To be the Richard you were proud of and to earn back your trust."

"You never lost my trust, Richard. Caring for your family was easy because they are my family too. Watching you suffer the way you did, keeping yourself away from the people who cared for you was one of the most difficult things I've ever had to do." His voice lowered. "And I am proud of you. For pushing through. For accepting the help. For finding the strength to be Richard VanRyan again."

His image became blurry as his words sank in. I had no idea how to respond. I felt his forgiveness and his belief in me. I cleared my throat, my voice raspy as I spoke.

"I don't know if I deserve that yet, but I'll keep trying to earn it."

I stuck out my hand and he gripped it, shaking it hard. He leaned down and hugged me, and the feeling of paternal affection filled me. I grasped his arms as he thumped my back and stood. We both wiped at our eyes and then he grinned.

"You know, Richard, one of the reasons we lash out at the ones we love is because deep within us, we know we'll be forgiven." He paused with a wink. "The way you lashed out, I must be one of your favorites."

We both laughed, the tension easing in the air.

"I think Gracie said there were cookies?" he asked, wiping his eyes again.

"Yeah."

"I need one or two of those. So will you when Laura has said her piece."

Shit. I had forgotten about Laura.

"Right. Okay."

"Once she's done with you, we'll discuss you returning to work."

"I still have a job?"

He smirked. "Of course, you do. I've been waiting as you so charmingly put it, 'for you to get your head out of your ass.' You can work from home until you're ready to come in. Your clients are waiting for you."

"What about Brad?"

He stroked his chin. "He's gone home to be with Laura's sister, about an hour north of here. He plans on returning soon—I hope."

I frowned in confusion. I had asked Katy a few times about Brad, and she said physically he was almost healed. Was there something I hadn't been told? I opened my mouth to ask when Laura walked into the room.

"I'll take it from here."

Graham clapped my shoulder on his way out of the room. "Good luck."

I swallowed as I looked at Laura. She planted her feet in front of my wheelchair and crossed her arms. Her normally warm gaze was frosty. Hurt. Before I could speak, she began.

"You hurt my family. Again. Even worse, you hurt your own family. Your beautiful little girls who need you. Your wife, who suffered from your rejection terribly. You turned your back on all of us. You were selfish, cruel, and frankly, rude. Do not ever speak to Graham in that manner again."

I could only nod. She was right. I was all those things.

"I know you were in pain. Confused. Scared. But you're an adult. You have words. In fact, Richard VanRyan, you have more words than most people, so I am shocked at your inability to use them."

"I know," I managed to mumble.

"Don't interrupt."

I held my tongue.

"As for Brad, his physical injuries are healing fine. But my nephew is still riddled with guilt. Your wife was gracious enough to assure him she doesn't hold him at fault, but you have yet to even speak to him. He is suffering. Unable to sleep. He can't get past this." She stuck her finger into my chest, pressing hard. "You're going to call Brad and you are going to talk to him. Do you understand me?"

I nodded, unsure if I was allowed to speak yet.

"You have a lot to make up for."

"I know." I caught her hand, holding it tight. "I'm sorry, Laura. I was out of my mind." I met her eyes, pleading with her to understand. "I have never been so scared in my life, and I didn't handle it well. Please forgive me."

Suddenly, I was encased in her arms. Surrounded by the elegant fragrance I associated with her.

"You scared us, Richard. We thought we'd lost you, and when we

got you back, you pushed us away. You shut all of us out. Even Katy."
Her grip increased, and I wrapped my arms around her waist,
accepting her embrace and her warmth. "You mean too much to us,
dear boy. Don't ever do that again, do you understand me? Never."

"I won't."

She pulled back and cupped my face. Her eyes swam in unshed
tears. "I'm mad at you, but I'm also relieved that you're coming to your
senses. Listen to me and hear what I'm saying. Families are stronger
together. I don't care what form your body is in, you are part of mine.
Do not disrespect that or decide to remove yourself again. Am I
clear?"

"Crystal."

She leaned down and kissed my forehead in a motherly gesture so
similar to the way Katy kissed our girls that it brought a lump to my
throat. I never had affection like that as a child. Getting it now as an
adult seemed odd, yet I liked it. I felt Laura's love in her actions. I reci-
procated by wrapping my hands around her arms, pulling her down,
and kissing her cheeks.

"Thank you, Laura. I'll try to be the man you seem to think I am."

She tweaked my nose. "It's the man you are." She stood. "When
you're not acting like a jackass."

I laughed at her mild curse.

"Now come have coffee and cookies."

"I have a call to make first."

"All right. Coffee after." She paused. "And I understand you do a
pretty magical thing with those parallel bars. Would you show us?"

I knew I could say no. But I also knew they wanted to encourage
me, and seeing me upright would show them how far I had come.

I winked at her. "Prepare to be dazzled."

∿

I had never tried to comfort a person still caught between being a
young man and a grown-ass adult. I had never reached out and
been the role model.

It was another lesson I was learning.

Brad was emotional. Filled with apologies. Begging for forgiveness. Once I broke through his stuttering words and barely held-back sobs, I set him straight.

"What happened was not your fault. You didn't put me in this wheelchair, Brad. None of it is your doing. You need to stop blaming yourself."

"I can't."

"You can. Get some help. I'll ask Randy to take you on. He is an amazing person to help you sort things out and get your head straight." I barked out a laugh. "If he can handle my shit, he can help you."

"But he's there."

"Yes," I agreed. "Which is where you need to be. You have a life waiting here for you, Brad. A job you're good at. Friends. Family." I huffed out a breath. "Don't let that day define you. Move past it."

"The guilt," he said quietly. "It holds me hostage. That I'm walking around, able to move and do things. While you're..." His voice trailed off, and I heard him swallow.

"I'm recovering. One day soon, I'll be walking around again. I'll pick up my life, and I expect you to be part of it. Hell, kid, we were making progress on your attitude and smart mouth. Don't leave me before I have you fully brought to heel."

He laughed, the sound relieving the tension between us.

"How are you doing otherwise?" I asked.

He drew in a deep breath. "I don't know if I can ever drive again. I have trouble getting in a car."

"I know that feeling. I get stressed too. But I'm working through it with Randy. Come back, and we'll work on it together."

"Yeah?" He sounded dubious.

"Yes. Your uncle wants you back, and so do I." I was surprised to realize I was telling the truth.

He sighed, the sound deep and filled with pain.

"Don't let that guy's bad choices dictate your life, Brad. Don't do it. You'll regret it one day."

"Okay. The cast comes off next week. I'll talk to Graham about coming back."

"Good man."

"Can I come see you?"

"I'd be disappointed if you didn't. Gracie would be too."

"I like her. She's a cute kid. Smart as a whip."

I grinned into the phone.

"Of course she is. She's mine."

∽

I looked at the piece of equipment in front of me with thinly disguised disgust. I pushed it away.

"Walkers are for old people."

"Or people recovering from spinal injuries," Colin retorted calmly, pushing the offending walker back in front of me.

"I don't want a walker."

"I don't care. You need to stop relying on the chair. Use the walker to get around. Once you're more relaxed, we'll start gait training. After, you'll move to a rolling walker. And after that, a cane."

"Why can't I have the rolling walker now?"

He rubbed his eyes. "Because you're still unsteady. This one gives you support. Once you've found your balance again, you get the rolling one." He indicated the other walker sitting beside the chair.

"Take the stupid basket off it."

Colin chuckled. "It comes in handy." He picked up one of Gracie's stuffed bears and set it inside. "See? You can bring a friend."

"Ha-ha." I picked up the bear and tossed it.

Colin crossed his arms. "Starting Monday, the parallel bars go. The wheelchair goes. This is what you use. You have all weekend to glare at it, curse my name, and act like a spoiled child. But it's happening."

I shut my eyes and counted to ten. Then I did it again. "Jesus. You've been channeling Aiden. Is it really what needs to happen?"

"Yes. It's the next step in your journey, Richard. One I know you want to happen as much as I want that for you." He pushed the walker in front of me. "Try it."

I stood, gripping the foam-covered handles. The familiar pain hit, and I stilled, waiting for it to pass.

"Go slow, Richard. One foot in front of the other. Use the walker for support."

It felt odd. My arms out in front of me instead of to the side. It took more effort and concentration. I walked a few steps and had to sit down in the wheelchair Colin pushed in behind me.

"Should it be that hard?"

He blew out a breath. "Everyone is different, Richard. The severity of your injury, the coma, it all contributes. I know it seems forever, but it's only been a matter of weeks. Two to three months before walking properly is not unheard of. Even longer. The fact that you are up, and this strong is good. We build—remember? Each day, one more rep, one more step until we don't have to count them. Until you can stand without thinking. Walk without concentration. It will come."

I sighed. "Okay."

He clapped me on the shoulder. "Let's get started. I know Gracie is anxious to get in the pool."

I laughed. My Gracie had been chomping at the bit all morning to go swimming. I promised her once I was done with Colin, I would go in with her. Katy would join us with Heather, who loved it when I swished her in the water. Gracie swam like a little fish thanks to the swimming lessons she started as a baby, and Heather was going to be the same. With summer fading away, the warm sun today made it perfect to hang in the pool and relax with my girls.

"Okay, let's get started."

❧

Gracie's huge blue eyes were filled with excitement as she watched me struggle to blow up the big pink flamingo I had ordered online and that arrived today. I should have thought this through better and ordered a pump too.

Katy smirked as I muttered my thoughts out loud, and she patted my leg.

"It's all right, my darling. You're full of hot air." She winked. "Blow."

I leaned forward, wrapping my hand around her neck and pulling her in for a kiss. I nipped at her bottom lip. "Cheek."

She grinned. "You do your version of a blow job, and if you're lucky, I'll show you mine later."

I sat back with a chuckle. "That's an offer I can't refuse."

"I didn't think so." She looked around the blanket she was sitting on. "Darn it."

"What's wrong?"

"I left the sunscreen for the girls in the house."

"Okay, I can watch them while you go grab it."

She stood, brushing off her legs. She was curvy and sexy in a halter top and shorts, the material dipping as she bent over to show the dimples at the base of her ass. Dimples I liked to touch as she rode me. I had touched them many times in the past few days.

She caught my leer and laughed as she tickled Heather's tummy. "Daddy thinks he's so sly."

Heather kicked her legs, grabbing at them with her hands as she chortled and gurgled at Katy.

"Be good for Daddy," Katy admonished.

I watched her walk away, the gentle sway of her hips enticing. The flamingo blew off my lap and skittered away behind me. I rolled the wheelchair back, cursing under my breath as I misjudged the edge and the wheel slid off the concrete, sinking into the grass beside it. The sudden shift in balance almost knocked me out of the chair, yet I managed to hold on.

"Daddy, look at me!" Gracie called.

I glanced behind me, unable to turn the chair around. She was on the swing, pumping fast and high.

Too high.

"Gracie!" I called. "Not so high!"

"It's fun, Daddy!"

"Slow down!" I commanded, feeling panic. "Stop, Gracie—*stop*."

Immediately, her legs stopped moving, the swing losing its momentum.

I exhaled in relief, turning around to look at Heather and make a comment about her daredevil sister.

Except she wasn't on the blanket.

I jerked my head, my heart stopping when I located her.

Crawling, fast and curious, she was right by the pool.

The next instant, she disappeared from my sight, the splash of water a deafening sound in my head—the one thing I could hear aside from my panicked breathing.

21

RICHARD

A scream from the house startled me as Katy rushed out the back door. There was no thought, no pain, and no effort in my movements. I was on my feet and headed to the water. In seconds, I was in the pool, grabbing Heather and lifting her to the side. Katy knelt at the edge, taking her from me.

I pulled myself from the water, dripping, panicked, and terrified.

Katy lifted Heather over her knee, patting her back.

"We need an ambulance. Where's my phone?" I managed to get out. "Where is my fucking phone?" I yelled.

Gracie gasped from beside me. "Daddy, bad word!"

I spied my phone behind Katy and reached for it as Heather began to cough and sputter, spewing water onto the pool decking. Then she started to wail loudly.

It was the sweetest noise I had ever heard.

"Oh fuck," I muttered. "Thank fuck. I'll call Mrs. Thomas, and we'll take her to the doctor."

"She's fine. She swallowed some water." Katy lifted Heather to her shoulder, soothing her. Katy's eyes were huge in her face. "Richard..." she breathed.

"I'm sorry, Katy. I was distracted, and she moved so fast." I yanked on my hair and stood, the movement awkward and jerky. "She was beside me one minute and in the pool the next. I'm so fucking sorry."

"Richard..."

"The wheel of that goddamn chair slipped... Gracie called... I looked, and Heather moved," I babbled. "How did she move so fucking fast?" I bent over my wife. "Is she going to be okay? Please let her be okay. I'll call the doctor and get her to come here. She can fucking bill me."

"Richard!" Katy practically screamed in my face.

I startled. "What?"

"First off, stop swearing. And second, do you not realize what just happened?"

"Yes. My neglect almost killed our daughter." I huffed.

How could I be so careless?

Katy shook her head. "Babies instinctively swim better than adults. She swallowed some water and her diaper is saturated, but that's not what I'm talking about."

I ran my hand over Heather's wet hair, pressing a kiss of remorse to her little head and inwardly thanking God, the heavens, and anyone else listening for my baby girl being okay. I pressed Gracie close to my side, keeping her safe beside me. "What are you talking about, Katy?"

She grabbed my hand. "You walked Richard. In fact, you ran. You were in the pool and had her out of the water before I could even call her name. And you're standing right now." She shook her head. "You're not even aware of it."

I looked at my feet, then at the wheelchair that was lying on its side, knocked over by the way I launched myself out of it. I felt Gracie's arms wrapped around my thigh.

I sensed the decking, hot and rough, under my toes.

"Holy fuck," I breathed out.

"You're walking, my darling. Whatever was holding you back blew out of your head when your child was in danger." She clutched my hand. "You did it, Richard." Tears glimmered in her eyes. "You did it."

I dropped to my knees and gathered all my girls in my arms.

And I wept.

～

The room around me buzzed with activity. Voices, people moving, talking to me, trying to get my attention. I held Gracie on my lap, keeping her close. She played a game on my phone, happy to be held by me.

My focus was on one thing. The doctor examining Heather. I had insisted, and finally Katy relented, seeing how upset I was about her. My wife glanced up, smiling as she lifted Heather to her shoulder. She tilted her chin, letting me know everything was okay. A fact that she was certain of, but I needed to be sure. She escorted the doctor out and I relaxed, pressing a kiss to Gracie's head. She looked up, wrinkling her nose.

"Hi, Daddy."

"Hey, baby girl."

She patted my hand. "Boo-boo better," she cooed. "Good."

"Yeah, Daddy feels better." I brushed a curl off her face. "How did you know?"

She pushed on my cheek with her tiny finger. "You Daddy again. You smile."

I dropped my head, pressing kisses all over her sweet little face. "I'll be Daddy from now on, okay?"

She giggled. "Otay." She lowered her head back to her game. That was far more interesting than the activity around her.

It hit me how correct Katy had been. Gracie didn't care if I walked. She didn't care if I'd been stuck in that godforsaken chair the rest of my life. All she wanted was me. My love and my closeness. To be there for her. A wave of shame hit me and I looked up, meeting Katy's gaze. We held a silent conversation across the room. She knew what I was thinking and feeling at the moment.

She always did.

With a gentle look and a slow shake of her head, she told me to let it go. Move on.

I gave her an imperceptible nod, letting her know I had "heard" her. She winked.

Colin crouched in front of me. "How you doing, Richard?"

I met his gaze. "Great."

"You ready to show off?"

"Sure."

Laura bent, smiling at Gracie. "Daddy needs to get up for a while."

Gracie frowned, cuddling closer, and I had to laugh. "Take the phone, Gracie. You sit over there, and once Daddy is finished impressing people, you can sit on his lap again, okay?"

She slid off happily and wandered to her favorite spot on the sofa, not even remotely interested.

While we were still outside, Katy had given me Heather to hold and made some phone calls. Not long after, Colin appeared, helping me up into my chair and wheeling me inside. Graham and Laura showed up, and then finally the doctor, who came as a special favor to Katy. She was the one I was most concerned with, and I refused to do anything until I knew Heather was okay.

Since my daughter was now happily snuggled into Katy and asleep, I knew I could lay my fears to rest.

Colin pushed the rolling walker in front of me, locking the brakes. I didn't argue or fight. I knew I needed the help. I gripped the handles and pulled myself upright.

I grimaced. "That was a lot harder than I expected. I mean, I *ran* earlier."

He nodded knowingly. "Adrenaline rush. Take your time."

With a deep breath, I released the brake. I didn't look down; I didn't think. I kept my eyes locked on Katy and walked toward her. It wasn't perfect, it wasn't easy or fast, yet I did it. I walked until I was in front of her, then I kissed Heather's unruly curls and my wife's soft mouth.

"Hi," I breathed out.

Katy beamed, her eyes misty with tears. "Hello. You seem taller than I remember."

"Thanks to you, I am." I glanced down at Heather. "She is really okay?"

Katy cupped my cheek, and I leaned into her palm. "She's going to be fine, Richard. And so are you."

I covered her hand with mine. "Yeah, I am. So are we."

She beamed. "We're gonna be great."

I kissed her again. She was so close, and she smelled enticing.

She smelled like home.

Colin clapped me on the back, startling me. I had forgotten anyone else was here. I turned and met his pleased gaze.

"Well done, Richard. I knew it."

I turned and looked at Graham and Laura. They were both smiling, their expressions proud. Laura's eyes glimmered under the lights, and even Graham's looked suspiciously damp.

"I'm training for a marathon next," I deadpanned.

Everyone laughed—myself included. My chest felt lighter, my head clearer, and my body felt more like *me*. I still had a lot of work ahead of me, but I now knew, without a doubt, I could do it.

I was ready to reclaim my life.

Richard fucking VanRyan was back.

Graham stepped forward and clapped my shoulder.

"That he is."

I chuckled, realizing I had spoken my words out loud.

Without a thought, I released the handles I was clutching and pulled Graham in for a hug. He hesitated, then gripped me hard, patting my back like a father would do to a son.

"I'm proud of you, Richard. You fought back. You did it."

The paternal gesture and his quiet statement made me hug him harder.

"Thank you," I said. "Thank you for everything."

He drew back, his eyes no longer damp, but wet.

"Thank me by coming back to the office. We miss you."

I gripped his shoulder and shook it. "Done."

I met Katy's watery gaze.

"I love you," I mouthed.

Her smile was my reward.

~

Katy crawled into bed with me, snuggled into my side, and rested her head on my chest. I groaned as I shifted.

"Are you all right?"

I nodded. "Colin warned me that getting the sensation back in my legs was going to hurt. He's fucking right."

Between rushing after Heather, walking for everyone, moving around the house with my walker, and sitting on Gracie's bed as I read to her for over an hour, I was exhausted. But I wasn't ready to sleep yet. Mentally, I was still wide awake.

"Do you want some pain killers?"

"No. As weird as it sounds, I want to feel it. I never thought I would get to this point, so aches and all, I'm going to go with it."

She laughed softly. "You're right, Richard. You are weird."

I dragged her up my chest, enjoying her little gasp of surprise.

"You wanna help me forget about the aches, Katy?" I murmured in her ear, biting her lobe. "Make me think about something else?"

She squeaked as I pulled her over top of me, making her gasp as I gripped her waist and lifted her in the air the same way I did Gracie. She stretched out her arms, her hair falling forward, brushing my chest.

"I'm flying!" she giggled. It had been a long time since I'd made her giggle. I loved hearing the sound.

I eased her down and kissed her. Lifted. Brought her back to my mouth. Lifted her again.

"Are you using me for reps?" she asked with a mischievous grin. "Or trying to impress me with your super strength?"

"Whatever gets me inside your sweet pussy," I replied, holding her high.

Her eyes grew round as I lowered her back to my mouth. I gazed into their blue depths, holding her until my arms shook.

"*Now*," she begged. "Have me now."

I lifted my head, capturing her mouth. I let her drop to my chest, wrapping my arms around her tight. I kissed her deeply, sliding my tongue along hers, moaning as a different ache began. Delving my hands under her camisole, I slid them over her curves, cupping her ass and grinding up against her. She whimpered, burying her hand in my hair and tugging on the strands.

"I can't get on top yet, but I want to be closer to you." I kissed the column of her neck, tracing the skin with my tongue. She sat up and pulled off her camisole, her full breasts on display. I cupped them, stroking my thumbs over her nipples, feeling her hair brush my thighs as she arched her back, pushing her breasts into my hands.

Impatient, I tugged on the lace that covered her center. It snapped in my fist, and I yanked the wisp of material away. She widened her eyes.

"You'll be replacing those, VanRyan. I liked that pair."

"I liked what they covered more." I teased between her legs, feeling her desire. I wrapped my hand around the base of her neck and brought her back to my mouth.

"I want to try something."

"Yes," she responded. "Anything."

I patted the bed. I wanted to be the one to move her, but I knew I had a way to go for that. She slid beside me with a sexy smirk. "Back or front?"

"Back."

As she moved, she yanked off my boxers.

"Eager, Mrs. VanRyan?"

She snuggled back to me with a sigh. "You have no idea."

Sliding my arm under her, I tugged her close. Cupping her face, I turned her head and kissed her. Long drags of my tongue, soft touches of my mouth. Deep, intimate moments where I mimicked fucking her with my tongue, and sweet, light tastes of her lips. I feasted on her, using my hands to touch her the entire time. The swell of her breasts that were made to fit into my hand, and my hand alone. I teased her nipples into hard points. I traced her curves—the gentle dip of her waist, the flare of her hips. The sweet, wet lips of her pussy opened as I tugged at her leg and lifted it over my hip. She whimpered my favorite noise as I teased and stroked her clit. Slipped two fingers inside her and thrust them until she moaned my name as I used my thumb to keep the pressure she needed on her clit. She began to move, meeting my movements, begging in her breathy whisper for more. For me. My cock.

I slid inside, burying my face in her fragrant neck. Grasping her hip, I rocked into her slowly and deliberately. Taking my time, feeling the grip of her warmth. I felt the flutter of her muscles, tasted the sweetness of her breath on my face, reveled in the look of desire and want in her eyes. The world, the pain of the past several weeks faded away. There was only her. Only us.

"Richard," she pleaded. "I need you."

My orgasm built, tendrils chasing up my spine, exploding in shards of ecstasy as I stilled. I came hard, my mouth open on her skin, my breaths short, heavy gasps, unable to articulate the moment with words.

Katy clutched the back of my neck, riding out her own bliss. Her low keening was a prayer of joy. The celebration of our coming together, the culmination of our need for each other.

One I would never deny again.

She collapsed into my chest, her skin damp against my own. I kissed her shoulder, her neck, and lifted her hand to my mouth, feathering kisses to her palm.

"God, I love you, Katy VanRyan," I murmured into her hair.

She hummed, kissing my forearm that held her close to me.

"I love you," she responded. "I love you so much, Richard."

I lifted the blanket over us, not wanting her to get cold. I grazed my hand over her side, tracing the curve of her hip and indent of her waist.

I spoke low into her ear. "You're too thin, baby. This has been difficult on you. I'm sorry."

She sighed, her breath a soft breeze on my skin. She played with my wedding band, twisting the platinum around aimlessly. "I don't want to dwell on it, Richard. You're moving forward. We'll do the same. We'll go to counseling and put it behind us."

"But—"

"No more apologies. I know how bad you feel. You've proven it. Forgive yourself now, and move forward with me."

"I'll move anywhere as long as it's with you."

"I'm right beside you, Richard. I always have been, and I always will be."

I dropped another kiss to her shoulder. "Good. Still, it's time for me to take care of you again. Be the husband I should have been all this time."

"Why don't we look after each other and call ourselves what we really are?" she asked. "Equals."

"Because in this relationship, Katy, you're so far ahead of me, I struggle to catch up at times."

"Then I'll stop and wait. How about that?"

I traced a finger along her cheek, seeing the love in her eyes. The one that always was there for me. Even when I was too blind to see it.

I pressed my mouth to hers.

"Perfect."

~

TWO WEEKS LATER

"Today's the big day, eh?" Maddox's voice filled my closet.

"Yeah," I said, tugging on my shirt. "Brad went back to work last week, and today is my first day back."

"You're not jumping in full time, are you?"

"No. I'll work from home too, the way I have been the last couple of weeks." I selected a tie—Katy's favorite one since I had worn it when we got married—and flipped up my shirt collar as I tied the knot. "But it's time to start back. I'm a lot stronger, and I need to get back into a routine." I chuckled. "And Katy needs me out of her hair."

He laughed. "I am sure Dee would sympathize with her. I drove her crazy when I was recovering."

There was a commotion in the background—voices and the sound of a loudspeaker, then it cut off as suddenly as it started.

"Where are you?" I asked.

"Sorry. I walked into the building. The café is busy, and I stepped back out. I have a meeting outside the office."

"Love those."

"Yeah. Listen, I wanted to call and wish you the best for today."

"Thanks, Mad Dog. Appreciate it."

"I'll give you a shout later."

He hung up, and I looked in the mirror. I'd had my hair cut, and my scruff was tight to my face—the way Katy and Gracie liked it. I studied my reflection, noticing a few new gray hairs and some wrinkles around my eyes that hadn't existed before the accident. I ran a hand over my head with a grimace. I had lots of scars both inside and out that I would carry with me always.

The past two weeks had been intense. New physio, gait training to learn how to walk again, plus additional leg strengthening. Counseling—alone, and with Katy. We worked through a lot of issues my behavior had brought up for us as a couple, and we planned on continuing. Randy helped me deal with my anger, and then we started on my history. He made me see how I still allowed my past to dictate my behavior at times, and we were now working on that together.

It was going to take a while.

I slid on my suit jacket and flexed my shoulders. It felt a little tight with the added muscle I had put on thanks to Aiden and Colin. I would have to get some new suits made or lose some of the new layer of muscle.

I was sure Katy would vote for new suits. She was enjoying the new muscles—every chance she got.

Her voice interrupted my musings. "Can I help with those cuff links?"

I turned slowly and smiled. "Perfect timing, Mrs. VanRyan."

She handed me a mug of coffee and slid the disks in, snapping them into place. She grinned as she ran her hand down my tie.

"My favorite."

"Big day needs a big tie."

She frowned. "A half day—right?"

I stroked her cheek. "Katy, I'm good. I swear. Alan signed off on this, Colin gave his okay, and I'm ready. If I get tired, I'll come home. I won't get there until ten, and the car is scheduled to pick me up at five. Don't worry, baby. I've got it."

"I do worry."

I slipped my arm around her and pulled her close. "I know, and I love you more because of it. But it's all good." I kissed her head. "I'm okay now, so you can relax."

She sighed, some of the tension leaving her body.

Katy had her own scars left from the accident. I'd started walking on my own around the neighborhood, going for longer periods of time every day. She worried every time I walked out the door. One day, I was so lost in the thoughts in my head, I sat down on a bench and I lost track of time. I was gone for over two hours. She had sobbed with relief when I got home, her body shaking with the force of her tears as I held her and apologized. I had forgotten my cell on my dresser, and when she couldn't reach me, her panic had overtaken her. Now I made sure my phone was with me and I checked in.

We both had to recover in our own time.

She stepped back with a smile. "You look good."

I winked. "I know."

She shook her head, walking out of the closet. "Oh, go fuck yourself, VanRyan."

I threw back my head in laughter.

There was my Katy. My smart-mouthed, beautiful wife.

I grabbed the cane leaning against the dresser and followed her.

The car pulled up outside The Gavin Group building. I drew in a deep breath, feeling oddly nervous. There was no reason to be nervous. I had been working from home the past couple of weeks. At first, I sat in on a few calls with Graham, Jenna, and Adrian. Then the BAM boys got in touch directly, and I began to work. I spent a few hours every day on a new campaign, which meant I was teleconferencing daily with them, the office, and many of the staff at The Gavin Group. They saw my face, they had already expressed how pleased they were to see I was well enough to work, so it was all good.

But they hadn't seen me walk. I looked at the cane clutched in my hand. I needed it to keep my balance. My gait was better, although still not perfect. I couldn't walk long distances yet, or drive. I got tired easily, and my pacing changed when I did. Still, I was able to get rid of the walker I despised and use a cane.

I recalled the day Katy handed me a gift of a cane. It was hand-made, dark wood with stylish trim and my initials etched into the curved handle.

"I had it made especially for you. The gentleman hand-carves them to your height, arm, and leg length."

"I don't plan on using it for very long," I informed her, raising my eyebrow.

"You can keep it for when you get old and you need it to chase me around," she replied with a wink. *"Or use it to threaten Gracie's and Heather's boyfriends if they get out of line."*

That made me growl, and she laughed. The girls weren't allowed to date until they were thirty.

"You hate the silver metal one Colin gave you from the clinic, and the ones the drugstore had were purple with butterflies or a horrid plaid. I thought you would prefer this elegant one, but if you want, I could go get the other one. The purple would set off your eyes."

I pulled her down and kissed her. "I know what you're doing, and I love you for it. I'll keep the elegant wood one."

"I thought you would."

The cane and all the limitations would have frustrated me and caused some sort of outburst before, but now I accepted it. Every day, I got a little better. A little stronger. A little less reliant on the cane. One day in the near future, I wouldn't need it. But I was living in the now.

I had a beautiful wife. Two sweet little girls. A great job. And friends who stuck by me, proving that family isn't always blood.

I was a lucky bastard.

Using the wooden cane my wife bought me, I stepped out of the car and walked into the office, my head held high and my shoulders straight.

Richard VanRyan was in the building. And I was ready to take on the world.

~

"Great work," Graham mused. "This is spectacular."

"Thanks." I smirked, reaching for my coffee. "I thought it was bloody brilliant."

Jenna chuckled, easing back in her chair, crossing her legs, and shaking her head. "I see your ego didn't suffer in the accident."

"Nope. Alive and kicking. Just like the rest of me." I lifted a shoulder. "Well, most of me."

Graham looked over the file in his hand, his glasses perched on the end of his nose. "Look how far you've come, Richard. You once thought you'd never see this day."

I waved my hand. "I know. It's fine. Katy tells me the cane adds another layer of sexiness to my persona. I'm good with that."

Jenna coughed out a snigger and stood. "On that note, I am out of here. I have some errands." She paused at the door. "Welcome back, Richard. I'm glad you're back—even with the ego."

She hurried away before I could retort. She had been emotional this morning, and I had teased her about it all day.

Brad appeared in my doorway, lifting his hand to knock. I waved him in, trying not to laugh as I remembered our first introduction. We had come a long way since that fateful day. When he returned to Victoria, he came to the house, and we sat in my den and talked for a long time. I hated the guilt he still harbored and refused to let him leave until he understood the only person blaming him was himself. I convinced him to see Randy, and it helped him a great deal.

Since that day, he was a regular visitor at the house and Gracie's new best friend. She loved it when he came over, and he had, in fact, babysat a few evenings for us. He watched Disney movies with Gracie, played with Heather, and Katy was his confidante. She adored him, and he returned the affection.

"What's up?"

"I got those designs we talked about." He handed me his tablet, and I scrolled through the images.

"Brad, these are awesome."

"I was wondering about tweaking the red. Making the logo stand out a little more."

I nodded in agreement. "Good eye. Yes. Do that."

I swiped again, stopping at the next image. It was a selfie of Brad and June—one of the new girls in accounting. Young, pretty, with blond hair and dimples so deep you could stick a dime in them, she beamed up at Brad in the picture. His arm was around her and his expression filled with happiness. I glanced up, raising my eyebrow.

His cheeks flushed, and he held out his hand for his tablet. "Sorry, I forgot about that one."

I grinned and refused to hand it over. "Pretty girl. You look happy."

Graham chuckled. "I know they're dating, Richard. Laura and I like her. We have no company policy about interoffice dating."

I started to laugh as I handed Brad back his tablet. "Good thing, Graham. Most of your executives are married to each other, and I can think of four other couples without even trying."

He grinned and stood. "What can I say? Great place to work and fall in love." He clapped Brad's shoulder on the way out. "I'm leaving in thirty minutes. I'll take you home."

Brad still couldn't drive. He froze every time he got behind the wheel. I was tense as soon as I sat in a car and had yet to attempt to drive. I was so worried about other drivers I knew I would be distracted. It was a hurdle we both had yet to overcome.

"Is this a bank?" I scoffed. "Everyone taking off early? Yeesh, I'm supposed to be the one on restricted time."

Graham shook his head. "Plans, Richard. I have big plans." He waved as he walked out the door.

"How long have you been seeing June?"

Brad sat down in front of my desk. "A few weeks. We had gone out once before the accident. She came to see me in the hospital and stayed in touch the whole time I was gone." He smiled as he looked down at his tablet. "She's been amazing."

"She is one of the rare ones."

He nodded, his eyes shining. "I think so."

I chuckled. I recognized the look. The kid was a goner.

"Katy know about her?"

"Yes, she's been very supportive."

I wasn't surprised—of course she would be. Katy wanted to see everyone happy, so she'd be thrilled to know Brad found someone.

"You'll meet her officially later," Brad started, then stopped and swallowed. "I mean, I'll bring her to meet you sometime."

"Sounds good. Arrange dinner with Katy one night."

"I'll do that."

"Email me the designs, and I'll make some more notes."

He headed for the door. "On it."

What felt like a few moments later, my phone buzzed. As I glanced at the screen, I was shocked to see almost an hour had passed. I had lost track of time.

I answered Katy's call. "Hey, sweetheart."

"How are you feeling?"

"Good."

"You coming home soon?"

"Yeah—shit. Sorry. I got caught up. The car is probably waiting."

She laughed. "I already asked them to pick you up at five-thirty. I knew this would happen."

I smiled as I stood, shutting off my computer. She knew me too well. I heard a voice behind her, muffled yet familiar.

"Who's there?" I asked.

"A delivery guy. I got a few groceries delivered that I forgot earlier."

"Sounded like Mad Dog."

She chuckled. "A little far away to bring me groceries."

"I suppose so. Okay, on my way."

"See you soon."

～

In the car, I rolled my shoulders and rubbed at my legs. I hadn't realized how hard it was to sit for an extended period of time. I decided to take Colin up on his suggestion of a treadmill in my office. I could walk and stretch when I needed to.

The car pulled onto the street, and I glanced around in puzzlement. There were a lot of parked cars.

"Someone's having a party," I stated dryly.

Leon, the driver, nodded in agreement. "So it would appear."

"Let me off here." I could use the short walk.

I stepped out of the car, still frowning in confusion. Ahead of me, I could see that my front lawn was once again covered in signs. There was no election going on, no candidates glad-handing around.

What the hell were they?

I walked closer, my lips quirking as I read the various placards.

～

> Richard VanRyan
> I'm not running for anything
> I just wanted a sign

> Richard VanRyan
> World's best husband

> # Richard VanRyan
> # World's best Daddy

That one had a picture of me holding my girls. It was my favorite.

All of them made me smile.

But one made me throw back my head in amusement.

> # Richard VanRyan
> # I'm kind of a big deal

The memories it brought back made my body tighten.

There was no doubt who was responsible. My smart-mouthed, brilliant, wonderful Katy.

I looked up to see her standing on the driveway, wearing a large grin.

"Care to explain?" I asked, walking toward her.

"A little welcome home after your first day back."

I laughed, indicating the yard. "I'm not sure all the neighbors needed to be in on the occasion."

She waved her hand behind her. "I think I'd disagree."

I turned and gaped at the people waiting.

Graham and Laura. Jenna and Adrian. Adam, Julia, and their kids. Brad and June. Colin. Mr. and Mrs. Thomas. Other neighbors.

The entire BAM office. Bentley, Aiden, Maddox, Reid, and their spouses. Sandy was with them, smiling broadly at me.

That explained the noise I heard when Maddox talked to me this morning. He was at the airport, coming here to surprise me. The reason everyone was leaving the office early. They were *all* here.

All the people I considered family.

Katy slipped her hand into mine. "Welcome home, Mr. VanRyan."

"I don't understand."

She smiled, looking shy. "It's my celebration of you. To show you how proud we all are of you."

"For me, Katy? All of this for me?"

She nodded. "All of this for you."

"Why?"

"Because I wanted you to know how much you're loved."

I blinked, my eyes suddenly not focusing properly. I cleared my throat.

"And you thought signs were in order?" I teased, needing to lighten the moment.

"What's a party without signs?"

"I helped put 'em up!" Gracie exclaimed, running toward me.

I bent down and picked her up, holding her with one arm. I kissed her cheek. "I bet you helped Mommy with all of this."

She patted my face with her tiny hands. "Thelbation, Daddy! Dere's suppa and cake!"

"Now that's what I call a party."

Gracie squirmed, and I set her down, laughing as she ran straight past Maddox to Brad. Mad Dog was going to be pissed off over that.

I looped my arm around Katy and kissed her. "Thank you. This is incredible."

She smiled my favorite smile—the one she had for me alone.

I kissed her again. "I think *you're* incredible," I said against her lips.

She winked and tugged on my hand.

"Come say hello to your guests."

I followed her, trying to take it all in.

I had come full circle from the last time I found signs on my lawn. My life had changed—I had changed. And despite the pain we went through, the struggles, and the way it happened, I wouldn't trade now for anything.

My future was brighter than ever.

And I would never take it for granted again.

EPILOGUE

CHRISTMAS

RICHARD

The house was quiet. The girls were finally asleep, and once they were down, Katy and I had finished getting out the gifts and arranging them all under the tree. We sat, admiring the way the lights glimmered off the shiny paper and the way I had hidden the rocking horse Gracie had wanted so much behind the tree, its nose sticking out of the branches. I knew once she saw it, nothing else would matter.

I could hardly wait to see the look on her face, hear her excited squeals, and feel the kisses she would rain all over my face when I dragged it out for her. Heather was still too young to understand what the day was about, but she would love the colors and sounds. I already predicted the big stuffed teddy bear would be her favorite. She loved soft things she could hold.

I drank a scotch while Katy sipped a cup of hot cocoa. She looked sleepy, her eyes fluttering shut more than once.

I chuckled. "Go to bed, sweetheart. I'll do the stockings and be up soon."

The stockings were my favorite part. Katy did most of the shopping for the girls, and she handled my stocking, but I did the rest. I loved shopping for little things to fill up the festive socks. I always bought something extra for each girl, and all of Katy's gifts, but the stockings were my "thing."

Before Katy came into my life, Christmas had simply been another day of the year. I had no one to celebrate with, no concept of the meaning of the season, other than a boom for the advertising world. She changed all that for me and showed me what the season meant. How special it was. When Gracie came along, the meaning became clearer than ever.

Christmas was about family.

And this year, it was more special than ever. I had come so close to losing all of it, and my gratitude knew no bounds.

Katy smiled at my urging and ran a hand through her hair, looking sleepy and sexy all at the same time.

"I might have a bath."

"Are you sure you won't fall asleep in the tub?" I smirked. She did that a lot. I often went upstairs to find her dozing in the tub. It was a good thing the new Kindle I gave her last year was waterproof since it ended up in the bath with her on occasion.

"No, I'll keep it short." She stood and stopped by my chair, leaning down and kissing my mouth. I lifted my hand to her thighs, stroking the backs of her legs, kissing her back. It was a soft kiss—one filled with love and sweetness.

"I'll be up soon."

She drifted her fingers over my cheek. "Okay, Santa."

I captured her hand in mine, pressing a kiss to her palm. "Love you."

Her eyes widened, the vivid blue still as captivating as it had been when I first fell in love with her. The warmth and love that filled her eyes had melted my soul, warmed my cold heart, and could still ignite a fire within me with one glance.

"I love you, Richard. Come to bed soon."

I nodded, feeling overcome. "I will."

I watched her walk out of the room, memories filling my head. From our rocky start, to our fledging love, the challenges of the past year, to the tower of strength we now were, she was a miracle to me. One that saved my life and changed me completely.

Before her, I was nothing. With her, *because* of her, I had the world.

One I had come precariously close to losing this past year.

I shook my head and stood. I knew if I allowed it, the past would swamp me, and there was no room for that in my life anymore. My life was Katy and my girls.

And I had stockings to fill.

I walked to the den, my gait steady, my legs strong. I no longer needed the cane, although there was a slight drag to one leg; it was still getting better. Katy assured me it was barely perceptible, and I worked with Colin regularly to make sure it vanished completely.

In the den, I found all the bags I had hidden away from prying eyes. Katy was worse than the girls, and she loved to snoop. Luckily, she was too short to find the bags I hid in the upper cabinets of the closet. Back in the family room, I added Katy's gifts under the tree and the extra surprises I got for the girls, including the huge teddy bear for Heather. I knew Katy would sneak down in the night to add some gifts for me. She had already taken my stocking, and I knew she would fill it before she had her bath and bring it down later. She always wanted the day to be special for me as well as the girls. It was one of the reasons I loved her so much. She knew my past and what Christmas had been for me as a child. She tried every year to wipe away more of those terrible memories with good ones.

Carefully, I filled the stockings. Heather's was easy—socks, simple toys, a couple of onesies, and a few chew rings and some of her favorite cookies that Katy approved of. As she was still teething, everything was fair game. Gracie's was more fun—toys, candy, girly things for her hair, frilly socks, some little games we could play together. It was full to overflowing when I rehung it, and I hoped the hook was strong enough to keep it safe overnight.

Katy's stocking, I filled with bath products, hair clips, kitchen gadgets, and some gift certificates for places she loved—Starbucks, White Spot, and her favorite salon. I added a couple of handmade ones for a massage and a few date nights. Those were always a big hit. In the toe of the stocking, I tucked a tiny box. The sapphire earrings were delicate and beautiful—much like my wife. The vibrant blue color reminded me of her eyes. I knew she would love them.

Into the branches of the tree, I slid another box. The matching ring would make her shake her head and mutter about going overboard, but she deserved it. She deserved nothing except the best, and I wanted to see the shimmering blue and clear of the gems on her hand. The elegant band would look good with her wedding rings and further mark her as taken.

The caveman in me liked that.

Satisfied, I cleaned up, turned off the lights, leaving the tree on. I stood back, admiring the scene, and snapped a picture. It turned out well, so I quickly sent it off to Maddox in Toronto, with the caption of *"Merry Christmas from my house to yours."*

I wasn't surprised when he replied right away—he was a night owl and he would no doubt be enjoying his Christmas eve with Dee.

"All the best, my friend. Merry Christmas to you and your family. See you soon."

I shot back a fast reply. *Can't wait.*

Maddox and Dee were coming to visit in a few days. I was looking forward to having him here. This time, it was all fun—he had no need to kick my ass. His friendship was a gift I had never expected in my life. I never had friends until Katy changed my world. I had business acquaintances, lots of enemies, but never a real friend.

I had confessed to him one night while I was in Toronto on a business trip what I said to Katy in the hospital and admitted my feelings of shame over it. He had stared at me and threw back his head in laughter.

"You are such an asshole at times."

"I'm aware."

He shook his head, still amused, and sipped his whiskey. "Even if you were stuck in that damn chair the rest of your life, your wife would never look at another man the way she looks at you, Richard."

"I wasn't thinking clearly."

He sobered. "No, you weren't. You were really fucked up, not that I blame you. So if you need forgiveness, you have it." He chuckled. "But the bill is on you tonight."

And that was that. He never spoke of it again, and I let it go. I had to let a lot of things go in order to move ahead.

I sighed, pushing aside the memories, and returned to my den for one last item. I slid the thick envelope into the tree branches where it would wait for Maddox and Dee. Maddox thought they were only spending a few days here, but with Bentley's blessing and Dee's permission, I had arranged a short cruise for them. They would depart from Victoria, and it would take them to San Francisco. A hotel and excursions were booked, then they would return on another boat and fly home. All first class, all designed with Maddox's interests at the forefront. Dee's enthusiasm had been evident, and her assistance in making sure I picked all the right things for them to do, invaluable.

"Maddox will love it!" she had gushed. "What an awesome gift!"

I had to admit, I was looking forward to seeing his face when he opened it.

I headed upstairs, checking on my girls. I pulled Gracie away from the edge of the bed and tucked her blanket around her, knowing in an hour she'd be starfished across the bed again, her blankets on the floor, but her favorite lambie tucked tight against her. Heather was a ball of sweetness in her crib, her tiny lips pursed as she slept. I kissed them both repeatedly, my love for them overwhelming tonight. I slipped into our bedroom. Katy was a huddled mass under the covers. I hoped she had put on some socks. She had the coldest feet at night, and she loved to use my legs to warm them up. I would find out soon enough, I supposed.

I jumped into the shower, knowing the morning would be crazy and I wouldn't have time. I toweled off my hair, then opened the bathroom door, flicking off the light. It took me a second to register the difference in the bedroom.

There were candles lit everywhere, the scent of cinnamon and spice heavy in the air. Katy was no longer asleep under the covers. Instead, she lay across the comforter, looking very wide awake, and dressed as an elf. A sexy, naughty elf. She lounged on the bed, one leg bent provocatively, her dark hair tumbling over her shoulders, and her blue eyes alight with mischief. She was sexy and sweet, all in one package. In her hand, she held a Santa hat, which she tossed my way. I caught it, allowing the towel I had draped around my waist to fall to the floor, my erection kicking up at the sight of her sensual tableau.

"Merry Christmas, Mr. Claus." She winked. "I think it's time Santa got a little present."

I donned the hat, grinning. "Oh, little elf, Santa has a present for you, all right. But there isn't anything little about it."

She giggled and patted the bed. "Why don't you come over here and let me decide that." Her smile grew wider. "Maybe we can disprove the myth that Santa only comes once a year."

I didn't need a second invitation. I stepped closer to the bed. "Well, fucking ho, ho, ho to me."

I gazed down at Katy, unable to stop my leer. Her shapely legs were encased in silky sheer stockings that stopped mid-thigh with a frill of lace. The red and green stripes emphasized the curves. Her transparent camisole was trimmed in white fake fur and held together with a small bow, which wasn't going to last long. Her full breasts spilled over the lace, her nipples already hard under the thin, diaphanous fabric. She bent her knee back, her bare pussy already glistening in the low light.

"You lost your panties, elf."

She shook her head. "I was saving you time."

"How...*thoughtful* of you."

Her eyes gleamed. "They were just getting all...*wet* anyway."

I braced my arms on the bed, grinning at her. "Is that a fact?"

Her voice dropped, the color I loved deepening her cheeks. "I always get wet when I think of you."

I dropped my head and breathed in deeply.

Jesus. I loved it when she talked dirty.

When I glanced up, a low laugh escaped from my lips as I took in the curled slippers with bells on the toes and the jaunty elf hat she had perched on her head.

"I like your slippers," I teased, tapping the end, making the bell tinkle.

She wiggled her toes with a lazy grin. "I thought you might like to ring all my bells, Santa." She tapped her lips. "I was thinking of licking your peppermint stick."

I grew harder, my cock twitching at the thought of her lips wrapped around my shaft. "What a naughty little elf you are," I mused. "You might get coal in your stocking this year."

"I was hoping for your cock in my sock instead," she deadpanned, then giggled at her words.

I blinked and joined in her mirth. I knelt on the mattress, swinging myself over her body, hovering, bracing my weight on my forearms.

I leaned down close. So close I could feel her breath, light and sweet, drift over my face. "God, I love you, Katy VanRyan."

She lifted her head, meeting my mouth. Our lips moved and caressed. Easy and soft. Then as usual when we were together and alone, desire took over and my need for her blossomed into a fiery want. I slid my tongue inside her mouth, claiming it. Claiming her. I moved one arm behind her back, lifting her close, using my free hand to shred the bow in the front. I needed her skin against mine. She wrapped her legs around my hips, cradling me. Our kisses grew deeper. Longer. More frantic and needier. I dragged my mouth down her neck, licking and biting at the soft skin, sucking at the juncture between her neck and shoulder.

"Jesus, Katy, I want to fuck you. Make love to you. All at once."

She cupped my face, her lips swollen and wet from mine. "Then do it, Richard."

I sat up, pulling her with me. Our chests pressed together, her hard nipples rubbing against the hairs on my skin. I cupped her ass, holding her tight. "Which one first, baby?"

Her lips brushed against my ear. "I want my taste first, Santa. Your cock in my mouth. After, you can do anything you want." She bit down, tugging my lobe. "Anything."

I groaned, letting her push me back. I fell to the mattress, opening my arms in surrender. "Do your worst, little elf."

She licked and bit her way down my chest, her teeth teasing my flesh as she soothed the pinches away with her tongue. She knew how much I loved for her to play with my nipples, licking and sucking at them until they were hard points under her tongue. She slid down my body, wrapping her hand around my aching cock.

I pressed my head into the mattress as she tongued the underside in a long, slow lick. I groaned low in my chest as her mouth closed around the crown, taking me deep. Her hands were everywhere, cupping my balls, stroking my nipples, scratching at my thighs. Her talent knew no bounds as she sucked me, alternating between light, teasing swipes of her tongue and deep-throating me to the brink. She slid her hands under my ass, clutching at the cheeks and going deeper than ever. I hissed as the pleasure, dark and deep, tingled down my spine. I never lasted long in her mouth—a fact that she was extraordinarily proud of.

"Katy, baby," I moaned, fisting her hair in my hands and tugging gently in warning.

She growled low in her throat, the sound reverberating around my cock. Pleasure spiked, and I came. And my wife, my naughty, sexy elf, took it. She swallowed, humming and moaning around me like it was the greatest thing on earth.

Which I knew to be untrue.

Talk about false advertising.

Still, she stayed until she drained me of pleasure and energy, then lifted her head with a salacious look.

"How about that, fly-boy?"

I groaned as she flopped onto my chest, once again running her fingers over my nipples. I nuzzled her head. "You are in so much trouble."

She hiked her leg over my thighs and straddled me. I could feel the warmth of her center, and despite the fact that I had already come, I knew it wouldn't be long before I was buried inside her. She peered down at me, her hair a mess, her cheeks flushed, and her silly elf hat still firmly in place.

Reaching up, I tugged the pom-pom, pulling the hat off her head. I wrapped my hand around her neck, guiding her face down to mine and kissing her. She tasted of me, of her, of us. I wound my hands into her thick tresses, kissing her harder, my need for her already building. She shivered and I rolled, pinning her under me. I kept kissing her as the heat of my body soaked into her and she loosened, her muscles at ease.

It was my turn to loom over her.

"My turn, Katy, my naughty, *naughty* little elf." I ran my fingers down her side, earning me another shiver—but this time, it was one of pleasure. "You've been very bad."

She winked. "I have, Santa."

"You know what happens to bad elves?"

She bit her lip and widened her eyes dramatically. "What?"

I lowered my face to hers. "They get a tongue-lashing. And fucked. Hard."

A smile broke out on her face. "In that case, maybe I need to list all my bad acts."

I chuckled. "Santa sees all, knows all." I lifted her leg to my shoulder. "I checked the list, Katy. I checked it twice. Your name appeared on every page."

Her arms fell open, her body undulating on the soft sheets.

"Good."

Her skin glowed in the candlelight, soft ivory under my fingers. I tugged the striped stockings down her leg, pulling them and her cute slipper off and tossing them over my shoulder. I repeated the action with her other leg, resting them both on my shoulders as I gazed down at her.

She was a vision in the flickering light, her full breasts rising and falling in rapid succession as her breathing picked up, getting faster with every passing second. I slid my hands up her torso, running my thumbs over her tight nipples. She arched into my touch. I turned my face, kissing the delicate skin behind her knee where I knew she was the most sensitive. I traced the dip with my tongue, and did the same to the other leg, grinning against her skin at the tightening of her muscles.

Leisurely, I licked, kissed, and bit my way up her thighs, alternating between the two, using my fingers to trace and tease. The quiet whimpering sounds falling from her lips became louder and more frequent as I hunched closer, my thumbs resting on either side of her center. Gently, I pulled her lips apart and closed my mouth around her, flattening my tongue and sliding it over her clit.

She bowed off the bed, her body taut. I worked her with my mouth, long, hard strokes followed by soft flicks of my tongue. I slid one finger inside her, then two, working in tandem, bringing her to the edge only to back off, wanting to lengthen her pleasure.

She clutched the back of my neck, her fingers restless and pulling at my hair. She moaned my name, begging for more, pleading with me. Her pussy was tight around my fingers, and my cock grew harder, wanting to feel the warmth of her. I sped up my actions, giving her what she wanted, fucking her fast with my fingers and concentrating on her hard nub until I felt her body shake, overcome with ecstasy, as she spasmed and gasped, coming hard.

Before she had a chance to recover, I was inside her, welcomed into her body in a hard thrust of need that made us both gasp in pleasure. I moved in long, powerful strokes, gripping her hips, holding her against me as I claimed her. Her noises spurred me on, her soft moans and pleas fueling my desire. She was hot and wet—her pussy gripping me with the intensity of her need. I changed my angle, hovering over her, bracing myself on one hand as I wrapped the other arm under her shoulders and pulled her mouth up to meet mine. Our tongues slid together, mimicking the same timing as our bodies. Katy trembled as I ran my hand over the swell of her ass, hitching her closer. I slowed my movements, my thrusts becoming leisurely. I rolled my hips, hitting her exactly where she wanted. Needed.

Loving her the way I knew she desired.

She cried out at the new angle, her body taking me even deeper. I groaned, the sensations already too much. She was all around me tonight, filling me up with emotions and making my body ache for her.

"Come for me, baby. I'm not going to last much longer, and I need you to come first," I begged. I slid my hand between us, pressing on her clit in light touches the way she loved. *"Please."*

She cried out, gripping my shoulders, coming around me. Her blunt nails dug into my skin as she arched and writhed. Her muscles fluttered and clamped down around me, drawing an orgasm out of me. Like liquid fire, it lit up my nerves, my balls tightening, and I exploded, drowning in the ecstasy I only ever experienced with my wife. Ecstasy that was not only physical but filled with a depth of emotion that took me to a whole other level.

I buried my face into her neck, riding out the waves of bliss. Words fell from my mouth, garbled and low, her name repeated often, until I was spent. Until I collapsed into her, unable to move, think, or feel anything except her softness and warmth.

Moments passed and I rolled us to the side, unable to separate from her but knowing I needed to lift my weight away. I nuzzled into her hair that was wild and messy from my hands. Kissed her neck that I had licked and bitten in my passion. Stroked the skin on her back that was damp and warm from our coupling. Held her close until we both stopped trembling and could form a sentence.

"You are amazing." Was all I could muster. "I'm the luckiest bastard on earth."

She snuggled closer. "Oh, Richard—that was…just…wow."

I chuckled into her hair. "Wow is a good word." I glanced over at the clock. "Hey, it's past midnight. Merry Christmas."

She looked up, her blue eyes tired, sated, and happy. "Merry Christmas."

I tucked her against me. "Go to sleep. Gracie is going to come roaring in here in a few hours, demanding we get up. It's gonna be a long-ass day." I yawned. "But what a way to start."

She sat up, her eyes luminous in the candlelight. "I wanted to give you my Christmas gift now."

"That wasn't it?"

"No, there's more."

She looked excited and nervous all at the same time. Her fingers twisted and clenched on her lap. Her toes wiggled in anticipation.

"Must be some present. You're practically vibrating."

"It is."

"Not a new tie or some funky Maddox-like socks?" I teased her.

She shook her head, if anything, looking more nervous now than excited.

I grinned. "Okay, Mrs. VanRyan. Lay it on me."

She reached into the drawer and pulled out a small bag. It was festive and glittery, tissue paper hiding the contents. She slipped it into my waiting hands. "Merry Christmas, Richard."

I pulled on the tissue paper and opened a small package. It revealed a ball of yellow fluff. I frowned in confusion. It was too small to be a scarf, and the color was pastel. I fingered the wool, noting the softness.

"Ah," I muttered. "It's a...?" I let my voice trail off and looked up at Katy. Her eyes were damp, and she was biting her lip in one of her nervous tells.

"Look closer."

I pulled on the ball, more confused as it separated into two bundles that fell to the mattress. I picked one up, studying it, realizing it had a shape.

A small bootie.

Like a baby bootie.

Exactly like a fucking baby bootie.

I snapped up my head, meeting Katy's teary gaze.

"Katy?" I breathed.

She pressed a small blue stick into my hand. It was familiar since I had seen one like it twice before.

"A baby? You're pregnant?"

She nodded.

I pulled her to me, encircling her in my arms. She wrapped her legs around me, holding me close. "Sweetheart," I murmured. "How far along?"

She leaned back. "The night we went dancing to celebrate your ditching of the cane. So, a couple of months."

"Oh." I grinned as the memory hit me. "The elevator."

She waggled her eyebrows, looking adorable. "The elevator. I forgot to take my pill. I remembered the next day and took it. I've done that before and we've always been okay, but this time I had also been on antibiotics..." She shrugged. "Add in your super sperm and bang! I'm pregnant."

I winked. "I don't know about super sperm, but it was quite the bang if I remember correctly."

She giggled, still sounding nervous.

I cupped her face and kissed her, rubbing my thumbs in small circles on her cheeks. "I don't care how it happened. I'm thrilled, sweetheart. Beyond thrilled." I kissed her again. "In fact, throw away those pills. I'll handle it from now on, or you can just keep getting pregnant. We make awesome babies."

She laughed and flung her arms around my neck. "Maybe it will be a boy this time."

I felt a little tug on my heart as I thought about having a son. A little guy I could hang with. Teach about football and cars. Girls.

"As long as it is healthy, I don't care," I stated.

Katy grinned. "Liar. I saw your eyes light up."

I shrugged. "Maybe. If not, we'll keep trying. A baby with a penis is bound to show up at some point."

She rolled her eyes at my teasing.

"Are you feeling okay?"

She lifted one shoulder. "It's been easy so far. No morning sickness. Not even a little nausea. I feel a bit tired, but other than that, I'm good."

"You saw the doctor?"

"Yes. I have an ultrasound soon."

"I'm there."

She smiled. "I knew you would be."

I tugged her back to my chest, holding her tight. "Thank you, sweetheart. Best gift ever."

She snuggled close, and I shifted, laying us both down and drawing up the blankets. She was asleep in seconds, leaving me to stare at the fluffy balls of wool.

I thought of the past months.

The terrible pain, drama, and worry were behind us. The shadows and clouds dispelled.

Ahead was clear and bright.

A baby.

A new life to join us and make my life even more complete.

I looked down at my wife—the center of my universe and the reason I was the man I was today.

She was my greatest gift.

~

I parked the car and turned to Katy with a grin. "This feels familiar."

I was glad to be back to driving. It took a while to get my fears under control and my confidence back. I was more cautious than before the accident, but I took some defensive driving classes and they helped. I no longer had to be driven places, and I didn't break out in a sweat when I got into a car.

Katy brushed the hair back from her face. At sixteen weeks, she was already glowing. This had been a different pregnancy for her. Little morning sickness, except she was tired all the time. And she was already showing more than she had with the other two girls.

I love her baby bump and watching the changes that happened with her body. The way her breasts filled out, the swell of her tummy as my child grew within her, the soft expression she wore as she absently ran her hand over her stomach, not even realizing she was doing it.

"Third time's the charm, they say." She winked as I opened her door and extended my hand to help her out of the car. "Are we going to find out the sex this time?"

We hadn't with Gracie or Heather. I knew this time she wanted to know, and I had no objections. We needed to plan the nursery and move Heather, so I nodded. "Why not? Surprise today or in a few months—I'm good with either. It'll make some decisions easier, I suppose."

"Okay, then, Daddy. Let's find out."

The waiting room was busy, but once we were called in, I helped Katy into her gown and to get settled on the table. The paper crinkled as she shifted on the bed, nerves making her restless.

I kissed her forehead and held her hand. I was excited too, so I couldn't sit down. Standing would have to suffice, although I wanted to pace. The room was too full of equipment to allow that.

Suzanne came in, her face beaming. "Hello, you two." She had been with us for the birth of both girls, and Katy trusted her completely. She was a great doctor and an even better human being. We were both very fond of her.

She bustled around, getting all the equipment she needed. "We ready to say hello?"

Katy bit her lip, already tearing up.

I cleared my throat. "We'd like to know the sex this time."

Suzanne looked surprised. "That's different for you."

Katy sighed. "This whole pregnancy is different."

Suzanne asked a bunch of questions, made notes, did an exam, and finally smiled. "All looks good. It's your third, Katy. Your body reacts differently each time."

She pulled the ultrasound machine closer. "Let's have a look."

I chuckled as she squirted the gel on Katy's tummy, making her squirm. Katy always reacted to the cold. I kissed her and watched as the wand moved back and forth, and the image became clearer.

"There's your baby." Suzanne smiled, clicking and measuring. I held my breath as she turned on the sound, and I heard the heartbeat. The odd noise filled the room, the fast, steady sound like music to my ears.

"You're sure you want to know?"

"Yes!" Katy and I exclaimed.

"It's a girl," Suzanne announced.

I laughed. "I'm surrounded. My own little harem."

Katy's eyes were focused on the screen. She tilted her head, looking confused.

"It all looks good…" Suzanne's voice trailed off.

I frowned at the subtle change in the noise. It was faster, like an echo of itself, the strumming continuous.

"Well, look who's been hiding," Suzanne mused and glanced over at us. "There's the reason this one is different, Katy." She grinned and winked at me. "You did good, Richard." She peered at the screen intently.

"It's twins. And the second one is a boy."

I blinked. Looked at Katy. Back at the screen. Blinked again.

There were two babies.

We were having two babies.

And one was a son.

I was having a son.

This generation of VanRyan men would know he was wanted and loved. I would teach him about family. Graham would be a real grandfather to him. Maddox and Aiden would be horrendous influences on him, and I would pretend to be outraged and secretly enjoy every moment of their adventures. Laura would spoil him.

He would have everything I didn't as a child.

All my children would.

I wasn't sure I had ever whooped in a doctor's office until that very moment.

But I did—and loudly. Loud enough to make Katy jump and the doctor laugh.

I kissed Katy. Kissed her for the gift of two more children to love and the son I secretly wished to have. Once again, she made my dreams come true.

"Thank you," I said against her lips. I tasted salt but didn't know if it was from my tears or hers. It didn't matter.

"You did it," she whispered back.

"*We* did it." I kissed her again, my happiness knowing no bounds. "*We did it.*"

~

SEVERAL MONTHS DOWN THE ROAD...

The hospital halls echoed with the sound of my footsteps as I hurried down the corridor. I stopped by the desk and met the amused gaze of Shelly. She had been on duty every time one of my kids was born, and she was used to me by now.

"How is she?'

"You were gone fifteen minutes. She survived."

I glared at her and held up a large bag. "I got enough ice cream for everyone. Unless they're rude."

She snagged the bag from my hand with a laugh. "Good thing I'm not. I hope you brought spoons."

I chuckled as I moved past her, needing to get back to Katy.

Katy's ice cream craving had been constant this time. I couldn't keep it in the house. I'd fill the freezer, and by the next day, I had to stop at the store again.

Today, after giving birth to our children, she had asked for some. Given everything we went through today, she could have anything she wanted from me, and ice cream was easy. Even if I hated leaving her for the briefest of moments.

I opened the door to Katy's private room, smiling at the sight in front of me. Katy was asleep, her cheek resting on her hand. Her face was pale and wan, but a smile still played on her lips. She was exhausted.

The latter part of her pregnancy had been fraught with problems. Katy was tiny, and carrying one baby was hard enough, never mind two. And my son seemed determined to make sure she knew he was in there and growing. Constantly active, larger than his sister, he was a challenge. The entire pregnancy was. After a few scares in the second trimester, bed rest was ordered and a date for a cesarean set. Somehow, Katy held on, and today our children arrived, healthy and happy at thirty-six weeks. Suzanne was pleased and expected their stay in the NICU to be a matter of days, not weeks. I already had a hotel suite booked close to the hospital. The girls were in the care of Mrs. Thomas, Laura, and Brad and June, who loved spending time with them. With the help of a nanny I had hired, they would be well cared for until Katy and I brought their siblings home. It would be a few days before the girls could see them, but I had sent pictures, and they were both excited.

I sat down, running my finger along Katy's cheek. She would be upset if I brought her ice cream and she didn't get to eat it.

Her eyes fluttered open, and she grasped my hand with a smile. "Hi."

"Hey, sweetheart."

"Did you get it?"

"Yes."

"Did you see the babies?"

I kissed her cheek. "Yes. They're doing great. You can get up and see them tomorrow."

"Mm'kay."

I opened the lid, dug out a spoonful and tapped her lips with the cold treat. "Here."

She opened her mouth and hummed around the mouthful. "Mmm. Salted caramel."

I took a large mouthful myself, enjoying the sweet and salty tang together. I knew I wouldn't get much of it, but I would steal what I could.

"Richard?"

I leaned forward. "What is it, sweetheart? Are you in pain?"

She shook her head. "I was wondering if you'd decided on a name."

I fed her some more ice cream. "I think so. How about you?"

We had decided we could each name a baby. No discussion—the other person had to accept the choice. It had been Katy's idea, which made me laugh. I highly doubted I would object to her choice. Or her to mine. We were too close for that to happen.

"Yes. Once I saw her today, I knew."

"Me too. You go first."

She smiled. "Gertrude Hermione VanRyan."

I tried to stop my horror from showing through. I failed.

"*Gertrude?*" I gasped. "Katy, what the hell?"

She giggled, the sound welcome. She had been kidding.

I took a huge mouthful of ice cream to punish her, ignoring her pleading eyes.

For a minute. Then I fed her some more.

"Penny Elaine VanRyan."

I nodded. Penny for her adopted mother, Elaine for Mrs. Thomas, who was such a huge part of our family. I leaned close, kissed her, and gave her the last mouthful of ice cream. "Perfect."

"Now you."

I took in a deep breath. "Gavin Riley VanRyan."

Katy knew how much those two men meant to me. She held out her hand and repeated my word.

"Perfect."

"I thought so."

"Graham will be touched. As will Maddox."

"I hope so."

"I was going to add Aiden, but the name seemed too big."

She nodded in understanding.

"Maybe the next one."

Her eyes grew round. "Ah—"

Laughing, I tossed the empty container away. "Teasing."

"Maybe we could get a dog instead or a cat."

Her words made me laugh harder. "Aiden, the dog. Somehow, it works. Bentley, the cat. They're always a little snootier."

She shut her eyes, weariness overtaking her again. "You train those ones."

I ran my hand along her brow, smiling at her little sigh of contentment.

I bent close and kissed her cheek.

"Sleep, my Katy. I'll be here when you wake up."

"Love you," she mumbled.

I looked down at her, already asleep.

My beautiful Katy.

"Love doesn't even begin to cover it," I told her, dropping another kiss to her sweet face. "There isn't a big enough word."

I opened the front door and waved Katy inside. I followed with the babies, each held securely in their carriers.

They were as different as night and day.

Penny was tiny, quiet, with a hint of red in her little curls that went well with her name. She had a sweet temperament and loved to be held. Her eyes promised to remain blue—like her mother's

Gavin was larger. Long and lean, bald as an eagle, and eyes that became hazel very quickly—like mine. And his temper matched. His demands were fast and loud. Food. A new diaper. Lift him up. Put him down.

Find his sister.

Penny was the one thing that seemed to calm him. I had a feeling these two were going to rule the house.

Gracie raced toward us, excited and anxious. Heather waddled behind her, a sunny smile on her little face. Laura and Graham followed behind them, happy to see us. I set down the carriers and scooped up my girls, kissing them and letting them love on me. I lowered them to Katy's level so they could kiss her. She couldn't lift them yet with her incision still healing, but once she sat down, they would be all over her. There were lots of squeals and hugs, then we went into the family room.

It felt good to be there—to finally bring our children home. To have them all under one roof.

Graham lifted Gavin from his carrier, holding him up.

"My God, he is big."

I laughed. "His lungs match."

Laura held Penny, running a finger over her cheek. "So sweet," she murmured.

Katy snuggled our girls, who were thrilled to have her home.

"Where's Tess?" I asked. A friend of Laura's, Tess was a kind, loving woman whom I'd hired to help out Katy. The girls had loved her right away, and she seemed to fit in well. She lived close and would be here full time for a while, until Katy decided what she needed. We were lucky to have found her.

Graham chuckled. "She was making dinner, so you didn't have to worry. She'll be out shortly—she was visiting with Elaine, and they were swapping recipes. I think they were going to get some coffee and snacks ready."

"Great."

Gavin let out one of his snuffly yells. His arms flailed, and his face turned red. Graham looked perplexed, then made a face and handed him to me. "Duty calls."

"It's all yours if you want it."

"Nope," he insisted. "Perks of being Gramps. I turn them over to you when they smell or get too loud."

Chuckling, I took Gavin and headed upstairs to the nursery.

Gavin grizzled into his fists, gnawing at them and making his frustrated noises.

"Like that, is it, my boy?" I asked. "Hungry too?" I kissed his brow. "Don't worry, Daddy's got you."

I loved feeding him. The way he burrowed close and suckled. Snuggled in and slept after being burped. Katy had experienced a problem breastfeeding with Heather and had made the decision to bottle-feed this time, so I got to feed one while she fed the other. I found it a great bonding time and hated sharing.

That was the perk of being *Daddy*.

∾

The house was dark when I made my final round before going to bed to check on my children.

I un-starfished Gracie and covered her back up, kissing her head.

I rescued Heather from the bottom of her new big-girl bed and laid her back on top of her pillow. She wouldn't stay there for long. She loved to roll lengthwise and rarely slept where she was supposed to.

Penny was asleep, her tiny chin moving as she slumbered, but no noise escaping her mouth. Gavin stirred as I got close, and I stood beside their shared crib, stroking his head until he fell asleep. He made a low grunting noise that made me chuckle.

In our room, Katy was asleep. I knew we'd be up in a couple of hours and that I needed to do the same, but my mind didn't shut off.

I thought of my past in comparison to my future.

One so cold and devoid of emotion, I became the same way. The other bright with promise and happiness.

My blessings were long.

Four children I never thought I would have.

A home filled with light and love.

Family and friends I cared for. Who returned the sentiment.

And a wife who gave it all to me simply by being herself.

Warm, loving, and real.

Because of her—I had it all.

Life was good.

And the future?

I could see it all. The first days of school, watching my kids grow, holidays, vacations, joy, tears, kisses, hugs. Love. Growing, laughing, sharing, learning. Together.

I glanced over at my wife, my need to see her loving gaze too strong to ignore.

"Katy, sweetheart," I urged quietly. "Wake up."

Her eyes fluttered open.

"What is it? Are the babies—"

I shook my head, cutting her off. "No."

She must have seen something on my face, because she cupped my cheek.

"What is, my darling?"

I swallowed the thickness building in my throat. "I wanted to tell you I love you. God, I love you, Katy VanRyan."

She stroked my face with her fingers. "I love you."

I brushed my mouth along hers. "Thank you."

She smiled, knowing and understanding. She always did.

I tapped the end of her nose. "Now go to sleep. My children will need to be fed soon, and I can't do it all myself, you know."

She snuggled closer, carefully moving until she was comfortable.

"Go fuck yourself, VanRyan."

I chuckled. That was exactly what I wanted to hear. What I needed to hear.

And she knew.

Because, yeah, it was Katy.

My future.

ACKNOWLEDGMENTS

As always, I have some people to thank. The ones behind the words that encourage and support. The people who make my books possible for so many reasons.

This book would not have been possible without the help of some medical professionals who took time from their busy schedules to answer questions, provide feedback, and make corrections to this story.

I especially want to thank Colin Oczkowski for his patience, time, and assistance.

To my readers—you asked for more Richard and Katy. I hope I did their story justice.

Lisa, thank you for your editing brilliance and patience. You make my words flow.
I love your comments and knowing I make you laugh.

Beth, Trina, Melissa—thank you for your feedback and support.

Carrie, my UN ladies, Ayden, Jeannie, Freya—
I love you and am honored to call you friends. You humble me.

Peggy and Deb, thank you for your support and keen eyes.

Melissa—you take my post it notes, scribbles, and thoughts and turn
them into covers I adore. Thank you!

Karen, my dear friend and PA. Life wouldn't be the same without you.
You make this journey fun and exciting. Our shared love of words
have blossomed into one of the most important and special
friendships of my life. Love you to the moon and back.

To all the bloggers, readers, and especially my promo team. Thank
you for everything you do. Shouting your love of books—of my work
—posting, sharing—your recommendations keep my TBR list full, and
the support you have shown me is so appreciated.

To my fellow authors who have shown me such kindness, thank you. I
will follow your example and pay it forward.

My reader group, Melanie's Minions—love you all.

And always, my Matthew. You are my world.

OTHER BOOKS BY MELANIE MORELAND

Vested Interest Series

Bentley (Vested Interest #1)

Aiden (Vested Interest #2)

Maddox (Vested Interest #3)

Reid (Vested Interest #4)

Van (Vested Interest #5)

Halton (Vested Interest #6)

Insta-Spark Collection

It Started with a Kiss

Christmas Sugar

An Instant Connection

The Contract Series

The Contract (The Contract #1)

The Baby Clause (The Contract #2)

Standalones

Into the Storm

Beneath the Scars

Over the Fence

My Image of You (Random House/Loveswept)

ABOUT THE AUTHOR

Melanie Moreland

New York Times/USA Today bestselling author Melanie Moreland, lives a happy and content life in a quiet area of Ontario with her beloved husband of thirty plus years and their rescue cat, Amber. Nothing means more to her than her friends and family, and she cherishes every moment spent with them.

While seriously addicted to coffee, and highly challenged with all things computer-related and technical, she relishes baking, cooking, and trying new recipes for people to sample. She loves to throw dinner parties, and enjoys travelling, here and abroad, but finds coming home is always the best part of any trip.

Melanie loves stories, especially paired with a good wine, and enjoys skydiving (free falling over a fleck of dust) extreme snowboarding (falling down the stairs) and piloting her own helicopter (tripping over her own feet). She's learned happily ever afters, even bumpy ones, are all in how you tell the story.

Melanie is represented by Flavia Viotti at Bookcase Literary Agency. For any questions regarding subsidiary or translation rights please contact her at flavia@bookcaseagency.com

Connect with Melanie

Like reader groups? Lots of fun and giveaways! Check it out Melanie Moreland's Minions

Join my newsletter for up-to-date news, sales, book announcements and excerpts (no spam): Melanie Moreland's newsletter

Visit my website www.melaniemoreland.com

Made in the USA
Columbia, SC
19 September 2020